THE PRINCESS OF THE REBELLION

THE PRINCESS OF THE REBELLION

THE MIRRORED CROWN: BOOK ONE

JESSICA R. LEMORE

In loving memory of Matthew John Battista.
Until we meet again.

CONTENTS

1

THE DREAM

For as long as she could remember, the same dream plagued Lana. A few nights a month, it crept upon her in the dark, sneaking into her subconscious and taking root. Tonight had been one of those nights, and she gasped for breath when she awoke. She sighed with relief when she found that she was in her bedroom, far away from the nightmare.

A gust of wind blew in from the open window, and the thick lace curtains danced as the streetlight outside flickered. Lowering her bare feet onto the floor, she winced with surprise when she found the carpet was cold to the touch. She reached for her bathrobe and wrapped it around herself.

As she walked to the open window, she paused when the streetlight outside lost its glow and bathed her in darkness. When she moved the curtains aside, she saw that the lights that lined her road were all off. She shivered from the cool night air and tied her bathrobe tighter.

A boom of thunder resounded, and a flash of lightning lit up the sky, giving her a clear view of the street. She dropped the curtains and stepped back when she saw a man staring up at her from the sidewalk. When the lightning flash disappeared, she approached the window again but saw only darkness.

Before she had time to fasten her window shut, another rapid succession of lightning lit up the sky again, giving her enough light to see that the man had disappeared—if there was even a man to begin with. She threw the curtains into place and jumped back into the safety of her bed. Once she pulled the blankets up to her chin, she thought about the dream. Long ago, it terrified her, but it had become so frequent it lost its frightening influence, a battle that had taken many years. She closed her eyes, flashes of the dream appearing before her.

Once again, she was standing in a large room reminiscent of an ancient cathedral. To her left were huge vaulted windows that framed the ominous sky. The only door was behind her. Above the doorway was a jeweled map, outlined in gold.

Across the room, two beautiful thrones decorated with rubies, sapphires, and diamonds were before an enormous stone fireplace that contained engravings of fantastical creatures she had only read about. The hearth of the fireplace was framed by two etched dragons. Their tails were converged, and their eyes of pearl seemed to dance and glow when the fire was lit, creating the illusion of their eagerness to emerge. The curious thing about this fireplace was that the dragon on the left was missing a pearl eye but, even with the exception of this small extraction, still seemed perfect. It appeared as if these creatures, once alive, were entombed.

She was always drawn to the middle of the room. Its focal point was a white bassinet festooned with red roses and adorned with lace. A woman with long black hair, olive skin, and green eyes gazed into it. Her pale gray dress sparkled from the flames in the fireplace whenever she leaned over to admire the tiny infant inside.

The three gentlemen around this woman were always involved in a heated argument that terrified her. She had been drawn to the man nearest the captivating woman—his brown eyes glimmered as he brushed his wavy hair back out of his face. The man wore a black cloak with a small silver dagger sewn on the top left.

Sitting on one of the bejeweled thrones was an older man with long white hair and a scraggly white beard. He wore a gold crown and a gold cloak and always looked so sad. Standing behind the thrones was another man almost identical to the one standing next to the woman. He had the same shoulder-length brown hair, brown eyes, and tan skin, but he was wearing a dark purple cloak.

To her right was a red velvet curtain. Numerous charts, maps, and portraits hung on the walls, but she never had a chance to look at them in detail. The fight began too quickly for her to pay attention to anything else.

None of the figures gave the slightest indication that they were aware of her presence. As had occurred in all her previous dreams, the argument escalated, and the men began shouting at one another. As the scene unfolded, she was compelled to watch the woman as she huddled next to the bassinet, as if fearful for the safety of its occupant.

Lana could never tell what the argument was about because she could never quite hear what was being said but knew it would always end the same. It was like watching a movie she had seen many times before. The older gentleman stood up from his chair and walked to the man in black with the aid of a wooden cane.

As much as it pained her, there was no willing this man to avoid the deadly fate that lay before him, and as much as she wanted to block the horrific scene that was about to unfold, she couldn't turn away. The older man slowly made his way to the man in the black cloak. The only sound that could be heard was the soft thud of the cane as it struck the floor.

When the man finally stopped walking, he put his right

hand on the shoulder of the man in black and used his left hand to brush away the cascade of white hair that had fallen into his face. After he exchanged a few words with the younger man, he kissed his left cheek, at which point the man began to cry. The older gentleman approached the woman, placing his hand on the tiny child, and there appeared to be a quick flash that brightened the room.

The flash subsided, and the man in black wiped the tears from his eyes, pulled a short knife from deep within the folds of his cloak, and plunged it into the older man's back. A piercing scream escaped the old man's lips. Lana watched as the man wiped the bloody knife on his cloak and returned it to its sheath. With the evilest laugh she had ever heard, the man in his solemn black cloak continued to pace the room, looking at the remaining occupants as the old man slumped to the floor.

After a moment, the man in black allowed his gaze to settle on the man in purple, who was kneeling by the lifeless body. Suddenly, he sprang forward and attacked the man in purple, which caused the bassinet to lurch forward. As the woman reached protectively for the tiny child, a gun was fired from the shadows behind the red velvet curtain. The bassinet tipped over, and the baby landed on the floor next to the motionless woman's outstretched arms.

At this point, just as the man in black runs over to the fallen woman with a dreadful scream, she always awoke, wishing she could have seen the aftermath of the chaos she had experienced. What had become of the woman and the little baby? She had dreamed of them so often they felt real to her.

As she looked around her room, she noticed movement out of the corner of her eye and glanced at the full-length mirror by her closet. To her horror, as the lightning lit up her bedroom and the thunder rumbled, a figure emerged from the shadows deep within the mirror. She immediately sank into her bed, wishing to wake from the dream she appeared to be in. The figure pushed its way out of her mirror with great difficulty.

She closed her eyes, hoping when she reopened them the figure would be gone. She wondered if the lightning was playing tricks on her or if it was just a figment of her imagination. Upon reopening her eyes, the figure emerged from the mirror.

She tried to scream, but her breath lodged in her throat. Beads of sweat trickled down her forehead as her heart rate sped up. The man took a calculated step towards her, trying to assess if she was awake.

Finally, she began screaming. The man took another step forward and held his hands out. Gold glitter fluttered all around her, and she felt at peace, as if everything was going to be all right. Her eyelids grew heavy as the man stepped into the hallway.

Lana wanted to scream again, to warn her parents, but couldn't even keep her eyes open. The last thing she heard before drifting off to sleep was the thud of footsteps as the man crept downstairs.

2

FRAZIER WOODS

The morning was calm and clear when Lana awoke. Birds were chirping, and all signs of the storm had vanished into a beautiful spring day in Mt. Sinclair, New York. As she rolled out of bed, she rubbed her forehead, trying to soothe her headache. Even though she had just awoken, she was still drowsy.

She threw her long, curly brown hair into a ponytail and stepped up to her full-length mirror. She froze as visions of a man stepping out of it appeared before her. She looked past her reflection, looking deep within the mirror, expecting to see the man. She touched the cool glass, but nothing happened.

As she looked around her room once more, she decided to put off making the bed. She needed to talk to her parents. She stepped into the hall and walked down the stairs, looking for anything out of place. She made her way to the kitchen, still in her hot-pink flamingo pajamas.

"Good morning," her mother said. "Your breakfast is ready."

Her mom was already dressed for the day, and her shoulder-length blonde hair was curled. She sat at the table, and her mother placed a plate of scrambled eggs and toast in front of

557444

her. Her mother never had been much of a cook. In fact, scrambled eggs was one of the few things she had mastered without burning the kitchen down. Her father was always the chef in their house.

"Are you all right?" her mother asked. "Why aren't you dressed?"

"I feel like I'm losing my mind. I thought I saw a man come out of my mirror last night."

Her mother sat at the table and smoothed a wrinkle out of her thin, blue sweater. "That sounds like some dream."

Lana nodded absentmindedly and took a sip of water. She turned to her mother again.

"I had been dreaming about the fight."

She didn't have to elaborate. She used to wake up crying when she was younger. When her parents had asked what was wrong, she had responded that the fight woke her up. Since then, they had always referred to it as "the fight."

"We've been over this before," her mother began, offering her a weak smile. "It's not real."

As if to signal the conversation was over, her mother took a sip of coffee. Lana took the hint and continued to eat her breakfast in silence, knowing she had to be right. It had only been a dream. She knew people didn't walk out of mirrors.

A minute later, her father walked into the kitchen, looking at his phone. A sigh escaped his tightly pursed lips as he sat.

"What's wrong?" her mother asked as she took another sip of coffee.

Her father swiped his forefinger on the screen, and she knew he was on the local news app. Her parents were obsessed with the local news. Her father looked at her mother as he increased the volume and placed the phone on the table.

"Residents of Mt. Sinclair's east side are urging the local sheriff's department to increase their patrol around the area's high school," the news reporter stated. "Numerous complaints have been filed regarding a trio of men. This group, dressed all in black, has been seen looking through windows of the first-floor classrooms. Ken O'Brian will have more on this story tonight at six."

Lana rolled her eyes. She attended Mt. Sinclair High School on the east side of town, and the school had been abuzz with rumors. Theories were running rampant from both teachers and students alike and ranged from the mundane to the bizarre. Everything from routine safety inspectors to men-in-black completing top-secret government business was discussed with great fervency that bordered obsession, and she was tired of hearing about it.

Her mother and father exchanged a worried look. When a commercial for a local cleaning service began, her father reached for his phone and stopped the broadcast.

"It's time to get ready for school," he said. "I'll be driving you today."

Lana frowned. She was tired of her parents treating her like a child.

"I can take the bus," she said emphatically. "I've been taking it since I started going to school."

"Were you listening to the news?" he asked, running his hand through his brown hair. "I would feel better if I dropped you off."

"I would feel better if your father dropped you off too," her mother chimed in.

"I'll be fine on the bus. I've *never* seen those men at school!"

Lana didn't want to be driven to school. While she loved her parents, she was often embarrassed by them. Last year, when she was in eighth grade, her father volunteered to chaperone a school trip to the zoo. To her chagrin, he dressed up as a safari leader and insisted she wear a matching costume. She knew this was just his way of adding a little humor to life, but he didn't understand how other people perceived this humor. Everyone at school still liked to tease her about her *crazy* father.

She pushed away her half-eaten plate of food and looked at him. "Are you going to sit with me in class too? Maybe we can eat lunch together."

"Not funny," he said, adjusting the black-and-white checkered tie around his neck. "Hurry up and get ready for school. I don't want to be late to work."

She stood up from the table without another word or glance at her parents. She had a plan. As she made her way to her bedroom, she knew that she had to get dressed fast if she wanted it to work.

Fifteen minutes later, she was showered and dressed. Mt. Sinclair High School's strict dress code took all the painful decisions on what to wear away. Dressed in a white shirt, navy-blue pants, and white sneakers, she studied herself in the mirror.

"So much for expressing our individuality," she muttered bitterly.

To complete her forced ensemble, she put her wet hair into a ponytail, grabbed her books, and crept her way downstairs. As she tiptoed to the kitchen, she heard voices. She adjusted her orange backpack on her shoulder as she listened to her parents.

"Cindy, she will be fine." Her father's frustrated voice echoed out of the kitchen. "Better yet, *we* will be fine."

"I think Lana would be safer if we pulled her out of school." Her mother's voice cracked as she stifled a cry. "The bureau doesn't seem to care."

"We can't pull her out of school," her father said. "We're not even sure these guys know who she is yet. They're just scouting, looking for possibilities. This isn't the first school they've checked, and if all goes well, they'll move on to the next."

"They've been there before," her mother retorted. "They're not moving to the next."

Lana heard her parents move to the opposite side of the kitchen, near the pantry. They continued talking but had lowered their voices. She wanted to continue eavesdropping but had to leave if she was going to catch the bus.

She tiptoed to the backdoor. She gently closed the door behind her and ran along the side of the house to the front yard. She checked her watch and noted the bus was due to arrive any minute.

When she reached the front yard, she ducked underneath the bay window, so she wouldn't be seen by her parents, and ran. A few feet ahead of her, the bus pulled to the curb. She sped up and was the last to board, just barely saving herself from tripping up the stairs. Her phone vibrated in her pocket, and she ignored it, knowing it was her parents.

Before she could find a seat, the bus lurched as it pulled into traffic and made its way to the next stop. She sat on the nearest empty bench. Cooper Gibson was sitting to her left, across the aisle. Her cheeks blushed, and she quickly turned away so he wouldn't see. She tried to think of something witty to say, but nothing came to her.

She had been working up the nerve to talk to Cooper for months, ever since he asked to borrow a pencil in English class. She turned to look at him and smiled when she saw that he was watching her. He turned back to the open textbook on his lap, and she pulled out her phone. Before she had a chance to look at it, she heard a familiar voice, and her stomach dropped.

"Hey, Laughs, why were you running?"

Lana ignored the voice. She unlocked her phone and saw she had a voicemail from both her mother and father, along with several text messages.

"Were your weird parents trying to dress you up as a witch?" the voice continued. "We're talking about the witch trials in history class, and it wouldn't take much for you to dress up as one, would it? Paste a wart on your cheek; you already have the ratty hair."

Her next-door neighbor, Nick Jacobs, was sitting in the seat behind Cooper. He had begun calling her Laughs years ago, which he got from her last name, Laughlin. As Nick told it, laughing was what everyone felt like doing after spending a day with her and her family.

Everyone within earshot began snickering, except Cooper. That's what she liked about him. If he didn't agree with something, he didn't go along with it just because it was the "cool" thing to do.

Mrs. Winston, the elderly bus driver, pointed to the handmade sign posted above the windshield. *NO TALKING* was stenciled in thick block letters. No one really paid much attention to the sign. She could hear those around her giggling and knew it was aimed at her.

"Hey, Laughs, isn't that your crazy father following us?" Nick asked loudly, standing up to get a better look out of the back window.

She turned around, and her spirits plummeted. It was her father, and when he saw her looking at him, he began frantically waving. She prayed he wouldn't follow the bus the whole way to school.

As the bus stopped to pick up the next batch of students, she peered out the back window and saw her father bobbing his head back and forth to the music he was listening to. Two young girls, both already experienced in the fine art of snobbery, held up their noses as they walked by her, still alone in the seat. She wondered how it had come to be that even the younger kids wouldn't sit by her. Then she heard Nick's shrill voice.

Five minutes later, Mrs. Winston pulled the bus to the sidewalk of Mt. Sinclair High School. In a rush, students began making their way up to the school. She gathered her belongings and stepped off the bus, only to come face-to-face with her father.

"Lana, you really shouldn't have run off like that," he said as he shook his finger in her face.

His tie was still hanging loosely around his neck, and she smirked. Before she had a chance to explain her reasons for wanting to take the bus, someone ran into her from behind. She lost her balance and fell to the grass. Nick feigned an apologetic tone and offered her his hand.

"Lana, I didn't see you there. Let me help you up."

She brushed him away and stood up, moving away from him in case he *accidentally* ran into her again.

"Hello, Nick!" Her father smiled. "I was going to invite your family to a barbecue this weekend. I hope you aren't busy. I know Lana hopes you can make it."

"No, I don't," she interjected, and her father shot her a warning look.

"Gee, Mr. Laughlin," Nick began, "I think we've already got plans. We have to go shopping and run some errands. But I'll tell my parents about the invite."

Lana didn't understand how her father could be so blind to his performance.

"I have to get to class, but it was nice to see you again," Nick continued.

"Why do you insist that I hang out with him?" she asked when Nick reached the school steps, joining his friends. "I can't stand him."

Around her, students were filing off the continuous row of buses as they pulled up to the school. She could already hear the whispers as her classmates pointed to her father and snickered behind their hands.

"Listen to me," he began. "I'm going to watch you walk into school, and then I have to go to work. I can't be late, so make it quick. I'll be here at three thirty this afternoon to pick you up. You are not to leave the building until you see my car."

"Fine."

She spun around and walked toward the doors, but her dad, always one to have the last word, yelled, "And you're grounded!"

With a wide grin on his face, Nick opened the door and said, "After you."

Lana walked past him and headed to class. She deftly listened to her morning lessons. In history class, she stared at the back of Cooper's head. She would have liked to be looking at the front of him but decided she had better be happy with what she could get. In math class, she thought about her friends, Ava and Trevor, and began counting down the hours until she could tell them about her parents' strange behavior. In music, she sat by herself and listened to Nick describing his plans for the weekend, which did not involve shopping, until a brief announcement over the loudspeaker caught her attention.

"Due to recent events, students will no longer be able to go outdoors for recess or gym class until further notice."

Mr. Jones attempted to calm the riotous class, but when it proved pointless, he dismissed them early for lunch. She threw her notebook into her backpack and stepped into the hallway to wait for her friends. Every day, Ava and Trevor met outside of her classroom so they could walk to the cafeteria together.

"Hey, did you hear that announcement?" Trevor asked as he made his way toward her, dodging groups of excited students congregating at their lockers.

Tall and pudgy, with short brown hair and brown eyes, Trevor barely fit into his pants anymore, as they were becoming too short since his recent growth spurt. His dad had left years ago, leaving Trevor and his mother on their own. His mom worked a full-time job as a phlebotomist at the hospital and was currently on the hunt for a part-time job to supplement their meager income.

"I've had an awful morning," Ava said, coming up from behind Trevor. "I forgot my Spanish book at home, which also had my homework in it."

Ava Graham and Lana had been friends for years ever since fourth grade, when Nick had made it his life's mission to torment them. They still weren't sure why Nick had targeted them; maybe it was because they were quiet and less willing to fight back. Trevor McAllister had joined them last year when he transferred from Stony Heights, which happened to be Mt. Sinclair's biggest rival. Since then, the three had become inseparable.

Ava dropped her backpack to the floor and threw her long black hair into a sloppy bun. Her brown eyes sparkled as she looked at Lana and Trevor, a wide grin curving her lips.

"Let's sneak outside for lunch," Ava whispered. "The quad will be empty. We'll have our pick of the tables."

"I'm in enough trouble as it is," she said, filling them in on her morning and her parents' insistence that her father drive her to school.

By the time she finished her story, they had gotten their lunch and sat at a table in the corner of the huge cafeteria. Ava and Trevor exchanged knowing glances.

"People don't walk out of mirrors," Ava said, taking a bite of her salad.

Trevor nodded; his eyes focused on something across the cafeteria. She turned to look and saw Laurie Huntington at the table near the window overlooking Lake Sinclair. She had her head back, giggling at something Nick said.

"I'm gonna go say hi to Laurie," Trevor said, standing up and brushing the crumbs from his sandwich off his shirt.

Lana's heart sank. She knew this would not end well. She watched Trevor walk over to Laurie, who didn't even acknowledge him. She didn't understand why Laurie had become so popular. She was pretty—tall and skinny with long blonde hair and green eyes, but she could be cruel.

Trevor shuffled back to their table crestfallen, and before Lana or Ava could offer words of encouragement, Nick walked by, his empty tray in his hands.

"Why would you think Laurie would want to talk to a loser like you?"

Trevor sat in his chair, and she reached for her friend's hand. "Don't listen to him."

"I'm fine," he mumbled, shrugging his shoulders.

She pushed away her uneaten lunch. She turned to Laurie again and saw her laughing with her friends. What would it feel like to be as popular as Laurie, to have everyone clamoring to be your friend, the members of the football team vying for your attention?

Ava stood up and Lana was pulled from her thoughts. She smiled at Trevor and they followed Ava to the doors. They dumped their garbage into the trash cans and made their way to the gym.

She walked in silence, following the joyful shuffle of students glad for their break from classes. When they reached the gymnasium, they saw the bleachers were down. Most of their classmates were sitting, playing games on their phones.

Ava walked to a ping pong table and picked up a paddle, brandishing it towards Lana and Trevor. When Trevor grabbed another paddle, she followed suit and stood across the table from her friends. She wished they could sit outside. The sun was shining, and there wasn't a cloud to be seen.

She looked for Cooper and saw him sitting by himself in the top row of the bleachers, reading a book. She tried to see what he was reading when the ping pong ball hit her in the cheek. Ava's eyes grew big, as if she couldn't believe that she had hit her friend. Lana looked around, thankful that no one had noticed.

When the bell rang, she made her way to the fourth floor for her next class. As she was coming up to the third floor, a cardboard box fell on her head. She tripped, which caused a pileup of students on the stairs. She angrily threw the box over the railing and saw Nick smirking at her from the fourth-floor landing. Students caught in the pileup sneered at her.

Drew, the school's maintenance man, ran up to her and asked if she was hurt, then explained that someone had taken the cardboard box from the top of his cart where it was stationed on the fourth floor.

"Are you sure you're okay?" he asked.

When she nodded, Drew took off running down the stairs in search of the missing box.

"Sorry, I didn't mean to throw it," she shouted after Drew, then turned to her friends. "I'm going to get Nick back one day."

When Lana reached her classroom, Mrs. Nowak, her Spanish teacher, was trying to calm the class, which never worked very well after their lunch hour. With gray hair and large glasses, Mrs. Nowak was her favorite teacher, as she was the most engaged. She made learning fun and usually started class with an inspirational quote.

Just as everyone was starting to settle down, Nick leaned across his desk and shouted across the room, "I saw you had a nice trip, Laughs. Next time send me a postcard."

The class burst into laughter. Her stomach sank, and she wanted to disappear. Cooper was watching her. When her eyes caught his, he smiled at her and then turned his attention back to his notebook.

She pulled her textbook out of her backpack and opened it, ready to forget about Nick and his childish antics. The rest of the afternoon flew by in a flash. Spanish, English, science, and art were all that she had to endure, and thankfully, nothing else embarrassing happened. The last bell of the day rang at three twenty, and by the time she said goodbye to Ava and Trevor, gathered her belongings, and walked to the front doors to meet her father, it was three forty. She searched the parking lot but couldn't find his car. She watched the last bus pull out of the lot and scanned the cars for her father again.

When she didn't see her father or their car, she pulled out her phone. She dialed her father's number and listened as it rang. When his voicemail picked up, she ended the call without leaving a message. She quickly dialed her mother's number, and it went straight to voicemail, which wasn't surprising, as her mother hated her cellphone and usually left it on her nightstand.

As she sat on the concrete steps, she opened her messages and began drafting a text to send to her father when she saw Laurie a few feet from her. She watched her demonstrate a new cheerleading move to a group of boys, which included Nick. Laurie sensed her gaze and turned to him, whispering in his ear. A moment later, she began walking toward her, a smile spread across her perfectly glossed lips.

"Your father was here a few minutes ago," Laurie said. "He asked me to tell you that there was an emergency, and you should take the bus home. I got distracted though, and I see that the buses have already left. Sorry."

Laurie skipped back to Nick. Lana knew her father wouldn't have told a random student to give her a message, but the buses had already left, and her parents weren't answering their phones. How long was she supposed to wait for them? She dialed her father's number again and sighed when his voice-mail came through the speaker.

"You've reached Tim Laughlin. Leave a message."

"Hi, Dad. I hope you're all right. I guess I'm going to walk home. I'll see you there."

Lana ended the call and stood up, hoping her mother and

father were all right. She walked past Laurie and Nick and heard them laughing. As she walked, she sent a quick text to Ava and Trevor.

Walking home.

A second later, Ava replied. *Where's your dad?*

Don't know. Laurie told me he left already.

You believe her?

She knew Laurie and Nick were pulling a prank on her. She couldn't see her father showing up to the school and telling Laurie, instead of one of her friends, that she should take the bus. She also knew her father had told her he would be there by three thirty, and it was already four. Since her parents weren't answering their phones, the only logical thing to do was walk home.

She sent another quick text to Ava and Trevor telling them that she was fine and would call them when she made it home. She made her way up Main Street, past the Mt. Sinclair Welcome Center. She thought about taking the shortcut home. It wasn't the safest route, as it cut through Frazier Woods and Capshaw Creek, but it was the quickest.

When she came to the corner of Main Street and Portobello Drive, she stopped walking, glanced at the white shingled house, and immediately ran across the street into the empty field surrounding Frazier Woods. Everyone knew that the residence of thirteen Portobello Drive was haunted by the restless spirits of an elderly couple who had been murdered. She had gone inside last Halloween and wished she could forget the entire incident. Doors opened and closed by themselves, and voices were heard murmuring in the attic, all which Trevor later blamed on mischievous upperclassmen.

Lana stepped in a mud puddle and frowned. Her white sneakers were now soaked. She found the path that would take her to Capshaw Creek and followed it down a hill, ducking underneath rogue tree branches. She shivered, stopping long enough to admire the family of deer that were grazing a few yards from her. When she continued walking, the deer ran away.

Soon the path began to dwindle, and she was forced to navigate her way through a maze of bushes, leaves, and tree branches. As she pushed her way through a particularly nasty bush, a branch snapped in her face. It had been covered with thorns, and blood trickled down her left cheek.

She placed her hand on her cheek, smearing blood on her fingers, when she heard a noise behind her. She turned around, surprised to see a man standing a few yards from her. He was wearing black pants, and a black long-sleeved shirt covered his arms. She thought of the news report this morning. The group of men seen looking in the windows of the school had been dressed all in black.

"Well, look who we have here, Marty." The man smiled, revealing the whitest teeth she had ever seen.

Another man stepped onto the path. Lana turned and began running. She reached for her phone and tripped over a fallen tree branch. It landed a few feet away, and she scrambled for it, hoping to reach it and call for help, when the first man yanked her to her feet.

The man panted, winded from chasing her. She knew she had to escape, but the man was very tall and easily outweighed her. She could think of nothing else to do but stomp her foot on top of his toes. The man released her, and she took off running, forgetting about her cellphone.

"You idiot, you had her!" the man she assumed was Marty shouted.

Lana was running faster than she had ever run before. Adrenaline pumped through her body as she slammed her way through branches and brambles scratching her skin. Her lungs screamed for air, but she kept on running. She didn't dare turn around for fear she would lose the precious time she had gained.

When she reached Capshaw Creek, she stepped on a huge rock covered with moss. She lost her balance and fell, landing in the cold water. A moment later, something heavy landed on top of her, pushing her deeper within the creek. She swallowed a mouthful of dirty water.

Her lungs felt like they were going to burst when a pair of strong arms pulled her out of the water. She coughed as her assailant slapped her face and threw her to the ground. She landed in the mud, hitting her head on a sharp rock, and she struggled to remain conscious.

"Marty!" the man cried out. "Where are you?"

Lana tried to sit up, but the man kicked her to the mud again. She felt her body go numb as the sharp rock dug into her back.

"What do you want from me?"

"You know why we're here," the man answered, searching for his partner. "Your father wants you back, Princess. It's been a long time since he's seen you."

"You have the wrong person. I don't know what you're talking about."

Her father would never send these brutal men after her. The man looked up the embankment, and someone hurled themselves toward them. The man was knocked into the creek with a tremendous splash.

Lana tried to sit up, but the pounding in her head was making her too dizzy. She heard someone calling her name as she closed her eyes and was swallowed up by darkness.

3

REFLECTIONS

Hours later, Lana slowly opened her eyes and found that she was in her bedroom. The light from her bedside lamp was too bright so she quickly shut them again. Her window had been left open, and she shivered. She tried moving off the bed but found she was too sore, so she remained still and listened to the conversation around her.

"When Tim came home without Lana, I was so scared," her mother whispered. "I knew something terrible had happened."

"It's a good thing you were watching her, Drew," her father said sadly. When he noticed that she was awake, he added, "Since she deliberately disobeyed me!"

The name her father spoke sounded familiar, as if she should know it. She opened her eyes. Her mother and father were standing near the bed, and Drew, the maintenance man at Mt. Sinclair High School, was at her desk. Drew realized the light was hurting her eyes and turned it off.

"What are you doing here?"

"Sweetie, he saved you." Her mother sat on the bed and took her hand, squeezing her tight. "He brought you home."

"Why did they attack me?" she asked, remembering the

men in Frazier Woods. "He said he was going to bring me to my father."

She narrowed her eyes at her father, waiting for an explanation. While she was glad she was safe, at home with her family, she had an uneasy feeling. Something felt off. The air felt tense, as if any moment a flame would appear, turning her well-ordered world to nothing but ash.

Her father exhaled deeply. "They *were* trying to bring you to your father."

Lana bit her bottom lip, trying to remain calm. Now was not the time for jokes.

"Why would they want to bring me to you? You should have picked me up like you said you would!"

"He should answer her questions," Drew warned.

"She's waited long enough," her mother snapped, wiping her hands on her jeans and nervously glancing at the mirror by the closet.

"I agree," her father said. "He'll understand."

"The bureau has alerted him." Drew tapped a pencil on the desk. "He should be here soon."

She looked at her parents, waiting for someone to fill her in. "Someone needs to explain what's going on."

"We can answer a few questions," her father finally said. "I'm not your father, and Cindy isn't your mother. We were, for lack of a better word, *appointed* to act as your guardians, but as you can see, this world has been breached."

Lana stared at him. She had never been so confused in her whole life. She pinched her arm to make sure she hadn't been dreaming and stared at the red mark left behind.

When no one said anything, she threw her hands to her lap in frustration. "Ha-ha, really funny."

"It's not a joke." Her mother looked at the mirror again, as if searching for something deep within the glass.

"Fine," she said, her voice growing louder. "It's not a joke. Then who are my real parents?"

Her mother's face paled, and a tear slid down her cheek. She looked at her father, and he held her gaze, unblinking. His face turned red, and he clenched his fists into a ball. Drew sighed loudly, clearly uncomfortable with the turn the conversation had taken.

When no one answered, she turned to Drew. "How do you fit into this?"

"I'm here to look after you," he answered, dropping the pencil. "I took over the responsibility of watching you while you were at school. You don't remember me when you were in elementary or middle school, do you?"

"You're kidding, right?" she asked angrily. "This isn't funny."

"I left my jacket at work," her father said, moving closer to the bed. "My phone was in the pocket. I had an awful day, and I forgot it."

"Well, that explains why you didn't answer your phone, but why didn't you pick me up?"

"There was an accident on Hemlock. Traffic was backed up. I couldn't even turn around. I was going to run to the school when the person in the car behind me let me use their phone."

"You didn't call me."

"I did." His voice fell as he continued. "You must have dropped your phone by then. It just rang."

She turned to Drew again. "How did you know where I was?"

"I was watching you," he answered matter-of-factly. "That's my job. When you began walking home, I grabbed my keys and left. I saw you enter Frazier Woods. I guess it's a good thing I followed you."

"I knew Laurie was lying," she said, her voice catching in her throat. "She and Nick must have had a good laugh watching me walk home. What happened to those men?"

"Don't worry about them," her father brushed her off, further angering her.

"What do you mean don't worry about them? That'll be hard to do with all my bruises."

"I didn't mean it like that. They've been taken care of."

"I left them in Frazier Woods, worse for the wear," Drew added. "Once you were safe, I alerted the bureau. They'll take it from here."

"The bureau?" she asked, searching the deepest recesses of her mind for what he was referring to. She had never heard of that particular organization.

"You'll learn of the bureau later," Drew said, shooting a warning glance to her mother and father.

"Lana," her mother said after a moment of silence. "I'm sorry I didn't answer my phone. This is my fault."

"You never answer your phone, Mom." She gave her a weak smile. "We all know you hate it. I hadn't been expecting you to answer."

"Well, now I know why people are glued to them," she said. "If something had happened to you, I don't know what I would do."

The room was silent, as if her parents were thinking of an alternate reality, one where Lana had been abducted. It was so quiet she was uncomfortable.

"Can someone just tell me the truth? What's going on?"

Before anyone could answer, something caught their attention from across the room. A dark shadow appeared in her full-length mirror. The shadow grew into a man, and her mother ran over to the mirror and began wiping the glass with the sleeve of her sweater.

Her jaw dropped as the man from last night stepped out of the mirror. He was wearing a gold crown and long gold cloak. As she studied the man, she was shocked at how familiar he seemed. A moment later, as the man brushed himself off, she recognized him from her recurring dream. This was the man that had cried when the man in black stabbed the older man.

Lana's heart raced. She turned and saw her parents and Drew bowing. She didn't know what to do, so she remained seated on her bed and stared at this strange new guest. He had the same shoulder-length brown hair and brown eyes, although he always wore a dark purple cloak.

The stranger looked around the room, glancing at her mother, father, and Drew, finally settling on her. With tears in his eyes, he walked over to her, put his right arm upon her left shoulder, and smiled. She was uncertain of what she should do but felt so drawn to this man, so comfortable with him, that she returned his smile.

"My dear, you have grown into a beautiful young woman," he said, a tear sliding down his cheek. "I have waited so long to talk to you."

Her world had turned upside down. Even though she had seen the man step out of the mirror last night, it had been easy to pass off as just another dream or a trick of the shadows. Now that she knew it had been real, she didn't know what to think and was overwhelmed.

"As the bureau has told you, Lana isn't safe here anymore," her father said, speaking to the man from the mirror. "Earlier today, she was attacked by rebels. If Drew hadn't been following her, she would be theirs."

"Not theirs—his," the man muttered.

"She already knows they're not her parents," Drew said, looking nervously at her mother and father.

Her father rushed to explain. "We had to tell her. She had been ambushed!"

The man nodded his head absentmindedly, as if thinking of other matters. As much as it pained her, the day had been no joke. Everything had been the truth.

She looked at the man standing before her. Was he her

birth father? She turned to her mother and father and felt sick to her stomach. She couldn't believe that they had lied to her for so long.

"As you can see, she is fine. Tired and full of questions, but otherwise in good health," her father ended.

The man was silent for a moment, processing what he had been told. She grew impatient, waiting for someone to give her the answers she desperately needed.

"I'm sure you have a lot of questions," the man said.

"Are you my father? How did you appear from my mirror? Who were those men that attacked me?" Like a flood, the questions came spilling out of her, unable to stop them.

"No," he chuckled. "I'm not your father. I'm your uncle."

Lana didn't know how to process this information. She didn't have any other family besides her mother and father. Both her parents had been only children, and their parents had passed away before she had been born. Like a ton of bricks, the realization hit her that everything her parents had told her had been a lie. Were they really only children? Did they have any other family?

"You're my uncle?" she asked slowly, enunciating each word.

"My dear Carlecia, I am your father's younger brother. My name is Ramos."

"Who's Carlecia? Where's my father? Why did those men want to bring me to him?"

"Your birth name was Carlecia Morgan," Ramos replied. "We gave you a new identity when you were sent into hiding as an infant. I know Tim as Grayson, Cindy as Jacqueline, and Drew as Contlay. These identities were assumed in order to protect you from your father and his rebels."

"His rebels?"

"Your father, my brother, Alderic, has been imprisoned for the past fifteen years for a series of terrible acts, murder among the worst."

"Where's my mother?"

"Kalinia died fifteen years ago. When you were only a baby."

She tried to comprehend what she had been told, but it felt like too much. How was she supposed to process that her parents weren't really her parents? That her birth father was a murderer?

Drew stood up and excused himself. She wondered where he was going and if she would see him again. She hadn't thanked him for saving her life, but other questions came to her, questions she needed answers to.

"Why did those men say they were going to bring me to him? What does he want from me?"

"I imagine his rebels are trying to help him escape," Ramos answered. "We had to send you into hiding because Alderic believes you know the location of a weapon that our father had hidden before his death."

Lana was silent, slowly coming to terms with the events of the day. How could she know the location of his weapon? She had supposedly been just a baby when she had been sent into hiding.

"Carlecia," Ramos said, and she interrupted him.

"My name is Lana."

"I know this is hard for you," he said, stepping closer to her. "It's time you returned home with me. You'll be safer there."

"This is my home." She spread her arms wide, gesturing around her bedroom. "If I'll be safer with you, why was I sent here in the first place? I'm staying here. I'll go to school tomorrow. Everything will be normal, and," she turned to the two remaining people on the floor and began to cry, "you can still be my parents."

"They found you," Ramos said. "I believe you'll be safer with me, in Bridian, where the army can protect you."

"Where's Bridian?" she asked, placing her hand on her quilt, tracing the outline of the daisies. "I've never heard of it."

Lana picked out the quilt last year before the new school year. She had been nervous to start high school, and her mother took her to the mall. In addition to a few new outfits, she picked out the quilt. It made her smile every time she saw it.

"You wouldn't have heard of it," Ramos said kindly. "We're from another dimension, a planet named Telorian. Bridian is the city you were born in. You're a Princess of Bridian."

"We're aliens? I'm an alien Princess?"

Her mother giggled, breaking the tension, and Lana turned on her. "Why didn't you tell me any of this? You told me I must have dreamed him stepping out of the mirror last night. That it hadn't been real."

"I'm so sorry," her mother said. "I couldn't tell you the truth."

"I asked them to keep it from you," Ramos added. "I wanted you to have a happy childhood, away from your father and his rebels."

"I wanted to tell you," her mother said. "I wanted to tell you the truth."

"It was real," Lana said, the pieces coming together. "I was the baby. Why have I been dreaming of this?"

"We believe my father imprinted the location of Alderic's weapon in your mind," Ramos answered. "The dream you've been having is the night that it happened."

"You know about it?"

Ramos nodded. "Grayson and Jacqueline keep me updated on everything."

"What makes you think that he imprinted the location in my mind? What does that even mean?"

"I saw the flash," he answered sadly. "Right before Alderic murdered our father, King Nicodemus. He hid Alderic's weapon, and it has remained hidden for fifteen years. He put the location in your mind. You just have to learn how to access it."

"This is a lot to process," she looked at her parents, feeling betrayed by the two people she loved the most.

"Why don't you take a few minutes to change," Ramos agreed. "I know it's a lot, and I don't want to overwhelm you."

She was numb. Her mother bent down to kiss her forehead. Her father gave her a feeble smile and walked out of her room. Ramos followed her parents, and she noticed the familiarity he had with their house. How many times had he visited?

When she stood up, her legs felt weak. She made her way to the bathroom and flipped on the light switch. As bright light filled her vision, she looked at her reflection in the mirror on the vanity. She touched the glass, but nothing happened.

As she glanced in the mirror again, she noticed the many bruises and scrapes on her face. Her right eye was purple, and she had a long thin scratch cutting through her left cheek. The blood had long since dried and crusted over. A shooting pain seared through the back of her head, and she instinctively placed her hand over the area that hurt the most and was dismayed to find two very large goose-eggs. To add to her disappointment, she had a thin layer of mud surrounding her ears from the grimy creek.

She quickly showered, threw her wet hair into a bun, and changed into a pair of jeans and a sweater. After brushing her teeth, she made her way downstairs, hoping the charade would be over. When she walked into the kitchen, she found her parents and Ramos gathered around the table, a heavy silence surrounding them.

"How do you feel?" her mother asked, handing her a cup of tea.

"As good as can be expected."

Lana sat at the table and looked into her tea, the steam swirling in a thin mist. "Where did Drew go?"

"I'm sure he's packing," Ramos said. "We'll be leaving soon."

Looking directly at her uncle, she asked, "How did you travel through my mirror?"

"There are many ways to travel between dimensions," he began. "As you saw, mirrors are one way. Naturally occurring portals are another. In this dimension, places such as Roswell, Loch Ness, and the Bermuda Triangle are just a few gateways to other worlds."

She looked at the clock on the stove, surprised to see it was nearly three in the morning. She stifled a yawn, and her father took her mother's hand, squeezing it reassuringly.

"Are you married, or was that part of the act?"

"No, we're not married," her mother answered. "We've been friends for a long time though."

"And loyal friends to me as well," Ramos added.

"I don't know what to call you anymore." She took a sip of her tea. "Mom and Dad are so natural."

Her parents turned to Ramos, as if waiting for him to take the lead. Her mother looked as if she were fighting back an answer as she opened her mouth, but no sound came out.

"Jacqueline and Grayson are your parents," Ramos said. "My brother was never a father to you."

Her mother stood up and hugged her, kissing her on the cheek. Her father took her hand. Lana savored the moment, glad for the normalcy of the gesture.

"So, how do you know which mirrors are portals? Or are all mirrors portals?"

Ramos shook his head. "No, every mirror isn't a portal. Every dimension's archivist keeps a master list. Most of the mirrors are coated in a very thin layer of film so unsuspecting people won't fall through, which makes walking out of them difficult."

"Why didn't I ever go through my mirror?"

"We've always coated it when King Ramos left," her mother answered, sitting in her chair.

"I usually visit Grayson and Jacqueline a few times a year," Ramos added. "They were expecting me, so they wiped off the protective coating yesterday."

"And recoated it after he left," her mother added sheepishly, as if she had been caught doing something she shouldn't have.

"I never woke up during any of your visits? I mean, besides last night?"

"Sleeping dust," Ramos answered.

Lana glared at her parents. She couldn't believe they had kept the truth from her for so long. She was angry and didn't know what to think. Everything was being thrown at her so fast.

"Why did you use my mirror?" She turned back to Ramos. "Why not use a mirror in another room?" Suddenly, another thought took root in her mind, one that terrified her. "Were you watching me through the mirror?"

"No," he answered. "You can't watch someone through a mirror between dimensions. We put it in your room because it was comforting to know that you were only a slice of glass away from Bridian. I'm the only one that knows about the mirror, so it was safe."

"I never thought I'd say this," her mother looked around the kitchen sadly, "but I'm going to miss this place."

Her father smiled. "I will too."

"Do we really have to leave?" she asked, suddenly feeling very emotional. She looked around the kitchen, remembering the many family dinners it held.

"Yes," Ramos said. "The rebels know you're here. It makes sense to bring you home to Bridian."

Lana took another sip of her tea and thought of her friends. She wished she could see them again. It wasn't fair that her life was being uprooted, through no fault of her own.

"Did you hear something?" her father asked, standing abruptly from his chair.

Before anyone could respond, a loud bang resounded on their front door. Her father flew out of the kitchen, and her mother grabbed her arm, pulling her to her feet.

"Go to your bedroom," she whispered, pushing her toward the staircase. "Lock the door and don't let anyone in."

Lana ran upstairs. When she reached her bedroom, she closed the door behind her and locked it. Her heart was pounding, and she was breathing in big, heavy breaths. She set her head on the door, trying to calm her nerves.

She felt a cool breeze behind her, but before she had a chance to turn around and close the window, she heard someone laugh. She spun around and saw a man dressed in black a few feet from her. Too late, she realized that she had locked herself in her bedroom with the enemy.

"That wasn't so hard," a familiar voice growled.

She recognized Marty, her first attacker's accomplice. He grabbed the front of her shirt and pulled her away from the door. When he let her go, he reached into his pocket, revealing three opaque stones in the palm of his hand. She felt so drawn to them she took a step towards him.

Lana knew she should scream. Her window was open, and someone would hear her but was torn in two. She knew she should jump out of the window, do anything to escape, but all she wanted was to take those few steps and grab the stones.

She dropped to her knees. Looking up, she noticed the smile on Marty's face turn into a look of bewilderment. He took a faltering step backward. During his confusion, she began screaming.

"Shut up!" He ran to her, pulling her to her feet.

Marty dragged her to the window. She elbowed him in the stomach as hard as she could. When he recoiled, she tore herself free, ran to her door, and tried to unlock it, but he grabbed her around the waist and lifted her into the air.

"Nice try," he sneered, throwing her back to the ground. "You're going to pay for that."

As she lay on her carpet, she saw her pink and purple polka-dot umbrella and knew she had to try something, anything to get out of the horrible mess she was in. She reached for her umbrella, turned onto her back, and swung as hard as she could, slashing her makeshift weapon across the man's face as he knelt next to her. The force of the blow was enough to tip him over. She quickly got up, opened the door, and ran downstairs.

When she reached the first floor, she turned into the kitchen and came face-to-face with her father. He pushed her to the floor, hiding her from view. She looked up and saw that he had a wooden baseball bat in his arms. She heard Marty running down the stairs, but when he reached the bottom, her father stepped around the corner and swung the bat at him. He hit him in the face, which sent him careening to the ground. The stones flew out of his hands and landed at her feet.

Lana picked up the stones. Her father grabbed her hand and pulled her after him, leading her back upstairs. Her mother and Ramos appeared behind them.

"FIND THE GIRL NOW!" a voice bellowed from the kitchen.

When they were inside her room, her father slammed the door shut, locking it. Ramos stepped into the full-length mirror, disappearing. Once he had vanished, she walked up to the glass, looking for him. She had just enough time to take a deep breath before her parents pushed her into her reflection.

4

RETURN TO BRIDIAN

Walking through the mirror was the oddest sensation Lana had ever felt. It seemed as if she were swimming through a sea of silver. She lost sight of Ramos and could only hear her parents struggling behind her as she clutched the three stones in the palm of her hand. She had to find a way out of the mirror soon. She was slowly suffocating.

A rectangle of light appeared before her, and she walked toward it. She saw Ramos and grew excited. Moments later, a pair of hands grabbed her, pulling her through.

Once she emerged from the mirror, she noticed she was in a very large room. The walls were stone, and the only piece of furniture was the mirror she stepped out from. Her parents joined them, and Ramos pushed the portal backwards.

The force of the push managed to shatter the glass as the outline of a man started to appear. She looked at the jagged piece of glass that landed at her feet and noticed Marty looking up at her. A shiver went through her as she thought of his partner, the first man that attacked her in Frazier Woods.

"It's very easy to get lost traveling between dimensions," Ramos said. "You did very well."

She returned her gaze to the shard of glass at her feet and was relieved to see that Marty's image had vanished.

"That's seven years bad luck," she mumbled after a tense moment of silence.

"People bring themselves bad luck by believing in superstitions." Ramos smiled. "How could breaking a mirror really bring bad luck?" He brushed the broken mirror into a pile with his foot and continued, "Belief in superstitions actually causes bad things to happen. Your mind is a very powerful tool."

Lana thought about this, and it did seem to be true. When she complained about having a bad day, it ended up ten times worse, and when she thought about the good that had happened, the bad seemed to vanish. As she was thinking, she started playing with the three stones she had taken from Marty. She rolled them between her fingers as she glanced at her parents, surprised to see them glaring at the stones she held.

"Where did you get those?" Ramos asked, his eyes narrowed in concern.

She looked at her parents again, wondering if she was in trouble. When they turned away, she answered.

"I took them from the guy he knocked out with the baseball bat." She gestured to her father. "I think his name was Marty. Why?"

"Let me have a closer look at those," Ramos said, extending his hands toward her.

As she walked toward him, she noticed her mother step backwards, averting her eyes. When the stones were no longer in her possession, she felt sad. The look on her uncle's face told her she would not be getting them back. She wasn't even sure why she wanted them. They had no value to her.

"What's wrong?"

"I'm afraid I'll need to keep these," he answered, slipping the stones into his pocket.

Her parents looked relieved as he did this but still retained their distance from Ramos. She thought of ways to steal them back and then came to her senses. She had never stolen anything before and wasn't going to start.

She narrowed her eyes at her father. "I thought I wouldn't have to worry about being attacked?"

"There must be a traitor in the bureau," he answered. "We alerted them. They should be in their custody."

Her mother took Lana's hand and squeezed it reassuringly, letting her know that everything would be all right. When her mother dropped her hand, she looked at the shattered glass on the floor, and a pit formed in her stomach. Would she ever see Mt. Sinclair again?

"Where are we?"

"We're in Bridian. In fact, this is the castle you were born in," Ramos said as he gestured around the room. "I'll show you to your bedroom, and then we can eat breakfast."

"I'd like to know more about the stones." She was tired of the secrets and just wanted answers.

"They were created with black magic," Ramos answered. "They're commonly referred to as the Stones of Medora, since they were made in the caverns of Medora."

"Stay away from them," her father added. "They're dangerous."

"Alderic and his rebels used them to control people," Ramos continued. "They bring out your worst desires. They make you feel indestructible, like you can do anything. My brother gained followers with their addictive properties. I'm amazed that you managed to get away when he was using them against you, especially crossing dimensions. It takes years of practice to gain the self-control necessary to handle them."

Ramos looked to the floor. His face hardened, and his lips were pressed in a thin line. Her parents remained silent. Her mother's eyes were set on Lana and her father crossed his arms over his chest.

"There are very few people naturally immune to them," Ramos said. "I can handle them for short periods because I've had many years of practice, slowly increasing the amount of time spent with them in my possession. As you can see, Jacqueline and Grayson have not and are vulnerable to their effects. The rebels that used them against you must have had years of practice with them."

She looked to the floor. For some reason, she felt ashamed that she had been able to hold them when no one else could. Ramos walked to the door and opened it. He led them into a bright hall. A female soldier was standing guard, and she stiffened when she saw Lana and her parents but didn't say anything.

Ramos led them down the hall to the right. When they reached the end of the hall, he turned left. She was surprised they had yet to encounter anyone else. The halls were empty, and their footsteps echoed around them. She looked out the many windows they passed, trying to gather any information on her new home, but all she saw were trees, the green leaves blowing in the wind.

A moment later, Ramos stopped at a white door, opening it slowly. A large four-poster bed was on the opposite wall. Royal blue sheets adorned the bed, and giant fluffy pillows were resting at the head. At the foot of the bed was a wood chest, decorated with intricately carved designs. A huge dresser was in one corner of the bedroom, and two bookshelves, overflowing with books, were near the door. A fireplace was to the right of the bed. Her head flew in every direction as she tried to take in everything at once.

"This is my room?"

She took another step forward. She heard a rhythmic *tick* and noticed a huge grandfather clock against the wall to her right.

"This used to be your bedroom," Ramos said, looking out

the window to his left. "Although, the last time you were here, it looked a bit different. We've been updating it little by little."

"It's bigger than the room you grew up in," her father said sadly, putting his arm around her shoulders.

"I miss that room already."

Her mother left, her hands covering her mouth as a quiet sob escaped. Her father followed her mother into the hall.

"This has to be hard for them." Ramos crossed the room. "They raised you for fifteen years."

"They're the only parents I know, and nobody will ever replace them," she said as she sat on the bed.

"How are you feeling? About everything you've learned?"

"Well, I was worried there wouldn't be electricity," she said, smiling.

"Our world is very similar to the world you grew up in," he chuckled, walking back to the door. "You'll see. I'll have someone escort you to breakfast. I have some quick work to do."

Ramos walked out of the room. She allowed herself to sink deeper within the bed and began thinking, not about the strange events of the last day, but about her friends. She missed them terribly. It would have been nice to have been given the opportunity to at least say goodbye.

Lana continued to look around the room, her eyes settling on the chest at the foot of the bed. It was made of wood and stained with a dark cherry finish. She stood up and kneeled in front of it, disappointed when she found it locked.

She walked over to the dresser, opening each of the drawers in turn, looking for a key to fit the lock of the chest, but all she found were stacks of neatly folded clothing. As she closed the drawers, the bookshelves across the room caught her eye. She hoped no one expected her to read all the books they held.

She made her way to the grandfather clock and saw that it was much wider and taller than the grandfather clocks she was used to in Mt. Sinclair. She watched the swaying pendulum as it tried to escape the confinement of the dark brown wooden panels.

"Excuse me, I was sent to escort you downstairs."

Lana jumped. She had been so consumed in her thoughts she hadn't heard anyone join her. She turned around and saw a boy standing before her. He seemed to be about her age, and she smiled.

"You scared me."

"I apologize." The boy looked to the floor. "I was sent to bring you downstairs for breakfast."

The boy had short, curly black hair underneath a gray wool cap and striking green eyes. He was wearing a single white pearl around his neck. Without another word, he began walking, leading her through the intricate maze of the hallways.

"I'm Lana," she said, extending her arm towards him. "Obviously you already know my name since you were sent up here to get me, but, well, now you know I guess."

The boy stopped walking and placed his hand upon the cracked button that fastened his cloak at the neck. It seemed as if he wanted to shake her hand but couldn't bring himself to actually do it.

"My name's Terris," he said, then continued walking.

"It's nice to meet you," she called after him.

As she walked, she used the opportunity to glance at the many paintings and portraits on the walls. Cloaked people with faint smiles looked down at her. She wondered if she was related to them.

Many twists and turns later, the pair arrived at a huge stone stairway. Terris descended at a very fast pace and didn't notice that she was having trouble keeping up. When they reached the bottom, she followed him into an enormous dining hall. Two wooden chandeliers hung from either end of the room.

Three long wooden tables were situated in a triangle underneath the chandeliers.

"Over here, Lana." Ramos waved from the table furthest from the doors. "Usually there are more people, and we eat a bit later, but I thought it best to dine with family."

She took a seat between Ramos and a woman she had yet to meet. As if reading her mind, the woman looked at her.

"Hello," she said coldly. "I'm your aunt Charlotte."

The woman's long blonde hair was pulled into a bun underneath a beautiful gold crown, leaving tendrils to fall across her face when she moved. Her icy blue eyes, that perfectly countered her dark purple cloak, pierced her, making her very uncomfortable. Along with her parents, Charlotte, and Ramos, there were three more people also wearing dark purple cloaks sitting at the table. When Ramos noticed her glance at the three remaining people left to be introduced, he began a round of introductions.

"Lana, these are your cousins. This is Damon," he said, gesturing to the gentleman sitting across from her. He was very thin with sallow skin and brown curly hair underneath a small crown. "And this is Dominic," he continued, pointing to the boy sitting next to Damon who was smaller with the same brown eyes and curly hair underneath an identical crown. "And this is Deliah," he finished, gesturing to the girl sitting next to Dominic who had long curly brown hair underneath a crown, brown eyes, and a tiny freckle above her left eyebrow that perfectly mirrored the one on her own forehead.

Lana smiled shyly. She felt sick to her stomach. She hated meeting new people.

"What happened to your eye?" Deliah asked, placing her hands demurely on her lap.

"I had a long night."

"We were waiting for you before we served breakfast," Charlotte said as a cart rolled into the hall, followed by two older gentlemen and Terris, who were all wearing matching gray caps and cloaks.

She noticed the cart had not been rolling on the ground but floating in the air. The two men and Terris began lifting plates, silverware, napkins, and dishes full of steaming food onto the table.

When Terris set a glass of water in front of her she said, "Thank you, Terris." He looked at her for a moment before returning to his chore. "Your name's Terris, right?"

"Yes," he said with a bow. "If there's anything else you need, I'm at your service."

"It's best to leave them to their work," Charlotte interrupted and, in that moment, that one sentence, she knew she disliked her aunt very much.

"I think you should try a Choclochino. You'll like it." Her father poured a drink into a cup and stood up, walking it to her. "It's like hot chocolate."

She looked into the cup, watching the steam curl into the air.

"It's really good," Dominic exclaimed happily. "Can I have some too?"

"One cup," Charlotte replied, and then turned toward the two men and Terris. "You may leave now."

She felt uncomfortable. Why was a boy her age working and, better yet, why did her aunt talk down to him?

"Lana, how do you like your drink?" her father asked, trying to draw her attention away from her aunt.

She blew on the liquid before taking a tentative sip. "It's better than hot chocolate."

Deliah asked what hot chocolate was, and she grinned. She placed a piece of bread, eggs, and a sausage link on her plate. When she looked up, she saw her cousins avert their eyes, as if they had been caught watching her. She took a few bites of sausage and put her fork down, too nervous to eat.

She wondered what she would be doing in Mt. Sinclair if the rebels hadn't found her. She realized she would most likely be getting ready for school. It was Wednesday. She thought of Ava and Trevor. What would they think of her absence?

When Ramos dismissed everyone, she stood up and quickly walked out of the dining hall, pausing outside to wait for her parents.

"How was the cart floating? You saw that, right?"

Her father nodded. "There's magic here. You'll learn how to access it."

She didn't think she heard right. Her head felt like it was going to explode, and she wanted to talk to Ava and Trevor. They would help her make sense of it all.

"Is there a phone I can use? I want to call my friends."

"There are no phones here," her mother answered. "I'll send a message to their parents. I'll tell them we moved."

"Will I ever see them again?" She blinked back tears.

"I don't know," her mother answered. "Why don't you change, and we'll show you the Square."

"What's wrong with what I'm wearing?"

"It'll be easier to walk through town if you blend in," her father said gently. "No one wears jeans here."

"No phones or jeans?" she exclaimed, following her father as he started walking up the stone staircase. "Can we go back to Mt. Sinclair? I want to go home. I don't want to do this. I don't want to be here."

Her parents stopped walking, and her mother hugged her.

"This is all new," her mother said. "It's all right to feel scared."

"Once you settle in, everything will be fine," her father added.

Lana looked over the bannister. Her cousins walked out of the dining hall, arguing. Damon saw that she was watching him and looked away quickly. She turned back to her parents. If she had known that her life would change so drastically overnight, she would have spent more time with Ava and Trevor. She would have told off Nick and Laurie. She may have even told Cooper that she liked him.

"I just want to go home. I can't do this. I don't want to be a Princess. I don't want to be here."

"Well, whether you like it or not, you are a Princess," her mother said. "You can't change your birthright."

"You're safer here," her father said. "The army can protect you."

"Come on," her mother urged, taking her hand. "Change your clothes, and we'll show you around Bridian."

When they reached her bedroom, her mother went to the dresser and pulled out a pair of black pants and a dark purple top. She opened another drawer and pulled out a matching purple cloak. She handed the pile to her.

"We'll be right back," her mother said, closing the door.

She quickly changed, surprised that everything fit. She placed the cloak over her clothes and slid her feet into her sneakers. She wanted to keep something from Mt. Sinclair and didn't think they made her stand out too much.

She heard a knock on her door and went to open it, expecting to see her parents. Instead, she found Deliah and Dominic.

"We thought we would see if you needed anything," Deliah said, holding a large doll with long blonde hair. "And introduce you to Angelica."

Deliah placed the doll on the floor, and to her utter astonishment, it began singing. Lana screamed very loudly, before realizing that it was no doll. She was too lifelike. Dominic pushed Angelica away.

"No one likes her, Deliah. She always sings, and she's not even that good."

"Yes, she is!" Deliah stomped her foot.

With great curiosity, Lana watched Angelica stand.

"Don't kick me, or you'll be sorry," she said, her voice childlike.

"What is she? She can't be a doll."

"Angelica was a present from the Outcasts," Deliah said proudly, as if that answered her question.

Before Lana could ask what the Outcasts were, Dominic took his sister's arm, dragging her toward the door.

"Let's go, Deliah, this is boring."

"Dominic," Deliah said, her voice sugary-sweet. "Can't you see that I'm talking?"

Dominic dropped his sister's arm and sat on the floor, his head in his hands. She wondered where her parents were. She didn't think they would be gone so long.

"How old are you?" she asked after a moment of awkward silence.

"I'm fifteen," Dominic answered. "Deliah's thirteen."

"Is that what you wear over *there*?" Deliah asked, pointing to the pile of discarded clothes.

Lana didn't answer. She wasn't in the mood to talk about Mt. Sinclair when all she wanted to do was go back and forget the past day.

"Tell me what it's like over there," Deliah said musingly. "I've never been. Mom and Dad won't let me, or Dominic, go."

"Though they let Damon visit once, for two whole weeks," added Dominic, clearly interested in Deliah's question.

Before she could answer, they were interrupted. She had never been so happy to see her parents.

"Deliah, Dominic," her father said. "We just saw King Ramos. He's looking for you."

Deliah scooped up Angelica and marched out of the room. Dominic followed his sister, rolling his eyes behind her back.

"Let's go," her mother said. "It's supposed to rain soon."

Lana followed her parents back to the stone staircase.

When they were on the main floor, they walked straight instead of turning to go to the dining hall. When they reached a giant set of double doors, guarded by two soldiers, her father turned to her.

"It's very important you stay with us." When she nodded, he turned to one of the soldiers, a man with gray hair, and said, "We need a few soldiers to escort us to the Square."

The man left his post and walked around the corner. She studied the entryway as they waited. The walls were a white stone. Four tiny windows let in the sunlight.

"We have three soldiers that can accompany you," the man said, taking his place near the door. "They'll meet you outside."

When the huge double doors swung open, she saw the soldiers that would be accompanying them. Her father walked ahead to the soldiers and began talking, pointing to something past the drawbridge. A moment later, he rejoined them.

Lana held her hands over her eyes, squinting from the sun. She heard a splash of water and looked over the railing. A huge alligator-like creature swam past her, and she stopped walking, trying to see it better.

"What is that?" she asked, pointing to the monster in the water.

"That's a Monogrose," her mother answered without stopping to look. "They resemble alligators, although they're bigger and quicker. There are three of them that live in this moat."

She looked into the water again, and sure enough, two more of the beasts swam up to the first and began fighting—snapping their teeth, clawing, and biting one another. She ran off the drawbridge onto safer ground. The last thing she wanted was to fall into the water.

"Come on, Lana, Bridian Square is right up here," her father said, pointing straight ahead.

They had only walked a few feet when she noticed a huge fountain in the middle of a courtyard. A row of older houses and shops encircled the fountain, closing it off. A few people were milling about, either on foot or horses, but were too busy completing their own errands to notice her.

When she approached the fountain, she noticed that gold metallic sparkles were flowing from three circular tiers along with the water.

"This is amazing."

"It is," her mother agreed as she too marveled at its beauty. "I forgot how much I missed this place."

"This is the biggest fountain that I've ever seen."

"It's what's inside the fountain that's important," her father said, pointing to the wooden door built into its base.

To her astonishment, he walked up to the concrete and stepped into the pool of sparkles. He slowly walked to the wooden door and opened it. She tried to see what was hidden inside the concrete and marble but only saw darkness. Her father looked over his shoulder one last time before stepping into the doorway and disappearing into shadows.

5

THE MIRROR IN THE ABANDONED HALL

S he watched her mother step into the fountain. She held her hand out for Lana, who looked behind her at the scores of people entering and exiting the many shops that surrounded the Square but, for the most part, seemed to be ignoring them. As the wind eerily whispered into her ears and made the various shop signs rattle, she saw a young boy about her age trip down the steep steps of a somber looking store that had *Poklin's Variety* cleverly scribbled into the layers of dust on the windowpane.

Lana marveled at the fountain as she lowered her right foot into it, relieved to see that the metallic sparkles did not burn, and the water passed around her. She followed her mother into the dark doorway and met her father, who was impatiently tapping his foot inside the entrance. The three soldiers followed, and when they were all inside the alcove, her mother shut the door, startling her so much she jumped into her father.

"Sorry. It's dark in here!"

She noticed a row of small lights fastened on the wall. They seemed to descend deep into the floor. The circular room they were in had a set of stairs leading downward. The lights led the way.

"What's down there?" she asked, imagining all sorts of things—huge, creepy spiders topping the list.

"You'll see," her father said mysteriously.

She noticed that it got colder as they descended. After what seemed like an eternity, they reached the bottom, and she found herself in a large room filled with dozens of translucent orbs rotating in midair. The orbs were striking, each emitting a different colored hue and spinning.

"They're beautiful, but what are they?" she asked, thinking of all sorts of scenarios involving the magnificent orbs.

"These are the Orbs of Telorian," her mother answered. "They're portals to other dimensions."

"How did they get here?"

"They've always been here," her father answered. "The fountain was built to protect them."

As the soldiers spread out, she stepped up to an orb. She saw rolling green fields and groves of leafy trees blowing in the breeze. She moved to the next orb and peered inside. Flashes of lightning lit up a sandy landscape. When she stepped up to the next orb, she saw cracked, dry dirt and dying trees. She couldn't stop looking into the various orbs revealing outdoor markets under tents, palm trees, dusty walls, and complete darkness.

"Why is this orb black?"

"That's one of the chaotic worlds," her father answered. "Everything is constantly changing in that dimension. Nothing's stable. Look into the orb now."

As Lana peered into the once black orb again, she was astonished to see rocky terrain. Moments later, the rocky terrain disappeared, and an undersea world filled her vision. Then the orb turned completely black again. She glanced around the room once more in awe.

"Why are there different colored lights coming from the orbs?"

"The different hues represent the stability of the dimensions," her father answered. "What color is the one you were just looking at?"

"It's black. Even when the scene changes the outline remains black."

"The blue hues are stable, greens are moderately stable, oranges and yellows are fairly stable, followed by the reds and blacks," her father explained. "Stay away from the reds and blacks, they can be dangerous."

"Every dimension has its own version of our orbs," her mother added, gesturing for her to join her. "Come look."

Lana stepped closer to her. She was standing near an orb with a green hue. She looked into it and saw a stone wall.

"Where is this?"

"A chamber underneath the Great Sphinx of Giza," her father answered. "It contains orbs, like the ones you're looking at now."

"This is amazing."

Her father walked up to the spinning orb. He put his hands on either side of it, closed his eyes, and within seconds, it began to expand, becoming large enough to walk through.

"We'll be right back," her father said to the soldiers. He then turned to Lana. "You have to manipulate the energy surrounding the orbs in order to use them."

Her father stepped into the orb. She took a deep breath and followed. A moment later, she found herself in a dark chamber with spinning orbs. The orb they had stepped out of returned to its original size.

"We're inside of the Sphinx?" she stepped closer to the now shrunken orb and saw her mother waving back at her through its gauzy film.

"Technically, we're beneath it," her father answered, turning on a small flashlight he kept on his keychain.

The room had no doors and was very dark. In fact, the only other light than the flashlight was from the spinning orbs. She panicked, running her hands on the low ceiling, looking for the exit.

"Is this it? There's no way out?"

"No," her father said. "There's a trapdoor somewhere."

He stumbled in the dark, running his hands along the walls and ceiling. After a few minutes, he gave up, pointing the flashlight in her direction.

"I can't find the exit," he said. "We should get back anyway."

He stepped up to the orb they had come through, shut his eyes, and made it expand, as he had before. When the orb reached the appropriate size, she stepped into it and rejoined her mother.

"You missed Samoa Stanich," her mother said, looking at her father when he rejoined them. "We've only been back a few hours, and everyone's going to know."

"It's going to come out eventually." Her father shrugged his shoulders. "We might as well get it over with."

She felt the pit in her stomach again. What would happen when her birth father, and the rebels, found out she was in Bridian? Would they come looking for her?

Lana made her way back up the winding staircase, following her parents. The soldiers were behind her, silently observing. When they reached the top, her father leaned into the wall, forcing it open, and allowing them a passage out of the fountain's base. As they stepped into the light of day, and the fountain's spray of metallic sparks, she was astonished to see the once quiet Square was now bursting with commotion. People were running and screaming excitedly. The soldiers stepped in front of her.

Lana struggled to see what everyone was running from. She

froze when she saw a tall figure in a long black cloak. The hood of the cloak covered the person's head, leaving nothing but a dark shadow in place of the face.

One of the soldiers grabbed her arm and began running, dragging her out of the fountain. As she stumbled after him, she glanced back and saw a dozen more men and women, in the same long black cloaks, in different areas of the Square. Some were standing very still with arms folded across their chests while others chased frightened people into nearby shops.

"TELL YOUR KING THIS IS NUMBER TWO!" a man shouted as the remaining figures in black cloaks raised their right fists into the air then scattered throughout the Square.

The soldier kept running, dragging Lana with him. She heard her parents behind her. She wondered where they were going. The figures in black cloaks had been blocking the drawbridge, and the other two soldiers had stayed behind to help with the commotion in the Square.

"How are we going to get back in?"

"You're lucky I was available to accompany you," the soldier said, stepping up to an enormous tree. "Only the senior soldiers know about this passage."

The soldier pulled himself up the nearest branch. She stood with her parents and watched him climb to a knot in the tree trunk. He gestured for them to follow, and her father hoisted her up. When she was standing, she took a moment to regain her balance and plot a route up the tree. She hadn't climbed a tree in many years, and thankfully, the branch the soldier was waiting for them on was not too much higher than the one she was standing on.

When Lana joined the soldier, her parents began their ascent. She looked out from her new vantage point, grateful that no one had followed them. The soldier placed his hands on the knot in the tree trunk, lifting it on hidden hinges and revealing a passage. The tree was a very realistic fake.

The soldier crawled into the passage. When he gestured that it was safe to do so, she followed. As her eyes adjusted to the darkness inside the hollow tree, she saw she was standing on a tiny platform. The soldier was on a ladder, looking up at her.

Lana stepped onto the ladder and followed him deeper into the tree. When her feet touched solid ground again, she breathed a sigh of relief. She saw her mother descending the ladder and her father at the top. He closed the hidden door, extinguishing what little light had come through the hole and bathing them in darkness. He switched his keychain flashlight on and made his way to them.

"Who were those people in the black cloaks?"

"Rebels," the soldier answered. "They've been very active the last few weeks. Follow me, I'll lead us out of here."

She felt her mother's hand take hold of hers. Her father joined the soldier and used his flashlight to guide the way. They made their way down the stone passageway, walking very slowly. As the tunnel sloped downward, the temperature dropped, and she shivered.

"We're under the moat now," the soldier explained when she asked why it had gotten so cold.

When the tunnel began to slope uphill, the temperature rose. Lana found she was having trouble breathing in the damp, musty air and felt claustrophobic in the cramped tunnel. When they finally reached the end of the passage, the soldier slid a camouflaged panel of wall a few feet to the left. She gasped when she saw that they were looking into her bedroom. The pendulum on the grandfather clock had stopped moving, giving them enough room to squeeze out. When they were inside her bedroom, and the door was secured behind them, the pendulum started moving again.

"Thank you for the assistance," her father said.

The soldier turned to Lana. "You can lock this so no one can enter the room. Only a handful of us know about it, so you have nothing to worry about. It's new, built only a few years ago."

The man showed her how to lock the panel into place and bowed when he left. She felt uncomfortable when he bowed but didn't say anything.

"If the castle is ever attacked, use this passage and find a man named Emeric," her father said. "He's a friend. He lives in a city called Ganyon Falls."

"We should go talk to King Ramos," her mother added. "See if there's anything we can do to help."

"Don't use that passage unless you absolutely have to," her father warned.

Her mother hugged her, kissing her on the cheek. "Maybe you can read something. Relax a little. The last twenty-four hours have been quite stressful."

With one last look at Lana, her parents walked out of the room, leaving her in stunned silence as she contemplated everything she had been through. She took her mother's advice and walked to the bookshelf. She chose a random book, hoping it would relax her when she heard a knock on her door. She tossed the book on the bed and opened the door, surprised to see an older man holding a tray of food and a frosted glass.

"You missed lunch," the man said, bowing to her. "King Ramos asked that it be brought to your room."

She brought the tray of food and glass to her bed, placing them on the floor when she sat down. She picked up the book and studied the cover.

"This should be interesting," she thought as she thumbed through *A Simple Guide to Levitation.*

The first picture caught her eye. A table and four chairs were floating in the air, but what was extraordinary about this particular picture was that there were four people sitting on the floating chairs. She sat on her bed and began to read.

While levitating objects can be difficult, here are some simple guidelines to make the process easier. Remember that daily meditation is ideal for the enhancement of your natural abilities.

1. *Pick an object. Beginners often make the mistake of picking an object that is too big to practice on. Remember to save the big objects for the experts!*
2. *Close your eyes and envision the object. Don't just envision the front, visualize the back, top, and bottom as well.*
3. *Begin meditation, any meditation will do. This is an important step that every beginner must learn to master.*
4. *After sufficient meditation, open your eyes and concentrate on reaching two invisible hands towards the object of focus and 'lift' it into the air.*
5. *Practice daily, and you too can master the phenomenon of levitation!*

She set the book down. Could she learn to levitate objects? She remembered that the breakfast cart had been floating. As she stared at the closed book, she thought about the steps she had read.

"Pick an object, meditate—no wait, close your eyes," she muttered as the book in her hands began to shake.

Lana had no idea what was happening and couldn't break her focus from the book. The shaking stopped, and the book began to rise. She watched wide-eyed as it rose higher and higher until someone knocked on her door, which broke her concentration. The book fell to the floor with a loud bang.

"Are you okay?" Damon asked, peering into her room.

"I'm fine," she lied, trying to catch her breath. "You startled me."

Damon looked at her with his eyebrow raised, as if he hadn't believed her, but she didn't feel like explaining what had happened. She could have imagined the entire incident. Damon swiped his chin-length brown hair out of his eyes, walked across the room, and sat next to her. His brown eyes pierced her.

Finally, she moved away from him and asked, "Did you need something?"

"I came to see how you were," he answered. "I heard you were in the Square."

"News sure does spread fast around here." She eyed the book on levitation curiously. "The rebels just stood there."

"Well, this can't be easy for you. If you need someone to talk to, I'm here."

Lana felt uncomfortable. He seemed disingenuous, as if he wasn't being sincere in his offer. Damon stood up and left without even saying goodbye, leaving her puzzled. As she contemplated his strange behavior, Deliah walked into her bedroom through the open door Damon had not bothered to close.

"What was Damon doing in here?" she asked, stepping into the room.

"I don't know." She shrugged her shoulders. "He said if I needed to talk, he was here for me."

"He doesn't talk to anyone. I can't even remember the last time he talked to me," Deliah said, and Lana could tell she was just as puzzled. "Anyway, Dominic is waiting for us downstairs. We thought we'd show you around."

"That's all right, I have things to do up here," she said. The last thing she wanted was to spend the day with the squabbling siblings.

Deliah took her arm, obviously not used to people telling her no. She didn't want to argue, so she followed Deliah out of her bedroom. They walked to a large mirror at the end of the hall, mounted to the wall. Deliah stepped into it, still holding her arm. She was surprised to see she had appeared in a new room instantaneously and realized it was because she was traveling a short distance.

Lana found herself in a small room with a dozen mirrors. Deliah dropped her hand and walked across the room to the farthest mirror. When she joined her, she looked into the glass and was amazed to see not only her reflection, but a stone hall just like the one they had stepped out of. However, as she looked closer, she saw it was not the same, and Dominic was pacing back and forth, arms behind his back.

"Can he see us?"

"I forgot you don't know the shortcuts," Deliah exhaled. "He can't see us unless we step closer to the mirror. All he sees is his reflection."

Deliah led her to another mirror, and she looked into it. An enormous room with cluttered counters was beyond the glass, behind her reflection. A handful of people were walking past the mirror. She even saw Terris walk by. She instinctively stepped backwards, not wanting to be seen.

"What room is that?"

"That's the kitchen," Deliah answered. "Come on, Dominic's waiting."

They walked back to the mirror Dominic was pacing in front of and walked through the cold glass.

"What took you so long?" Dominic demanded as soon as Deliah stepped through the mirror.

Before a fight could erupt, Lana answered, "Deliah was showing me the shortcuts."

"That gathering in the Square has everyone panicked," Dominic said, then began walking down the hall. "Is it true? Were you really there?"

Lana didn't understand how everyone had already heard

the news. "Nothing happened. People were running around and screaming, but the rebels just stood there."

"Well, it sure means something," Dominic whispered. "Hurry up."

"I thought you were going to show me around the castle?"

Dominic snorted then said, "First we're going to see what we can find out. It should be easy because most of the guards were sent to the Square."

They continued walking, passing many empty rooms, until Dominic stopped in front of a huge doorway. The door was shut, and nobody else was in the hall, save the three cousins.

"What are we doing?" she asked, not bothering to whisper, as no one was remotely near them.

"SHH!" Deliah and Dominic said at the same time, both putting a forefinger to their lips to signal the importance of silence.

Deliah and Dominic leaned against the door very carefully. Lana placed her ear against the wood and listened, surprised that she could hear inside the room.

"That was the second time," a man said angrily.

"The next one won't be as friendly. Something has to be done!"

"We can't beat them," another added. "They're coming out of hiding."

"The old fool had to die before he could tell us where it was hidden," the first man said.

"Old fool," Ramos repeated. "That old fool was once your King, show some respect, Damarius! It's remained hidden for the past fifteen years. I would rather it stay that way than be in the hands of my brother!"

"Forgive me, my King," Damarius said. "I didn't mean to offend you, but we're running out of time and resources. Who's to say they haven't found it yet?"

"If you were doing your job, then you would know if they've found it," Ramos said.

"We can't let them divide us," she heard her father speak up. "Don't you see that's what they're doing?"

The room fell silent, and outside the door, Lana, Deliah, and Dominic exchanged worried looks. She was going to leave when the conversation caught her attention.

"What about Carlecia? Alderic still wants her?"

She turned around and pressed her ear against the door again.

"She's safe here," Ramos said. "It would be pointless to send her into hiding again. Our army can guard her now. We know Alderic doesn't want her back simply because he misses her."

"The only thing he misses is the magic surrounding her," a woman said slowly.

She could feel Deliah and Dominic looking at her but was too focused on the conversation.

"How could any father do that to his child?" Damarius asked. "She'll be very powerful, perhaps more so than he is. Are you sure she's not already working with him?"

"She isn't working with him," her father sighed. "I've already gone over this. She just found out the truth yesterday. She's a good kid."

"Of course you think that, you've pretended to be her father for fifteen years," Damarius sneered. "Perhaps you're getting too attached."

"That's not necessary," Ramos interrupted. "It's good for Lana to see both Jacqueline and Grayson. This was all thrown on her so fast."

"Who's to say she's as innocent as we all think?" Damarius asked. "You said it yourself, the Stones of Medora held no power over her. NONE! Already the will for the Rebellion runs through her."

She felt dizzy. It was all too much. She slid to the floor as her cousins sprang to life. Dominic grabbed her hand and began running.

When they reached the end of the hall, she heard the door open. She followed Dominic around another corner and saw an enormous painting of a weeping willow tree over a peaceful lake. Dominic pushed her to keep running, but in their haste to get away, they didn't see Terris walking in the opposite direction, happily humming, until it was too late. They collided, and she fell into the picture.

She found herself in a large room, looking out into a backward picture of the lake. Deliah ran into the painting and knocked her back to the ground just as Terris was thrown in. When Dominic jumped in after them, he pushed the group away from the painting. Deliah and Dominic held their forefingers to their lips again with such urgency neither Lana nor Terris protested.

"I swear I heard something," a gruff voice said from the hallway.

"Come on," another said. "We have more important things to do than chase ghosts."

They exhaled a collected sigh of relief.

"That was close," Deliah whispered.

"Where are we?"

"Another shortcut," Deliah said while trying to catch her breath. "That mirror was painted to look like a picture though. All these years and I didn't even know."

"I knew," Dominic said. Although, from the tone of his voice, she knew he was lying.

"Was all that true?" Deliah asked, turning to Lana.

"Who cares," Dominic said before she could answer. "She doesn't remember anything anyway." Suddenly, he turned on Terris. "What were you thinking, barreling down the hallway like that?"

"I was on my way back to my room," Terris answered,

looking at the ground. "I finished my work for the day. I didn't mean to run into you."

"Let's just find a way out of here," Deliah said.

"We're not going back yet." Dominic looked around the room. "We'll be in trouble for listening to them."

"I'll go first," Terris volunteered. "If I'm caught, I'll tell everyone the noise was me."

"That would work," Dominic said.

"Who are you?" Deliah asked. "Do you work here?"

"No, Terris, you don't have to do that," Lana said, his smile turning into a frown when her cousin asked him who he was. "We either all leave together or find another way out."

"Who made you Queen?" Dominic asked. "If memory serves correctly, your father ruined that for you."

"Shut up, Dominic," Deliah said. "Lana's right. Besides, this was your idea. If anyone should go out there and take the blame, it should be you!"

"Fine, we'll go through that mirror then," Dominic said, pointing to another mirror across the empty room.

As she followed her cousins to the mirror, she realized all of this was beginning to feel normal. She had seen so many strange things already walking through mirrors no longer fazed her. When she approached the mirror, she saw the faint outline of a wall behind her reflection.

"Thank you," Terris whispered, startling her, "for talking to me and remembering my name. I have lessons with them. Every child living in the castle does. They've never bothered to get to know me though."

"Out of the way," Dominic said, pushing through them. "That hallway doesn't look familiar."

Dominic stepped through the mirror. He looked down both sides of the hall. When it looked clear, he motioned them to follow. First Deliah, then Lana, and finally Terris stepped through.

"Does this look familiar to you, Del?" Dominic asked his sister.

"No," she answered, sneezing. "It's very dusty."

"What about you?" Dominic asked Terris.

"No, it doesn't look like it's been used in a while."

"This must be one of the abandoned halls," Deliah said excitedly. "I heard Dad talk about them before. Bad things happened here."

"Grow up, Deliah," Dominic said, rolling his eyes. "If this is one of the abandoned halls, how did we get here?"

"That mirror was obviously disguised as a painting. Why do you think that was?"

"Let's look around, maybe we can figure out where we are," Dominic said, walking down the long hallway.

"What happened in the abandoned hall?"

Deliah and Dominic exchanged glances, and Terris looked to his feet. It appeared as if they were afraid of looking at Lana or answering her question.

"I, uh, we don't know," Deliah answered. "I heard my dad say that terrible things happened in the hall, so he had it closed off. All the doors were barred, and the mirrors sealed. We've spent years trying to find a way here."

"Deliah, we don't even know if this is that hall or not," Dominic said angrily.

"Well, I've never seen it before, have you?" Deliah asked, her voice growing higher when Dominic ignored her. "Does any of this look familiar?"

"Come on, let's see where the hallway goes," Dominic said.

The hall was dark and dreary. Not an ounce of light escaped any of the windows, as the dust covering them was much too thick. She saw a door and desperately hoped it led to a part of the castle near her bedroom. Dominic reached the door first and waited for everyone to catch up, then pushed it open. Lana's spirits plummeted. Before them was an empty room, save for a huge dusty mirror surrounded on either side by tattered red drapes.

"Great, there's no way out," she muttered.

The thought of walking down the abandoned hall again made her mad. She wanted to get away from her cousins as soon as possible.

"Maybe the mirror goes somewhere," Dominic said.

Everyone walked across the room. Deliah leaned over the dirty mirror and started blowing dust off it while Dominic held a tentative hand to the glass. She found herself holding her breath, but when Dominic pushed on the mirror, nothing happened.

"Nice going, Dominic," Deliah exclaimed, pushing her brother away from her. "Thanks to you, we have to walk all the way back to the painted mirror!"

"Stop fighting, this isn't going to help!" she said but was too late.

Dominic caught his balance and pushed his sister with all his strength, sending her atop the mirror. Glass shattered in tiny pieces, piercing Deliah's skin. Terris ran over to Deliah while Lana grabbed Dominic before he could hit his sister again.

She saw that her cousin had deep scratches on her arms, face, and legs, but when Deliah sat up, no one was looking at her anymore. When the mirror broke, a hidden room had been uncovered. Without a word, she stepped into the room, pushing aside the huge, dusty, red drapes.

Lana shuddered. Before her was the room she had dreamed about for the past fifteen years, with the two thrones and the enormous fireplace. She was standing in the very room where her grandfather and mother had been murdered.

6

FOOTPRINTS IN THE DUST

Lana took another step into the room as Deliah slumped to the ground. Dominic bent down, put his sister's arms around his shoulder, and tried to lift her. When that failed, he too fell to the floor, allowing his sister's head to rest on his shoulder.

"I'm so sorry, Deliah," Dominic whispered as tears gathered in the corners of his eyes.

After a moment of silence, Terris spoke up, "We should go back. She needs help."

"I'm fine," Deliah said slowly. "I just need to rest for a minute."

Lana frowned. Her cousin did not look well, but she desperately wanted to stay. The room looked exactly the way it did in her dreams, and she wanted to explore.

"Deliah, you're not fine," she said. "Those cuts look deep. We're going to have to carry her back the way we came," she said to Dominic and Terris, but something caught her eye. "Someone's been here recently."

"What?" Dominic and Terris asked in unison, momentarily forgetting about Deliah.

"Look, there are footprints in the dust," she explained, pointing to a row of prints across the room.

Lana could hardly believe what she saw. The room looked so dusty, as if no one had ventured into it in ages. She took a step closer, wondering why she missed the footprints when she had first entered the room, but on closer examination realized that they too had a thin layer of dust atop them.

As if reading her mind, Terris added, "We must have missed them because the prints are covered with dust, camouflaging them."

She followed the prints and came to a stop next to the huge fireplace when an unexpected voice startled them.

"What are you doing here?" Damon asked.

"You have to help us bring Deliah back," Dominic said, struggling to stand under her limp body.

"How did she get hurt?" Damon asked, glancing around the room, his gaze finally settling on Lana.

"She fell onto the mirror," Dominic answered, glaring at both Lana and Terris, daring them to contradict him.

Damon slowly walked over to Lana, who was still standing across the room by the enormous fireplace.

"You remember," he said with wide, unblinking eyes. "Tell me what you know."

"Damon, what's wrong with you?" Dominic shouted angrily. "We need to help Deliah!"

"You can tell me. We're family," he said, ignoring his brother.

"I don't know what you're talking about," she answered, fumbling for the right words. "We stumbled into the mirror with the picture of the lake and found ourselves here. We need to help Deliah. She doesn't look good."

Damon snapped out of his trance and rushed to his sister. He lifted Deliah out of Dominic's arms and cradled her in his own.

"Come on, I'll lead the way out."

Damon, Deliah, and Dominic left the room while Terris waited for her. She slowly followed her cousins, her mind working in overdrive. Had Damon been in the abandoned hall before? Whose footprints were in the dust?

"Is this the abandoned hall?" Dominic asked his brother.

"I don't know," he snapped. "I just stumbled here as well. If you tell anyone about this place, you'll get in trouble, so let's keep it our secret."

When they reached the painted mirror, Damon stepped back and allowed Dominic, Terris, and Lana through first. She had no idea why Damon was acting so strange and was very uncomfortable being around him.

"Remember, not a word of this to anyone," he said, breaking the silence when they had all stepped out of the mirror. "I'll bring Deliah to her bedroom. If anyone asks, we were playing Parsneakity."

Dominic nodded in agreement. Damon wasn't going to leave until they all had, so she nodded along with Terris. She didn't know what Parsneakity was but wanted to get as far from Damon as she could.

When Damon left, Terris began walking down the hall she and her cousins escaped from earlier. Dominic turned on his heel and began walking in the opposite direction. She reluctantly followed her cousin. He led her to a mirror that she recognized. When he stepped into it, she remembered it was the same mirror Deliah had shown her earlier and knew it led to the room of mirrors.

"I didn't mean for any of this to happen," Dominic explained when Lana rejoined him in the room with the polished mirrors. "I just wanted to see what everyone was so worked up about."

"I know, but obviously there was a reason they were talking

in secret. And you don't have to be so mean to Terris. He seems nice."

"Why do you care?" Dominic said. "He's not one of us."

"What do you mean *one of us*?" she asked, incredulous at her cousin's manners. "Because he wasn't born a Prince doesn't make him any less of a person."

She stepped into the mirror and found herself in the hall near her bedroom. When she was in her room, she slammed the door behind her. She looked around sadly. It felt as if she were in someone else's bedroom, living their life. Suddenly, the door opened, and her parents marched in, looking very angry.

"We were on our way up here to get you for dinner, and we ran into Damon," her mother said, crossing her arms over her chest. "What happened to Deliah?"

Lana shrugged her shoulders.

"What happened to her?" her father asked.

She looked to the floor. She hated lying but didn't want to get in trouble.

"Well, we were playing Parsnikity, and she got hurt."

"How do you play Parsneakity?" he asked, subtly correcting the name of the game.

She was at a loss for words. She had no idea what the rules of the game were or how it was played. She just knew it would not be that far-fetched to get as hurt as Deliah was, otherwise Damon wouldn't have told them to say she hurt herself playing the game. She looked around the room, giving herself a moment to think of something to say.

"We know you weren't playing Parsneakity," her mother said. "Damon fed us the same line, but I can tell it's a lie."

"You'll be starting lessons tomorrow," her father said. "That should keep you out of trouble. King Ramos is going to assign a soldier to you. I was initially against the decision, but now I know it's the right one."

"What do you mean? Someone's going to follow me around?"

"It's for the best."

"No." She crossed her arms over her chest. "I need to fit in. How am I going to make friends with someone following me?"

"You need to be protected," her father countered. "This is for the best. You'll see."

Lana didn't believe him, but there was nothing she could do. She didn't know how being followed by a member of the army was going to help her fit into her new life. If she couldn't go back to Mt. Sinclair, a small part of her hoped that maybe she could be a different person in Bridian, someone with lots of friends. If she was going to be followed by the army, she doubted that would happen.

She joined her parents for dinner and was happy to see the dining hall was as empty as it had been for breakfast. Besides her parents, Ramos, Charlotte, and Dominic, the table was empty. Deliah had gone to sleep early, and Damon hadn't felt like joining them, which was fine with her. Dominic was quiet throughout dinner, barely looking up from his plate. When Ramos dismissed everyone, she jumped up from her seat and flew out of the dining hall.

She followed her parents back to her bedroom, still upset with them. Once she brushed her teeth, she found a pair of pajamas in the dresser. She quickly changed and jumped into her bed. She closed her eyes but was overtaken with thoughts. How had she made the book levitate? Had Damon been in the abandoned hall before?

Sometime later, thoughts of Damon switched to those of lessons. The night before the first day of school, she always felt anxious, imagining what classes would be like and if the year would be any different than the last. What scared her the most was that she had absolutely no idea what to expect.

She tossed and turned the entire night, her mind

constantly reeling. After what seemed like hours of restlessness, she decided to take a walk, maybe even find something to eat. She opened her bedroom door and stepped into the cold hallway, bumping into a man wearing a dark blue cloak with a tiny gold and purple crest near the collar.

"Who are you?"

"My name's Grant," he answered. "I'm here to make sure you don't get into any more trouble."

"I was just going to find something to eat. I'm starving."

"You're in luck, breakfast is in half an hour," he said as he bowed and shut the door in her face, leaving her to ponder where the night, and her previous life, had gone.

After Lana showered, she dressed in a pair of gray pants and a short-sleeved white shirt. She was in the process of running her hands through her hair, in a feeble attempt to detangle it, when someone knocked on the door. She was surprised to see Deliah.

"I didn't think I'd be seeing you today."

"I'm fine," Deliah said. "Your eye looks better."

"Was there a man out there?" she whispered.

"Just Grant," Deliah replied in her normal, although loud, voice. "How long has he been there?"

She shook her head in disbelief. If he was right outside her door, she knew he had heard Deliah.

"I think he's been there all night."

Deliah shrugged her shoulders. "Come on, we have to go downstairs for breakfast. By the way, have you seen Angelica? I haven't seen her since yesterday afternoon."

"Nope," she answered as she tiptoed her way to the door and peeked into the hallway, glancing to the left.

"I'm still here."

"There's no need to worry about me," she said sweetly. "I'm going to walk down with Deliah."

"Orders are orders," Grant said. "Until I'm stationed elsewhere, I stay with you. Besides, I miss lessons."

Deliah stepped into the hall and shoved a stack of books at Lana. She glanced at the pile sadly. She wasn't in the mood for reading or school.

"I think these are the books you'll need today," Deliah explained. "Maris will tell you what to bring tomorrow."

"How long do lessons last?"

"It depends, usually a couple hours."

As they walked, she remembered the conversation they had overheard before they found the abandoned hall.

The only thing he misses is the magic surrounding her.

How could any father do that to his child? She'll be very powerful, perhaps more so than he is. Are you sure she's not already working with him?

What magic was surrounding her? What did her father do to her as a child? Why did they think she would be powerful? She didn't feel powerful. If anything, she felt weak. She was lost, confused.

"What do you know about magic?" she asked Deliah, leaning close so Grant wouldn't hear.

"This is about yesterday, isn't it?" Deliah whispered while pretending to study a portrait of a plump woman in an ugly blue dress. When Lana nodded, she continued, "I've heard that your father had his rebels infuse you with some kind of magic. I don't know much about it, but it can't be true, right? You seem normal enough to me."

Was it true? Had Alderic willingly handed her over so his rebels could infuse her with their magic? Would she turn out to be just like him? Maybe it was inevitable. The Stones of Medora held little power over her.

"Do you remember what happened when we found the abandoned hall?" she asked her cousin, trying to gain insight into Damon's behavior.

"Not really, I remember the fight with Dominic."

"Well, Damon found us," she began but was interrupted by a loud voice.

"Where have you two been?"

She looked down the staircase and saw Charlotte looking up at them, wearing a blue dress, strikingly similar to the one worn by the woman in the portrait.

"We've been waiting for you!"

"Sorry," Deliah mumbled as she picked up the hem of her dress and skipped down the stairs, joining her mother.

"Your face has a lot of healing to do," Charlotte said, taking Deliah's chin with her forefinger and thumb, inspecting her face. "How many times have I told you not to play that silly game? You are a Princess, and your appearance is very important. And you," Charlotte turned her attention to Lana, "your face doesn't look much better either."

Lana rolled her eyes and followed her aunt into the crowded dining hall. It seemed as if every eye was upon her when she walked in. She carefully made her way to the table. She didn't want to trip or embarrass herself in front of everyone. Ramos was sitting by himself, her mother was talking to Damon and Dominic, and her father was whispering to the man next to him. She tried to see who the man was, but her father blocked her view until she got closer.

"Drew!" she exclaimed when she stepped up to the table, which brought confused stares from both Charlotte and Deliah.

She sat down as Charlotte questioned, "Who's Drew?"

"It's good to see you!"

"I know your name is Contlay," she felt herself explaining. "But I guess I'm used to Drew."

"That's all right, the name grew on me anyway." Contlay shrugged his shoulders. "Do you think we can meet after your lessons?"

"I don't know when I'll be done," she answered, assuming he had news of Ava and Trevor.

"Don't worry about that, I'll catch up with you."

Once everyone was seated, Terris entered the room with six others. They were all dressed in gray cloaks and matching caps, the same style he wore the day before. Three floating carts slowly made their way to each table. Terris and another man escorted the longest cart to her own table.

"We don't know where King Simon stands," she heard Ramos whisper. "Langdon and his boy should be back tonight. I hope they come back with good news, for once."

"Give me the pencil, Deliah!" Dominic shouted, shifting her attention. "I have to finish my homework."

Lana looked at her cousins and found them fighting over a dark brown wooden pencil Deliah was twirling in the air. Dominic had books stacked on the table in front of him, leaving no room for his breakfast plate.

"Deliah, give your brother the pencil," Ramos interjected absentmindedly.

"Homework is to be done after class, not right before class," Charlotte scolded. "Perhaps if you had been doing homework instead of playing Parsneakity, Deliah's face wouldn't be bruised! What will people think?"

"I don't care," Deliah sighed dramatically.

Ramos stood up, prompting everyone else in the room besides those at his table to stand as well.

"My friends," he began, motioning those in gray to hold off serving for the moment. "It's with great honor that we breakfast together and an even greater honor that my niece has finally returned to our great city."

Everyone in the room looked at her again, and her cheeks flushed. Ramos motioned those standing to sit back down. Once the room was silent, he joined her at her seat, holding a shiny silver crown.

Ramos took Lana's hand and pulled her to her feet. The crown was encrusted with tiny diamonds. She felt awkward and uncomfortable standing in front of everyone, the center of attention. She looked at her parents and saw that her mother had tears in her eyes.

Ramos gently placed the crown on her head, and the room burst into a shower of applause. Once the applause subsided, Ramos walked back to his seat, and she sat, trying to blend back in. As the meal of eggs, ham, bacon, and bread was served, she wondered how long she was going to have to wear the crown. It felt heavy on her head.

"Dominic, move your books!" Deliah exclaimed. "I have no room to eat."

"Just think, you have to spend the whole day with them," her father joked.

Lana idly rearranged the food on her plate. She tried to remember her life in Mt. Sinclair, but it seemed like ages ago. She missed her friends terribly and wished she could go back.

Half an hour later, Ramos dismissed everyone. She followed Deliah and Dominic out of the dining hall, eager to leave Damon's presence. Even though they hadn't spoken, she caught him watching her.

"Where are we going for lessons?" she asked as she read-justed the crown on her head.

"The library," Deliah answered, as if she would know where that was.

Lana set off after Deliah and Dominic. As she followed her cousins, Grant walked beside her. She decided that if he was to follow her, for what was sure to be the rest of her life, she would at least learn something about him.

"How long have you been in the army?"

"Sixteen years," Grant answered proudly. "My father, grand-father, and great-grandfather were all soldiers for Bridian."

"Do you remember me?"

Grant nodded. "There wasn't a dry eye to be found the day you were sent into hiding."

She looked to her feet, unsure of what to say. Grant slowed his pace and took her books from her. As she walked, she thought up possible ways to show King Ramos she didn't need to be followed anymore. They soon came upon an enormous room; empty, save for three arches that led to three different halls.

"Hurry up!" Deliah called as she walked through the left arch.

Dominic was tapping his foot impatiently, reluctantly waiting for them. Once she and Deliah caught up, he turned on his heel and continued walking.

"I don't know what's wrong with him," Deliah said. "I asked him as we were walking, but he looked back at you."

"I don't like the way he treats other people."

"This is about that boy, isn't it?"

"He has a name, Deliah, and it's not just about him," she answered as they stepped into an enormous room.

Her breath caught in her throat. The library was beautiful, filled with leather bound books sitting on dark wooden bookcases. Heavy, plush curtains framed the enormous windows, and a huge fireplace took up the entire wall to her left with cozy couches and chairs before it.

Deliah began walking up a set of stairs before them. When they reached the second floor of the library, her cousin pulled her into a room to their right. She let her eyes adjust to the bright light and saw half a dozen people talking happily. All conversation stopped when her presence was detected, even Deliah stepped away from her.

Lana glanced around the room and saw four wooden tables. At each table were four wooden chairs. As she looked around the room, a tall woman with long brunette hair walked up to her.

"Hello," the woman said. "I'm Maris, your instructor."

She heard chairs being shuffled, and everyone took their seats.

"Please take a seat at the empty table." Maris pointed at a chair.

Lana walked to the lone table, followed closely by Grant. As she passed Deliah, she noticed her cousin avert her eyes and open one of her books. When she reached the table, she sat on the closest chair, turning her head so she wouldn't have to look at those curiously watching her.

"Let's take a moment to introduce ourselves to Lana," Maris said, looking at Terris. "Since she already knows Deliah and Dominic, we'll start with Terris and work our way around the room."

"Actually, I already know her too," Terris said, his cheeks turning red.

Dominic rolled his eyes, and the boy sitting next to Terris shouted, "Terris finally has a girlfriend!"

Terris stared at his clasped hands.

"That's enough, Ivan," Maris warned the blonde-haired boy. "Introduce yourself."

"I'm Ivan Pilkins," the boy said, not bothering to look up.

When he didn't say anything else, Maris said, "Please tell her something about yourself, your age, and why you are living in the castle will suffice."

Ivan exhaled loudly before continuing, "I'm fifteen. My father's an advisor to King Ramos."

Maris pointed to the boy sitting to Ivan's left.

"My name's Randy Watts," the boy said in a bored voice as he thumbed through the book in front of him. "I'm sixteen, and my father's a soldier stationed at the castle."

"I'm Marnie Martin," a bubbly girl with green eyes and long blonde hair exclaimed from Deliah's table. "I'm fifteen, and my mother is an advisor to the King."

The last person in the room to be introduced was a boy with black hair and brown eyes. He was sitting at Dominic's table, whispering excitedly in his ear. After a tense moment, he realized they were waiting on him.

"My name's Carter Linley," the boy said, his cheeks red. "I'm fifteen, and both my mother and father are soldiers for Bridian."

She looked over those in the room again, trying to remember everyone's names, as Maris walked towards her.

"Kiernan Emerson will be back tonight. He's sixteen, and his father is an advisor to King Ramos," Maris said when she was standing in front of her. "There are also a few younger children, but they have the day off. They come three days a week."

Ivan slammed his fist on the table while exclaiming, "Lucky little—"

"Enough Ivan," Maris interrupted over the peal of laughter that erupted from the class. "I'll be working with Lana today. Mrs. DeGette will be here shortly, so you have some free time to study silently. When she arrives, you'll each be quizzed on your homework."

The room was quiet as everyone opened their books and began to study. Lana drummed her fingers on the table, waiting for someone to tell her what to do. Maris sat next to her.

"We can't place you at a table until we learn your current abilities," she said. "Everyone is placed at a table according to how comfortable they are in their studies."

"Okay," she said nervously, wondering what exactly that entailed.

"We're going to work on levitation today." Maris made the pencil sitting atop the table rise, spin clockwise, and land on its pointed tip. "First, let's try meditation. Have you ever meditated before?"

"Well, I tried meditating yesterday, and I think I made a

book levitate," she whispered, hardly believing it even happened.

"Do you think you can make this pencil levitate?" Maris asked as she reached for the still upright pencil and placed it on the table horizontally.

"I can try."

Lana tried to remember what she read, but nothing came to her. She concentrated on the pencil, but nothing happened. Try as she might, nothing seemed to work.

"It's all right," Maris said, patting her arm.

"I did make a book levitate," she said, secretly doubting the incident happened at all.

"I believe you," Maris jumped to explain. "Levitation is hard."

Lana nodded, waiting for instructions.

"Close your eyes and relax," Maris said calmly. "Imagine yourself at a peaceful place. What are you picturing?"

"A beach," she said, still with her eyes closed and feeling very self-conscious. "Do you know what that is?"

Maris laughed. "Yes, we have beaches here. Picture it. The sun is shining high above you, and you can feel its warmth fill your body. You can feel the sand between your toes and hear the calm waves rolling onto the shore. Take a few moments to completely relax."

Just as she was starting to feel relaxed, she heard a loud crash and quickly opened her eyes to find a few books and papers on the floor. She saw Terris, his face flushed, as he put his head in his hands.

"What happened?" Maris asked.

"Nothing new," Ivan giggled. "Terris can't do anything right."

"Terris was trying to levitate his book," Randy explained as Terris's cheeks turned bright crimson again. "Ivan threw a pencil at him, breaking his concentration."

"Ivan, bring your chair to that corner," Maris said while pointing to the far-left corner of the room. "When Mrs. DeGette gets here, you'll be taking your quiz first, and you'll be receiving extra homework tonight."

Ivan gathered his belongings and moved to the empty corner. Terris pulled his sleeves up to his elbows and made the small book in front of him levitate shakily.

"Everyone, back to work," Maris said. "Mrs. DeGette will be here shortly. Remember what we went over, Terris. Lana, let's continue."

She smiled at Terris, which made his face turn an even darker shade of red. She tried to recall everything Maris told her and found herself back at the beach, the sun shining warmly, the waves gently crashing on the shore, and the sand beneath her feet.

"Focus on your breathing," Maris instructed. "Feel every breath you inhale and every breath you exhale. Feel your chest expanding and deflating."

She was beginning to feel very relaxed when Maris began a countdown.

"Ten ... nine .... eight ..."

She felt the warm sunshine radiate through her body.

"Seven ... six ... five ..."

She felt the sand between her toes, warming her feet.

"Four ... three ... two ..."

She heard the crash of waves against the shore and the screech of seagulls in the distance.

"Lana!"

She felt a whoosh of air and heard a loud noise before she opened her eyes. The table in front of her crashed to the ground.

"Well, that was very good," Maris said, staring at the table in disbelief. "You need to focus on where to direct that energy."

Her classmates were staring at her, most with wide eyes and mouths open in shock.

"Back to work," Maris said to the rest of the class as she waved her hands in a dismissive manner. "Lana, you have to concentrate in order to control the object. Here, try with the pencil."

She nervously glanced around the room, expecting everyone would go back to their work. They continued to stare, transfixed with her lesson. She closed her eyes and imagined herself at a beach again.

She allowed herself a few moments to enjoy the sights and sounds of her imagination, and then began to focus on her breathing. She felt every exhale, as well as inhale, and began counting down from ten. When she finally reached zero, she slowly opened her eyes and focused her energy on the pencil lying atop the table.

No one dared move. The built-up anticipation hung over the room, ready to explode at any moment. Lana imagined arms extending out from her body, reaching for the pencil. To her surprise, it began to vibrate, making a tapping noise on the table that broke the stone-cold silence. Without warning, the pencil suddenly shot into the air, zigzagging.

"Control it," Maris whispered.

She concentrated even harder on the pencil, pushing thoughts of everything else away as it hung in midair, floating high above Maris's head. Lifting out her right arm, palm up, she beckoned the pencil into her hand and then offered it to Maris.

"Good job. It usually takes years of practice to pull that off," she explained, clapping her hands excitedly.

Lana looked at her classmates and saw them watching her. The door opened, and an older woman marched into the room.

"So glad you're here," Maris said happily. "Ivan will be quizzed first."

Mrs. DeGette, a pleasant-looking woman with bright blue

eyes, sat and began shuffling papers. Maris cleared her throat loudly, trying to get everyone's attention.

"After you finish your quiz and turn in your homework, you may leave," Maris explained. "Ivan, you'll be staying after to tidy the room and receive your extra assignments."

Ivan stood up, pushed his chair away loudly, and joined Mrs. DeGette. The woman slid her glasses from atop her head to their rightful place over her eyes. Sensing her gaze, Mrs. DeGette introduced herself.

The next hour passed in a blur as Lana practiced levitation. After they took a break for lunch, Maris gave her a reading assignment on the history of Bridian, but she couldn't concentrate. Instead, she watched Ivan clean the chalkboard with a wet washcloth. Tiny particles of chalk were floating all around him, leaving white marks on his face while soapy suds were splashing onto his blue cloak and forming puddles at his feet.

"Very impressive," Grant said as he slid his chair next to her. "I'll have to watch my back."

"We'll see. It all depends on how close you'll be following."

The only people left in the room were Lana, Grant, Ivan, Maris, and Mrs. DeGette. She was anxious to leave and find her parents so she could tell them that she made a pencil levitate. She heard Maris approach her table, so she quickly glanced at the book in front of her, trying to appear as if she were reading her assignment.

"Nice job today," Maris said as she placed a folded piece of thick yellow paper on top of the book. "I wrote down all your assignments, so you're free to leave."

"It was nice to see you again, Maris," Grant said, standing up from his chair.

Lana rolled her eyes as she gathered her belongings.

"I'm going to have to follow you, Grant," she said impatiently. "I want to find my parents."

"You want to go, now?" Grant asked, still looking at Maris who seemed to enjoy his attention.

"Yes, I want to go. Come on."

She walked to the door. She knew if she walked far enough, he would have to follow. Sure enough, when she reached the door, she heard Grant behind her.

"You can't see your parents," he explained moments later, as if she had just spoken. "This morning, Grayson told me he would be attending meetings with King Ramos all day. Jacqueline too."

"Fine," she groaned, wishing more than ever she were back in Mt. Sinclair. "Just show me how to get to my bedroom."

Grant stepped in front of her, guiding her out of the library and through the many twists and turns of the castle.

"Why wasn't Damon in lessons?" she asked, relieved that she hadn't seen him.

"He's eighteen," he answered. "He graduated."

"Will you please tell King Ramos I don't need anyone following me?" she asked, stepping into her bedroom. "I didn't get in trouble at all today."

"Well, that's because you were in lessons, and I was with you," Grant answered as he pulled the door shut, leaving her alone in the cavernous room.

Lana didn't know what to do. Her bedroom still felt foreign, like she had encroached upon someone else's life. She heard a knock on her door. She sprang to answer it, hoping it was her parents.

"Hi," Terris said, glancing nervously at Grant, who was leaning against the wall with his arms crossed over his chest. "I thought you might need help with your homework."

"Come in."

"You were amazing today!" Terris said, looking at the floor.

"I still have a lot to learn."

Terris took a cautious step into the room. He clasped his hands in front of him, as if afraid to touch anything. She heard footsteps in the hall and looked to the door, surprised to see Dominic.

"What's going on here?"

"Hello, Dominic," she said dryly. "What do you want?"

"We're going to play a game, and we need more people," he explained as Deliah marched into the room.

"Oh good, two more," Deliah said. "That makes Dominic, Randy, Kiernan, Lana, Terris, and me."

She was going to tell Deliah that she wasn't interested in playing their game but stopped when she saw Terris's face. He had the biggest smile, and she realized he had only been invited because he was with her. If she bowed out, he would most likely be left out.

"It's not fair!" Dominic whined. "Randy's father is taking him to Poklin's tonight!"

"Get over it, Dominic," Deliah said. "I told him to meet us up here, so stop complaining."

Lana stopped listening. Out of the corner of her eyes, she saw that two more people had joined them. Randy and a very cute boy she had yet to meet, but assumed was Kiernan, had stepped into the room.

"I can't play long," Randy said. "My father's taking me to Poklin's later."

"No one cares," Dominic sneered, sitting on her bed.

Randy began explaining his plans for Poklin's, but she had heard enough. Instead, she discreetly studied the new boy out of the corner of her eyes as he walked up to her.

"You must be Carlecia."

She was mesmerized by his perfect white teeth, wavy brown hair, and vivid blue eyes. He was tall, about six feet.

"I—yes—no—Lana," was all she could muster as her cheeks flushed.

"Oh, that's right," Kiernan said. "Father told me you go by Lana now. I'm Kiernan."

"Nice to meet you," she stammered. "You weren't in lessons today."

Kiernan looked at her, his mouth turning upward in a smile. She wanted to disappear. She sounded like a stalker.

"I just got back," he answered. "Deliah found me in the foyer. She demanded I follow her up here. How could I say no?"

She smiled. Her hands felt clammy, and her cheeks blushed. She tried to think of something to say, but her brain didn't seem to be working. She heard Deliah trying to wrangle everyone into the hall, but she couldn't stop staring at Kiernan.

"Do you think it's all right if I talk to you?" he asked, looking over at Grant.

"Oh, don't worry about him." She waved her hand in the air, like it was a normal occurrence to be followed by a soldier.

"How are you adjusting?" he asked, stepping closer to her. "It looks like you're fitting in okay."

She tried to think of an answer. She didn't feel like she was fitting in very well.

"I'm adjusting," she answered. "It's a lot to take in at once. I didn't know about any of this until a few days ago."

"Lana, Kiernan," Deliah called, stomping her foot. "Let's go."

She looked at her cousin. She had her hands on her hips, annoyed that they weren't paying attention to her. She felt as if she had been caught doing something wrong. Kiernan laughed and she looked up at him. He winked, making her knees go weak.

She followed him out of the room. Deliah led them down the hall, and she tried to think of something to break the silence that had fallen on them.

"I don't even know how to play."

"I'll teach you," Kiernan said. "It's not hard."

Deliah stepped through the mirror at the end of the hall, followed by Dominic, Randy, and Terris. Kiernan stepped back, gesturing for her to step through first. When she emerged in the room of polished mirrors, she saw her sneaker had come untied. She was going to retie it when Kiernan stepped out of the mirror, bumping into her and making her lose her balance.

"Where are you going?" he joked as he caught her.

She stood up, embarrassed. Deliah narrowed her eyes at her. Lana couldn't believe she had tripped in front of him. She quickly tied her shoe and looked around the room. Two soldiers were near a mirror to their left, looking out a window. When they saw Grant, they waved him over urgently.

"Stay here," Grant said as he stepped over to confer with the other soldiers.

Kiernan leaned close to her, whispering, "You ready to win?"

"You get five minutes." Deliah stood in front of the group. "After that, good luck."

Beside her, Kiernan stepped closer to the mirror to his right. Deliah was still rattling off a long list of instructions. Grant was engaged in conversation with the soldiers, pointing to something outside.

"Go!" Deliah called out excitedly.

Kiernan grabbed her hand and stepped into the mirror, bringing her with him. When she stepped out of the mirror, he dropped her hand. He began running down the hall.

"Come on," he said. "That is, if you want to win."

Lana looked back to the mirror. She knew Grant was supposed to stay with her. Kiernan stopped running and turned to her, waiting for her to make a decision as Dominic stepped out of the mirror after them.

"What are you waiting for?" he asked. "Do you want to come with me? I can show you how to play."

She knew it was a bad idea to leave Grant but really wanted

to fit in. She never took chances in Mt. Sinclair and couldn't help but think that was why she didn't have many friends. She heard Dominic run in the opposite direction, away from them. She ran toward Kiernan. When she reached him, he began running, and she followed him to the end of the hall and down a set of wide stone stairs.

"I have the best hiding spot."

He led her to a dead-end. She was going to ask where they were going when he placed his hands on the wall. He slid a section of wall to the right, revealing a small room. He pushed her inside and then joined her. He slid the wall back into place.

Lana found herself pressed up against him. When he turned around, they were facing each other, and her heart raced. He fumbled in the dark, pulling out a small light.

"How'd you get the black eye?" he asked, shining the light on the wall behind her.

"I was attacked by rebels."

He leaned in closer, and her breath caught in her throat. He put his hands on her shoulders and spun her, so they had switched places. She was near the closed entrance, and he was near the wall.

"What do we do now? How do you play? Do you just hide?"

"It's a little more complicated than that," he chuckled. "You have five minutes to hide. Deliah will have to find us within the hour. If she finds a hider, then the hider has to help find other hiders."

"I've played this game before," she said.

"So you know the rest?"

"There's more?" she asked, placing her hand on the wall for balance. She was starting to feel claustrophobic and didn't know how much longer she would be able to stay in the cramped room.

"The hiders that were found can turn on Deliah. If they can take her down before she says *Parsneakity*, they can hide again.

If they fail, they're out of the game for good. The last one to be found in the hour wins. If everyone is found, and no one turns on her, Deliah wins."

"We didn't play it like that," she said. When he didn't say anything, she asked, "How long do you think we'll have to stay here? I don't like small spaces."

"I always win when I hide here."

She groaned. She didn't think she could stand to be in the cramped room for an hour. Kiernan bent down and fumbled with something on the floor. She nervously bit her lip. She heard a click and looked down. She watched him lift a door on the floor, setting it near her feet. He jumped into the hole in the ground.

"Come on." He shined the tiny light up to her. "I have an idea."

Lana sat with her legs dangling into the hole. She slid down, and Kiernan caught her, holding her tight. She wrapped her arms around his neck, not wanting to fall. His hair smelled like eucalyptus, and she inhaled deeply.

Kiernan gently lowered her to the ground. When she was standing, she took a step backwards, away from him. She saw that they were in a tunnel. Kiernan began walking, and she followed.

"Where are we going?"

"Poklin's."

"I can't leave the castle," she said. "I'll be in so much trouble."

"No one will even know. We'll get a drink and come back. By then, the game should be wrapped up, and we'll emerge as the winners."

"Isn't this cheating?"

"No one will even know," he repeated.

As they made their way deeper into the tunnel, she shivered as the temperature dropped. She knew she should stay in the castle but figured it couldn't hurt to get a quick drink and bring it back. Besides, she wanted to see Poklin's for herself.

"We're walking under the moat now, right?"

He turned to look at her. "How'd you know?"

"Just a guess," she answered, not wanting to divulge that this was the second passageway she had used since her arrival in Bridian.

The tunnel started to incline. She wondered if the alligator-like creatures had been swimming above her and was thankful to be getting farther from the moat. When they reached another dead-end, Kiernan cracked open another trapdoor in the ceiling, which let in a very thin sliver of light. After checking to make sure the coast was clear, he threw it open, flooding the tunnel with bright sunshine. After he climbed out, he turned to help her.

"Why don't the rebels use these passages to get inside the castle?"

"They don't know about them," he answered. "Most were built a few years ago, in case the castle was ever attacked. King Ramos had all those that they might know about sealed."

"Then how do you know about them?"

"When I'm bored, I explore."

They emerged near the forest. Tall, green trees surrounded them, and even though it was a sunny day, the forest was dark. She turned around, and Kiernan closed the door, covering it with leaves. The door was camouflaged to blend in with the dirt, and when it was closed, you couldn't tell it was a door.

Kiernan pulled the hood of his cloak over his head and did the same with Lana's.

"Less recognizable this way," he explained.

When he began walking she followed, hoping no one would recognize her. When they reached Bridian Square, they made their way to the backdoor of a shop. Hanging above her in faded green lettering was a sign that read *Poklin's Variety*

Store. She jumped when she heard a jingle. She glanced up and saw a small silver bell attached to the door.

She noticed that the shop was much bigger than it appeared on the outside. It was crowded with people. Children were running around while adults sipped drinks at the long wooden bar.

"Welcome to Poklin's," he said, his eyes twinkling with excitement. "Let's get a Choclochino."

"I don't have any money with me."

"My treat." Kiernan pulled her to the bar, past flying paper airplanes and shelves upon shelves of brightly colored candy. "There's Marnie."

Lana turned and saw Marnie, one of her new classmates. She groaned and adjusted her hood, making sure the crown was completely covered. She didn't want to be recognized.

"I'll be right back," he said, then walked over to Marnie, who was sitting at a tall booth with what looked to be her family, all of whom were drinking foaming beverages out of bamboo-like straws.

She watched him step up to their table and quickly turned around, hitting her head against a shelf that held a clear ball. She carefully picked it up, and flecks of gold and silver fell throughout the liquid inside. She flinched when she saw an old man missing several teeth and wearing a dirty brown cloak appear from deep within the ball, his brown eyes looking into her own.

"That's a Crystal Ball," a calm voice said, startling her. "I didn't mean to scare you."

"I wasn't scared," she lied as she carefully placed it back on the shelf.

A chubby man, wearing patched brown pants and a white shirt held up by rope-like suspenders, had joined her from the back of the shop. What was left of his black hair was cut short and circled around a bald spot atop his head, which made his dark brown eyes stand out and his plump cheeks shine.

"I don't remember seeing you before," he said, curiously glancing at her. "I know all the children of Bridian. They all come to my shop."

"Are you Mr. Poklin?" she guessed.

"Sure am," he answered, crossing his arms over his chest. "Who are you?"

"This is my cousin, Lydia," Kiernan said, rejoining her. "She's visiting, staying with us at the castle too."

"Well, in that case, you should try our new Rasmint Choclochino. Come on over," Poklin said, directing her to the bar and pushing her onto a stool.

A young boy to her right slapped a gold coin on the counter. With a wide grin, he withdrew a red lollipop from the jar in front of him.

"Thanks, Poklin." Kiernan sat next to her.

"Sure, we just had a delivery at the castle," he said, mixing ingredients into a tall silver glass. "Did you hear the news?"

"What news?" Kiernan asked.

Suddenly, she felt a hand on her shoulder. She turned around and saw the same man she had seen in the Crystal Ball. His brown eyes narrowed maliciously as he removed the hood from her face, exposing her crown.

"Well, look who we have here," the man whispered in her ear. "Carlecia Morgan. It's been a long time."

Everyone in Poklin's went silent. Even the little boy sitting to her right froze with his lollipop inches from his mouth. She looked at Kiernan one last time before the man lifted her off the stool by her cloak, dragging her to the backdoor of the shop.

7

THE DISAPPEARANCES

Lana began screaming, hoping someone would help her. Was the man a rebel? Where was he taking her? She heard Kiernan asking for help as well but couldn't see or hear if anyone was going to do anything besides watch.

When they reached the back of the shop, the man pushed her so hard she fell to the ground, hitting her head on the door and scraping her hands on the rough floor. She saw Kiernan rush towards her, but the force of the push was making her lightheaded. She slowly sat up just in time to see her attacker push Kiernan backwards into a shelf, sending multicolored candy everywhere.

"Don't mess with me, boy," the man growled as he pulled her to her feet.

When she was standing, she kicked the man, but he clutched her even tighter. A door leading to a backroom opened, but she couldn't see who opened it. The man's putrid odor was making her nauseous, as the combination of liquor, smoke, and body odor was too much to handle.

He threw open the backdoor and pushed her down the steps. She managed to free her right arm and blindly swing it behind her, hitting the man's face and startling him enough to loosen his grip. She began running as fast as she could. She saw the castle, but the drawbridge was up, and she didn't remember the woods well enough to find any of the secret passages.

Just as she was contemplating leaping into the moat and taking her chances with the beasts inside, the man jumped on her, sending her sprawling to the ground. She tried to get up, but the adrenaline racing through her wasn't enough to lift the heavy man off her. When she thought she would suffocate, the man pulled her up and carried her to the moat. Her hair was muddy, and she couldn't feel the crown on her head.

"Let me in!" the man shouted, hurting her ears.

After a tense moment, she realized he was screaming to the guards stationed atop the drawbridge. She silently scolded herself, as she could have been pleading with the soldiers for help.

The man removed the hood from her face. "Look who I have!"

The drawbridge lowered, and the man pushed her to walk. When they reached the doors, they swung open, and a soldier greeted them.

"I need to speak to King Ramos," her abductor said. "I believe he'll want to talk with me, since I found his niece."

The soldier looked at her, and his face paled. He quickly turned and shouted an order to another soldier. She wriggled her way out of the man's hold. When he reached for her cloak again, she pushed him away. She heard talking and looked up, finding her father, Contlay, and Ramos standing behind half a dozen guards.

"Thank you, Alexander," Ramos said.

Her uncle's eyes were red and puffy, like he had been crying. Her father's arms were folded across his chest, and his face was stern. Contlay showed no emotion at all.

"Let's get inside from the cold," Ramos added. "Where did you find her?"

"Poklin's," the man said, then spit onto the floor.

"I don't know what to do with you," her father said as he took a step backwards, finally turning and leaving them.

She was too ashamed to speak. It seemed as if all she had been doing lately was disappointing those she cared about.

"Thank you again, Alexander," Ramos said as he placed his hand upon the man's back, looking out at the Square.

"I knew who she was as soon as she walked in," the man said. "There's no denying she's Alderic's daughter."

"Yes, there's no denying that," Ramos agreed glumly. "We need a word with Lana, alone."

Alexander slowly made his way off the drawbridge. She wanted to explain everything, but when she tried opening her mouth, no sound came out. She still felt nauseous and shivered again, wishing she could change out of her wet clothes.

"No, you will listen!" Ramos exclaimed when he saw her struggling to speak. "You're being guarded for a reason. Why would you run away from us?"

Contlay opened his mouth, as if he were going to say something, but then thought better of it and looked over the rail at a Monogrose.

"I'm disappointed in you," Ramos continued, "and I know that Grayson is too. He's like a father to you and Jacqueline a mother."

Lana looked at the floor in shame. The last thing she wanted to do was disappoint her family, and one look around the room told her she had. Her father couldn't even stand to be in the same room with her anymore, and she knew her mother would be just as upset.

"Let's go," Ramos said, rubbing his forehead in frustration.

Contlay opened the door, revealing Grant. She kept her eyes to the floor as she ran her hands through her hair. She didn't have the heart to tell them she lost her crown, although she knew they could see she wasn't wearing it.

She walked in silence, barely looking up when they finally reached her bedroom. Ramos motioned her in and quickly shut the door behind her, leaving her alone in the room with just her thoughts, which were not good. Outside her bedroom, she heard voices and hoped Grant wasn't in trouble. She was beginning to like him.

Lana sat on her bed and cried. She knew she had messed up, and she had to make it right. She had hoped to make a fresh start in Bridian, but her plan wasn't working. She felt as if she were making everything worse.

When she fell into her pillow, she closed her eyes, thinking of Kiernan. Had he made it safely back to the castle? Her thoughts soon drifted to her friends in Mt. Sinclair. She missed them and wanted to go home.

A moment later, she found herself in the abandoned hall. The thrones were before her, the light reflecting off the gemstones. Her grandfather slowly made his way toward the bassinet. Suddenly, Alderic stabbed him in the back. Her grandfather's anguished scream pierced her ears.

Lana sat up. She saw that she was in her bedroom. Bright light poured in from the window. She fell back onto the pillow, thinking about the dream. She knew there was a reason she had it so often. She just needed to unlock its secrets.

She was still thinking when she heard her bedroom door open and close a moment later. Pretending to be asleep, she hoped whoever had joined her would leave. She was disappointed when someone sat near her feet.

"I know you're up," her father said tensely. "You used to pretend to be asleep to get out of chores."

She opened her eyes and saw her parents. Her mother was sitting near her, holding a tray of food, and her father was standing near the foot of the bed. She sat up.

"You missed breakfast," her mother said.

"Well, at least you can be in the same room with me now," she mumbled, looking at her father.

"I don't know what's gotten into you," her mother said as she set the tray in front of her.

Her father tossed the crown to the bed. "This was found by the moat."

She placed the muddy crown in her lap. She knew something was wrong; the look on their faces gave it away. Her father looked at her in silence for a moment, finally sharing unwelcome news.

"Your cousin is missing."

"Deliah's missing?" she asked, concern coloring her words.

A million thoughts raced in her head. Had Deliah followed her to Poklin's? Had she been abducted?

When he shook his head no, she asked, "Is it Dominic?"

"It's Damon," her mother answered. "No one has seen him since breakfast yesterday. King Ramos is worried about him."

Lana let this news settle. Now she understood why her uncle had been crying last night, and a pit formed in her stomach. She felt horrible for giving him more stress when he had been worried about his son.

"You don't happen to have anything to do with this, do you?" her father asked. "If you know anything at all, you need to tell me."

For a long moment, she couldn't answer. The fact that he believed she had something to do with her cousin's disappearance hurt her deeply.

"I don't know anything," she lay back down, covering herself with her blankets. "I've only talked to him a few times. He hardly talks to Deliah or Dominic either. Have you asked them, or am I the prime suspect?"

"Calm down," her father said. "Did you see him at Poklin's?"

"You really shouldn't have left," her mother added.

"We were playing a game and decided to go," she whispered, playing with the ends of her blanket. "I didn't think it would be a big deal."

"A big deal," her father repeated. "Very dangerous people are after you. They'll stop at nothing to find you."

"Lana," her mother began. "This isn't the way to make friends."

She knew her mother was right but didn't want to admit it. She drummed her fingers on her leg nervously.

"Let's just go home."

Her mother shook her head. "You know we can't."

"I don't know where his weapon is. I don't know why the rebels are looking for me. I can't help anyone."

Her father sighed. "You've been attacked before, so you know this is serious. You have to start thinking. Not just about yourself, but others as well. Kiernan didn't come back last night."

"He's not back yet?" She sat up. "Are you sure?"

"Very sure," her father answered. "I saw his father this morning. King Ramos sent a few soldiers to look for him."

"I'm sure he's fine," her mother added. "He has family in Bridian. He probably went to stay with them."

Lana wondered where Kiernan went after Poklin's. He hadn't mentioned going anywhere else.

"Have you checked with that man?" she asked. "The one who brought me back?"

"You're very lucky Alexander found you," her father said.

"Lucky?" she questioned sarcastically. "If he had just told me who he was, I would have come back with him. He practically carried me away, and he pushed Kiernan in the shop," she continued breathlessly.

"Alexander's brother is a rebel, and he blames your father for it," her father explained. "He may have been taking it out on you a little, but he did bring you back to us. You're lucky a rebel hadn't recognized you."

Her father bent down and hugged her. A moment later, she felt her mother's arms. She noticed the bags underneath their eyes and knew they hadn't been sleeping. Her life wasn't the only one that had changed in the last few days. Her parents had taken her, raised her in a new world for the last fifteen years. They were readjusting as well.

When her parents left, she showered and dressed in jeans and a T-shirt from Mt. Sinclair. After she cleaned the crown and placed it on her head, she sat on the bed. She lifted the lid on the breakfast tray but quickly replaced it. She wasn't hungry after all. She heard her door open and sat up, sighing loudly when she saw her cousins.

"I need a lock," she mumbled.

"Dad told us you were back." Dominic stepped into the room.

"I suppose you heard the news," Deliah added.

"Yeah, but I'm sure Damon's all right," she said, desperately wishing she could be alone.

Lana knew the news had to be about Damon, and judging by the way Deliah asked, it wasn't that he had been found.

"He's fine, Deliah," Dominic said. "He probably disappears like this a lot, just no one notices. He's always in his room. Tell me about Poklin's. You should have told me you were going. I would have gone with you."

"I didn't even know that's where we were going. Do either of you know if Kiernan's back yet?"

"No, and no one knows where he is," Deliah answered. "Soldiers went to Poklin's, but he wasn't there."

"He thinks he's better than everyone else," Dominic muttered. "He drives me crazy."

"You're jealous of him," Deliah said.

"What if Damon's in the abandoned hall?" Lana whispered. "He found his way there before."

"Why are you whispering?" Deliah asked.

"No one trusts me. Grant could be listening, or my room might be bugged."

"Bugs, where?" Deliah shrieked.

"Not real bugs," she said. "People might be listening to me. I can't check the hall, so why don't you two go?"

"Good idea," Dominic said, leading Deliah to the door. "We'll meet you in class."

She watched them leave and then quickly brushed her teeth. When she opened her bedroom door, she smiled at Grant. She was too embarrassed to say anything, so she began walking, hoping he hadn't been in too much trouble.

"How about we try something different today?" he said. When she turned to look at him, he continued, "How about you stay out of trouble? Go to lessons, eat dinner, go to bed?"

"That doesn't sound very fun," she said. "I'm sorry. I got caught up in the game."

He nodded. "Next time, tell me where you're going."

She followed him to the library and sat at the empty table. She placed her books in front of her. Ivan made another comment about Terris's girlfriend, but she ignored him. Randy was engrossed in a textbook on his lap, and Marnie and Carter were talking near the window.

Maris and Mrs. DeGette began class, and Deliah and Dominic ran into the room out of breath. They took their seats and spread their books out. Maris continued the lecture.

"The Revatto were sacred healers for the ruling families of Medora," Maris explained.

Lana was not in the mood for lessons. She bit her lip, wondering where Kiernan was and if he was okay. She had not made a good first impression.

"They moved into the caves of Medora during the Medoran

War," Maris continued. "They didn't want to be involved in the fighting. When King Thaddeus was killed, and Medora became a territory of Bridian, they stayed in the caves. Can anyone tell me why King Nacaro waged the war against Medora in the first place?"

Ivan raised his hand. "He was greedy?"

Randy chuckled. Maris didn't react. Her lips were pressed in a tight, thin line. When no one else answered, she continued.

"Land. King Nacaro wanted to expand Bridian."

"What happened to them?" Terris asked timidly. "The Revatto?"

"They're dead," Ivan answered before Maris could. He then pointed to Lana. "Her father killed them all."

Everyone turned to look at her, and she felt her cheeks flush. She wished she could disappear.

"Ivan, what have I told you about speaking out of turn?" Maris asked, stepping around her desk. "But you're right. Alderic did kill them before he was imprisoned."

Lana cleared her throat nervously. "Why?"

Maris shrugged her shoulders. "I don't know."

The class turned back to Maris, and she continued her lecture, explaining that the Revatto had been around for thousands of years. They lived with Medora's ruling King, or Queen, until the Medoran War. Lana tried to listen, but her head hurt. She wished she could somehow separate herself from Alderic. She didn't know how her birth father could be so evil.

After their lesson, they had a break for lunch. Deliah and Dominic ran to her table, startling her.

"Terris," Dominic called, waving him to join them.

"Someone was there," Deliah said excitedly.

"The abandoned hall?"

Terris sat next to her, and Lana took a sip of her dandelion tea. She didn't think she was going to like it. She had never heard of people drinking dandelion tea in Mt. Sinclair.

"We went to the abandoned hall again," Deliah explained to Terris. "We thought Damon may have been there. He wasn't, but someone had been there."

"The thrones were tipped over," Dominic added. "It looked like someone was looking for something."

Lana took another sip of tea, surprised that she liked it. "I wonder who it was and what they were looking for."

Deliah turned to Terris. "I suppose you heard that Damon's missing."

"I'm sure he's fine," he said.

"I was with Dad when he found out," Deliah explained. "Someone from Poklin's delivered an order for Damon that had to be signed for. We went to get him, and he wasn't in his room."

"What do you think he was doing in the abandoned hall?" Lana turned to Deliah. "I don't think it's a coincidence that he found the painted mirror by accident."

Deliah shrugged her shoulders. "I think we should search his room after lessons."

Randy slid his chair up to their table. "I still can't believe you won last night, Terris."

Terris's cheeks turned red, and he looked at the table. "It was nothing."

"No," Randy said. "You had us all fooled. I didn't think you would turn on Deliah."

Deliah rolled her eyes. "That wasn't very nice."

"Well, I don't think I won," Terris said. "Lana and Kiernan were never found. Technically, they won."

"Oh no." Dominic put his hands on the table. "They went to Poklin's. That's cheating. They're disqualified."

Maris called the class back, and Dominic groaned. The rest of the afternoon passed in a blur. She practiced levitation with Maris. She had mastered the small objects, like pencils and chalkboard erasers, and had moved onto her history book by the time class was dismissed.

She gathered her belongings and saw Terris, Deliah, and Dominic waiting for her at the door. Grant stood up from his chair and stretched his legs. When she stepped into the hall, she followed her cousins. Terris and Grant walked beside her. Behind her, she heard Marnie, Carter, and Randy talking excitedly about a party they were going to before they turned down another hall.

When Deliah and Dominic began arguing over the quickest way to Damon's bedroom, she looked at Terris and shook her head in disbelief. She couldn't believe how much they fought. When they finally reached Damon's room, surprising her at how close it had been to her own, she followed her cousins inside. Grant remained in the hallway, standing near the door, watching them. She looked around his room. It was very large, bigger than hers, and filled with books and papers.

A bed stood off the door, a dresser was against the far wall, a huge clock just like the one in her room was to their left, and three bookshelves took up most of the room. Clothes were piled on the floor, on the unmade bed, and hanging out of dresser drawers. She wanted to check if Damon's clock was a secret passageway as well but didn't want to draw too much attention. She didn't need everyone knowing the clock in her room was a passage.

"He could have at least cleaned up before he left," Dominic said in disgust.

Terris stood near the door while Deliah and Dominic poked around their brother's room. She found a clean spot on the floor near a bookshelf and sat. She wondered why Deliah and Dominic didn't seem genuinely more upset at their brother's disappearance. She couldn't imagine anyone she loved just disappearing, and if they did, she knew she would be a wreck. Then she remembered how cold Damon was towards his siblings. A pit formed in her stomach. She knew Ava and Trevor were probably wondering what happened to her.

She stretched her feet towards Damon's bookshelf, hoping her cousins were almost done with their search. As she stifled a yawn, she glanced at the bookshelf again. It looked as if someone had covered up the bottom shelf with a piece of wood that matched the material the rest of the bookcase was made of. She was sure she would have missed it if not for the fact she was eye level with it.

When she pulled the wood, it swung open on tiny hinges, revealing a stack of books. She was curious why Damon would camouflage the lowest shelf until she looked closer. *The Art of Black Magic* was stacked neatly on the shelf along with smaller books without titles.

She quickly grabbed the closest book and discreetly put it in her pants pocket. She shut the bookshelf door before anyone else could find the hiding place.

"What are you looking for?" Grant asked Deliah and Dominic.

"Nothing really," Dominic answered. "Just seeing if there's anything that might tell us where he went."

"I'm sure King Ramos has already looked. Why don't you put your books away? You have to get to the dining hall for dinner."

Lana stood up and followed her cousins out of Damon's room. She felt the book in her pocket. She didn't want to mention it to anyone. Her plan was to look at it later when she was by herself. It may have even been an old lesson book. If she found something of importance, she would let Ramos know.

When she walked into her bedroom, she dropped her books on the bed. She then made her way to the dining hall, trying to find it on her own. Grant had to readjust her route once, and she took that as a win.

She sat between her parents and scanned the room,

searching for Kiernan. When she didn't see him, she turned toward the door, waiting for him to walk in. Deliah and Dominic ran in a moment later, taking their usual seats, and Terris made his way toward the staff.

"How were lessons today?" her mother asked, taking a sip of water.

"Fine."

She listened to the conversation around her and continued to watch the doors, when her uncle's voice caught her attention.

"I'm worried about him, Charlotte."

"So am I," Charlotte said. Although, from her tone, it didn't sound as if she were worried in the slightest. "But there's nothing else we can do. He hasn't been gone that long."

"I could be out there searching for our boy!" Ramos slammed his fist on the table.

"Fine," Charlotte said as she folded a napkin over her lap. "We're making the announcement first though. We'll let our people know that we're still having your party, despite Damon's foolish behavior. It's tradition. Then be on your way. He's probably visiting friends. He's done this countless times before."

"It's as if you don't even care."

"He's my son too," Charlotte scolded. "This isn't the first time he's disappeared, and I'm sure it won't be the last. Remember the time he disappeared for two weeks and went to that—other place," she said, looking pointedly at Lana.

She quickly averted her eyes. She didn't want her aunt to know she had been listening. Her mind raced. Damon hadn't been given permission to come to Mt. Sinclair. She remembered Deliah had said that he changed after returning.

"Yes, but it's too dangerous now," Ramos said. "It's inexcusable for him to disappear like this without a word."

"He's eighteen, and ever since he found out about your *dilemma* concerning himself and Lana, he's been acting out."

"Don't blame this on me!" Ramos said, raising his voice again. "You know what's right!"

Suddenly, her attention was drawn to the doors of the dining hall. Alexander staggered in, heaving for breath, and covered in blood. Three frantic soldiers ran in after him.

"Alderic," Alexander said as he fell to the floor, pointing to Lana.

8

THE BOOK OF MATHIAS

No one moved. Even the trio of soldiers surrounding Alexander remained still. Perhaps it was the sight of the bleeding man that stunned everyone into silence or fear of the name he had uttered. The room remained eerily silent as Lana stood up from her chair, trying to see what happened.

Suddenly, everyone sprang to life. Young children began crying while men and women rushed to the aid of the fallen man. A soldier threw his arms around her, keeping her confined to the chair. She could hear the three soldiers with Alexander shouting, but the noise in the room was too loud to hear what they were saying.

Her father ran towards Alexander. Dominic stood up on his chair for a better view of the action while Deliah remained in her seat, staring blankly at the commotion unfolding before her. Lana looked for Terris, but every time she tried to stand, the soldier pushed her to her seat again.

Grant ran to her, shoving a handful of confused people out of the way. When he finally reached her, he began shouting orders to those around him. In one swift move, he picked her up and sprinted toward the doors.

From her new vantage point, she searched for Terris, but too many people were trapped in the chaos. When she saw Alexander's bloody body, she stiffened, temporarily ceasing her struggles to escape Grant's grip. Alexander was dead, although it seemed as if his eyes were eerily watching her.

When the crowd parted, she saw Terris. He was standing very still with his mouth hung open in shock. Time moved in slow motion as he placed a finger underneath his eye, as if wiping away a stray tear. She began shouting his name, trying to get his attention. Grant pushed his way through more soldiers, all rushing to get inside the dining hall. She heard Deliah crying behind her.

When they reached the main staircase, Grant said, "Don't worry, we're going somewhere safe."

"Where?" she asked as images of Alexander's lifeless body flashed before her eyes.

Grant didn't answer but rather focused every ounce of energy on sprinting up the steps. She slipped out of his arms and threw her hands around his neck, trying to stay in his grasp. She felt nauseous when she heard angry shouts behind her.

"Where are my parents?" she asked, surprised that they were heading towards her bedroom.

Grant remained silent. When they finally reached her bedroom, he dropped her to the floor. Deliah, Dominic, Terris, Ramos, and three soldiers rushed in after them.

She stood up, unsure of what was going on. Grant hunched over his knees, breathing heavy as Ramos began shouting. She felt so sick she placed her hand on her forehead and made her way to the bed, tripping over a box.

As she pushed herself onto her elbows, she glanced at the cardboard box, ignoring the commotion around her. In a greater state of confusion, she realized that there were four more boxes of the same shape and size scattered throughout the room.

"I don't need to be locked up!" Ramos threw his hands down in frustration. "Now I'm separated from my wife!"

"I'm sorry," one of the soldiers said, bowing low to the ground. "You need to be protected at all costs."

Grant silenced the man with a wave of the hand. The young soldier's cheeks flushed as he stepped backwards, inadvertently bumping into another behind him.

"It's our job to protect you," Grant explained, stepping closer to Ramos.

Just then, the door swung open, and her mother and Contlay burst into the room, followed by Charlotte. Deliah ran to her mother, throwing her hands around her waist and burying her head in her chest. Charlotte's cheeks were red, and her eyes narrowed, glaring at Ramos as another soldier slammed the door shut.

Her mother pulled her emerald-green cloak tighter around her shoulders and said, "Grayson will be up after the threat is assessed."

"The castle's under lockdown and is being searched," a soldier added. "Everyone's safe here."

"Why are we here?" Charlotte asked, looking around the room with a sour look on her face. "This isn't the usual spot."

"I wasn't really thinking," Grant answered. "I just knew I had to get Lana to safety, and it's better that you're all together."

Charlotte sighed loudly and Lana looked around her bedroom. How long were they going to be locked inside? While it was a big room, it seemed tiny with so many people crammed into it. Dominic slid to the floor with his head in his hands, and Deliah clung to her mother. Terris remained across the room, away from everyone else.

Having nothing else to do, she slid the nearest cardboard box closer as Charlotte pushed Deliah away and marched to Ramos. When she reached her husband, she pulled Contlay away by his cloak. Contlay stumbled backwards, almost tripping over his feet.

"How could you leave me down there?" she questioned, waving her finger in her husband's face.

"I didn't have a choice," he answered, stepping closer to Charlotte, who refused to back away. "They pulled me out of the dining hall!"

Grant cleared his throat, as if he were going to interrupt, but Charlotte jumped at her husband, proclaiming, "I could have been killed! If Jacqueline hadn't found me, I might be dead!"

"Now is not the time for exaggeration," Ramos said, putting his hands in the pockets of his cloak and walking away from his wife. "I have more important things to worry about at the moment, like the fate of our son! Do you understand the leverage my brother would gain if he found him?"

Charlotte began giggling. She could think of no other word to describe it. With the exception of Charlotte, the room was silent.

"Damon's an adult now, Ramos. He can look after himself."

Lana was too shocked to turn away and disliked her aunt more than ever. Ramos shook his head and rejoined Contlay. She didn't think that she would be able to stand the tension in the room much longer. She glanced at her cousins again, wondering how often their parents fought. Terris slowly walked toward her, as if afraid of joining her too quickly, when the door opened.

Her father stepped into the room. His cloak was smeared with blood and he glanced around the room sadly. She held her breath, waiting to see what was going to happen. She barely had time to think since Alexander had stumbled into the dining hall.

"The castle's secure." He took another step into the room,

closer to Ramos. "Alexander was attacked outside. Three soldiers found him and brought him inside."

"They should have discreetly brought this to my attention, and I would have dealt with the situation without causing mass panic!" Ramos bellowed angrily.

"I completely agree," her father said. "Apparently, Alexander fought his way into the dining hall. He wanted everyone to see what the rebels had done to him."

"Fool," Ramos muttered. "Where is he now? I should speak to him."

Her father looked to the floor sadly. She knew what he was going to say. She had seen Alexander as she was being carried out of the dining hall.

The room remained silent until her father spoke again. "He's dead."

Ramos fell to the floor and whispered, "Dead?"

Her father nodded, silently confirming the utterance, as he helped Ramos to his feet. She wanted to ask why Alexander had been attacked and why he said Alderic's name but didn't want to upset anyone. She knew now was not the time for questions.

"For the time being, I think Lana, Deliah, Dominic, and Terris should remain here," he continued to Ramos, as if no one else were present. "The soldiers are performing another precautionary search."

Charlotte, who had remained silent, began pacing the room, still angrily glaring at her husband from time to time. When it became clear that no one was going to address her, she stormed to the door.

"Since no one needs me, I'm leaving," she said as she brushed her hand over her lips, as if trying to remove her lipstick.

"I'll go with you," Ramos said.

Charlotte scoffed and turned on her heel, leaving the room

in stunned silence. Lana couldn't believe her aunt didn't even say goodbye to her children. Deliah and Dominic looked very upset.

Her mother hugged her. After a moment, she admitted first Deliah, then Dominic, into her fond embrace.

"I bet you're curious about the boxes," Contlay said after her parents and Ramos left. When she nodded, he continued, "I was able to bring some of your things back."

Even though she was exhausted, she was excited to have a few things from Mt. Sinclair. She eagerly stepped up to the closest cardboard box and carefully pulled the flaps away. Her breath caught in her throat when she looked inside. A few pictures were scattered atop her sketchbooks. The pictures were from her fifteenth birthday party. Her mom had insisted on having them printed. She glanced at a stray picture and saw herself with Ava and Trevor. The birthday girl was wearing a homemade crown Ava had made just seconds before the picture had been snapped, effectively capturing the moment for eternity. Their smiles were priceless.

She covered her face with her hand, not wanting anyone to see the tears that were forming. As she moved to the next box, Deliah and Dominic dove into the pictures. She heard their eager whispers as she removed the flap and saw some of her clothes. She moved to another box and found her jewelry, her blue daisy quilt, and some knickknacks.

She slumped to the floor amid her cousins' whispers as they shuffled through her belongings from another world. She wished more than ever she could go back to Mt. Sinclair to see her friends again and still couldn't believe how drastically her life had changed in the past few days. She wondered how long another search of the castle was going to take. She wanted to be alone so she could go through her belongings at her leisure.

She leaned against the chest at the foot of her bed. The more she thought about her life, the angrier she became. It wasn't fair that she had been uprooted, that her whole life had been a lie. She felt the lock of the chest digging into her neck and sat up, trying to open it again.

When the chest didn't open, she angrily kicked it. She reached into the cardboard box containing the knickknacks and pulled out a small replica of the Statue of Liberty. Without thinking, she smashed the statue against the lock of the trunk, trying to open it.

She could feel every eye in the room upon her but couldn't stop. She had too much angry energy to release and wanted to know what was inside the trunk. The fact that it was locked made her even more curious.

Suddenly, Grant was behind her, struggling to hold her back. He managed to dislodge the statue from her grip.

"What's wrong with you?" Dominic asked.

"What's wrong with me?" she repeated angrily, pointing to herself. "Everyone's been lying to me. My whole life has been uprooted. My parents really aren't my parents. I can't go anywhere without guards. My birth father is a murderer and is looking for me. Should I continue?"

"You're crazy, you know that?" Dominic took a step backwards.

She ignored her cousin and pulled her knees up to her chest, resting her head against them, when Dominic said something that caught her attention.

"There's an easier way to open that trunk."

Lana glared at him, waiting for him to explain. She wiped the rest of the tears from her eyes and watched him walk to the trunk. When he reached it, he sighed, as if he had better things to do, while pushing both ends of the lock together with his index finger and thumb.

"It's a trick lock," he explained as the trunk popped open. "I have the same one in my bedroom."

She glared at her cousin, wishing more than ever she could be alone.

"Well, don't you want to see what's inside?" he asked.

She crawled to the trunk. With shaking hands, she lifted the lid and peered inside. A sparkly gray cloak greeted her. She removed it, revealing a few scattered photographs atop a small silver box.

"What's inside?" Deliah asked.

She held the cloak up. "Just this cloak, a few photos, and a small silver box."

"What's inside the box?" Dominic asked, kneeling beside her.

Lana carefully lifted it out of the chest. The box creaked open to reveal a gold band with tiny green gems. She removed the ring and saw that the green gems formed the shape of two leaves.

"A ring," she answered, holding it up and finding an inscription on the inside. "There are letters engraved on the band."

She brought the ring closer to her eyes and read the inscription *K.S.R. & A.M.M.* After she read the initials out loud, she placed the ring back in the box. Her bedroom door opened, and Ramos rejoined them, accompanied by two soldiers.

"Everything's fine," Ramos said as Deliah ran up to him and threw her hands around his waist. "I'm going to take my children and Terris to their bedrooms."

Grant bowed. Terris walked up to Ramos, passing her with a smile. She wondered why he had been so silent but realized it was probably because he felt out of place. Terris was used to working, passing life without notice.

"Whose stuff is that?" Dominic asked his father, pointing to the trunk.

Ramos pulled Deliah off his waist and walked up to Lana. When he reached her, he put his hand on her shoulder and smiled.

"These were your mother's."

She clutched the small box in her hand so tightly her knuckles hurt. Ramos saw the box and gently removed it from her hands.

When he opened it, he explained, "This was a promise ring given to your mother from your father. She loved leaves. The very first time she met Alderic, she had been walking through the forest, looking at them. Their initials are engraved on the inside."

"What was her middle name?"

"Samara." Ramos took the ring out of the box and placed it in her hands. "Kalinia Samara Roberts was your mother's full name before she married Alderic."

She slid the ring on the ring finger of her right hand. When it was secure on her finger, he walked back to Deliah, wrapping his arm around her shoulders.

"Wait," Lana called out. When Ramos turned to her, she asked, "Why did Alexander shout Alderic's name?"

"We believe it happened on his orders," he answered. "Try to get some sleep."

She looked at the beautiful ring, cherishing it even more since she learned it had been her mother's. She heard the door close behind her and turned around, finding that she was finally alone in her bedroom. She folded the cloak on her lap, and the photographs in the trunk caught her eye again.

She brought the pictures closer and saw that they were black and white. In the first picture, three men were standing in front of the fountain of Bridian. She studied the picture and saw Alderic. He had his arms around the two men at either side of him. She had no idea who the man on his right was. Studying the man on his left, she knew he looked familiar but couldn't place him.

Lana quickly flipped through the rest of the photographs. Alderic and Kalinia, Kalinia and the man she couldn't place in the first picture, her grandfather Nicodemus with Alderic and Ramos. She couldn't help thinking that if those in the photos knew what fate had in store for them, they wouldn't be smiling.

She tossed the photographs back into the trunk and saw that she had missed one. She picked it up, and her whole body stiffened. The same man who had been standing next to her father in the first picture, whom she had recognized but couldn't place, was holding a baby. The fact that the man was holding her as a child was not what surprised her. She recognized him now. She carefully touched the picture and knew it was Contlay.

After placing everything back into the trunk, she placed her crown on the dresser, turned off the lights, and walked to her bed in a greater state of confusion. Too much had happened for her to process it all. She took off her cloak and snuggled into the covers, wanting more than anything to put the awful day behind her. She hadn't even changed into pajamas.

The hours seemed to fly as she lay still, afraid to shut her eyes for fear she would dream of Alexander's bloody body caught in the blank stare of death. She turned onto her stomach, hoping the change in position would help her fall asleep. Instead, she felt a pain in her thigh and realized she still had Damon's book in her pocket.

She eagerly sat up, straining her eyes in the dark room. The book was small and bound in leather. She brought it closer. On the first page, handwritten in ink, was *The Book of Mathias*. Her interest was piqued, and she jumped off the bed, scurrying over to the window in order to see more of the book through the light of the moon.

Lana sat on the floor and turned the page. She bit her lip nervously as she began reading the first page of tiny handwriting.

I carried his lifeless body back to Bridian. It was the hardest thing I ever had to do. The look on her face will haunt me forever. They took what little joy I had in this life and obliterated it.

That's why I did what I did.

The full moon was my companion that night. The forest was silent, and the water was calm. The lights from their city lit up the darkness beneath the glass-like surface.

When I stepped into the lake, I swam to the exact spot Gavril died. I emptied the bottle into the water and smiled for the first time in weeks. If the Revatto had known my true intentions, they never would have shown me their magic. It doesn't matter though. They'll be gone shortly.

The hair on Lana's arms prickled, and she shivered. She quickly turned the page and continued reading.

The story of my namesake, King Mathias of Medora, has always intrigued me. He was a great king, and Medora prospered under his rule. Until the death of his only son.

The one thing the history books all agree on is when Drunden died in battle, King Mathias was distraught. He never recovered. Medora suffered a harsh winter the following year. In the spring, the crops didn't grow, the water supply ran dry, livestock were found slaughtered, and a devastating earthquake tore apart the kingdom. King Mathias died a few months later. A terrible coincidence.

Or was it....

Rumors have been circulating for many years that King Mathias was so distraught he began practicing sacrificial magic. He would do anything to bring his son back. There are those that believe he called forth something dark, something evil.

With trembling hands, Lana turned the page. The words had a hypnotizing effect on her, and she couldn't put the book down.

They are real.

I have seen the demons, and they are glorious. The Revatto finally told me what I needed. Their predecessors had been present when King Mathias released them, and the knowledge had been passed along throughout the generations. The demons will be my revenge upon the Altarians. Murder cannot go unpunished. They will be sorry. Father is doing nothing, and for the sake of Bridian, he needs to be dethroned.

I know how to release them now, to bring their physical bodies into the world. I just need a way to tether them. To make them obey me. I was told it can't be me—I need an innocent. This world has already corrupted me. This is how King Mathias failed. They were bound to no one.

In two months' time, I shall have a child, a girl. At the moment of her birth, the innocent will be taken to Medora. Her life will be blessed beyond all others. She shall be the Princess of the Rebellion.

Once the demons are released, the Altarians will suffer. Tethered to my daughter, I will control them, make them obey my every command. I shall be unconquerable—King Mathias of Bridian, and soon, the world. I'll control the elements, release plagues—the possibilities are endless. All those in my way will endure their wrath. Only then will peace thrive.

Lana snapped the journal shut, glancing around the room as her heart beat rapidly in her chest. She knew that her parents and Ramos should read it. It seemed as if Alderic had written it, but his name had not been Mathias. What had happened to the author and his unborn daughter?

She listened to the swaying pendulum of the grandfather clock as she carefully made her way to the trunk at the foot of her bed. Aside from the clock, the room was silent. She had trouble seeing when she left the light of the moon and stumbled over one of the cardboard boxes containing a few possessions from her previous life.

Once she regained her balance, she continued toward the trunk. When she finally reached it, she placed her hand on the lock and, with shaking fingers, pushed the sides together. Once the lock popped, she lifted the lid for the second time that night, finding nothing but darkness.

She placed her hand inside the trunk. Tears formed in her eyes as she slowly withdrew Kalinia's cloak. As her heart beat louder within her chest, she dropped the cloak and twisted the ring on her finger, wishing she knew who Mathias was.

A million thoughts swirled through her head as she gingerly removed the pile of photographs. She couldn't bring herself to look at them again; it was all too much. She placed the photos in the journal, curious why Contlay had been with Alderic in one of them.

She pushed herself off the floor and shivered, either from the chill night air or thoughts of the horrible journal in her hands. She put Kalinia's cloak over her shoulders and clutched the journal tightly as she tiptoed her way to the door. When she opened it, she remembered Grant. Her mind raced as she thought of possible explanations for going to visit her parents in the middle of the night. She stepped into the dark hall, deciding that the truth was best.

She found Grant sitting on the floor with his legs spread out in the hall. He turned his head sharply when she shut the door behind her.

"Where are you going?"

"I have to see my parents." When he sighed, she continued, "It's important. I wouldn't go unless it was."

He stood up. "Do you know what time it is? Can it wait until morning?"

Lana shook her head. "Who do I need to ask to get you a chair?"

Grant smirked. He led her around a corner to a stairwell. She slowly made her way up the stone steps, trying not to trip over her feet in the darkness. Large, diamond-shaped windows lined the wall. Bright stars lit up the dark sky, surrounding the full moon. She stopped walking, shivering when a line from the journal came to her mind.

The full moon was my companion that night.

Suddenly, her attention was drawn to a light near the ground, making its way closer to the castle. A moment later, she realized that it was a lantern light. Grant joined her at the window to see what she was looking at.

The light stopped moving. She held her breath, not wanting to fog the window as she listened to Grant's heavy breathing beside her. She knew he was just as confused as she was.

"The drawbridge is up," he whispered. "There's no way in."

Lana looked through the window again, watching the lantern light disappear into the forest, near the secret passage she had used to go to Poklin's. She knew who was outside the castle and decided to put off talking to her parents. With a startled gasp, she ran down the stairs, eager to hear where Kiernan had been.

9

UNEXPECTED GUESTS

L ana tapped her foot impatiently as she shoved the journal containing the photographs into her pocket. When she realized the noise of her foot against the floor was echoing, she abruptly stopped. She leaned against the wall for support and watched Grant set the lantern near his feet.

It seemed as if they had been waiting for hours. She guessed that Kiernan was going to enter the castle the same way he left and had already explained everything to Grant, but she was beginning to think too much time had passed. She heard a noise and glanced at the wall to her right as it began to slide open. Grant gave a startled jump, almost knocking over the lantern. She pushed herself off the wall she was leaning against, glad that he hadn't made too much noise in his surprise.

Kiernan struggled out of the passage. When he noticed them, he ran back into the tiny room. She sprang into action, running to the wall and squeezing into the crevice after him. Once she was completely in the passage, she grabbed his hand, preventing him from jumping into the hole in the floor.

Kiernan struggled in her grasp and hot drops of liquid landed on her.

"Ouch," she said. "What was that?"

When he heard her voice he stopped struggling. She heard Grant and knew he was watching them through the thin gap in the wall. Kiernan threw the hood off his face, struggling to see.

"It was a Rasmint Choclochino."

"Are you okay? Everyone's been worried."

He rubbed his palm against his forehead, as if trying to decide what to tell her. Finally, he picked up a bag that had dropped to the floor.

"I have something for you. It's my apology."

Lana fumbled with the bag in his hands, finally getting it in her grip. She turned toward the light of the lantern and noticed it had *Poklin's Variety* stenciled on the front. She peered into the bag and saw a Crystal Ball identical to the one she had seen in Poklin's shop.

"What do these do?"

"They help clear your vision, your third eye," he explained with a smile. "Personally, I don't think they work. I look into them and see my reflection, but they are kind of neat."

"At Poklin's, I saw Alexander in one of these before he grabbed me," she said. Kiernan looked surprised, and she continued, "Thank you. Everyone's been worried about you."

"I knew Alexander wouldn't hurt you, and I tried to tell you, but I guess you couldn't hear me." He ran a hand through his hair. "After he pushed me to the floor, I saw him."

"Who?"

"Damon," he whispered.

"He's all right?"

"He's better than all right. During the commotion, someone opened the door to the backroom."

"What was he doing?"

He shrugged his shoulders. "I knew that you would be safe,

and I was curious what he was up to. He was acting strange, so I followed him. He ran out the front door into the Square. He finally stopped at an old house in the middle of the woods."

She remained silent, too stunned to speak.

"There were lots of people there," he continued. "I recognized Damarius Pilkins and a few people I've seen around the Square."

"How long did you watch them for?"

"I've been there the whole time, hiding in the trees. I had a close call when Damarius stormed out looking very angry."

"You have to tell Ramos."

Kiernan ran his hands on his cloak. "He's not hurt. If he's not back in a couple of days, I'll let him know."

"I really think you should tell him now," she said.

"What good would it do? Damon's probably not even there anymore."

"You said Damarius Pilkins was with him," she countered. "Clearly he knows where Damon is."

"That's exactly why I can't tell anyone. King Ramos will trust Damarius more than me. Damon is involved in something he shouldn't be, and Damarius will deny it."

"If Damarius is anything like Ivan, you're probably right," she finally admitted, her gaze drifting back to the bag at her feet. "When did you go back to Poklin's?"

"I was just there. I had a craving for a Choclochino. Actually, I still do."

"Lana!" Grant thundered from the hall. "Let's go, NOW!"

Kiernan grabbed her hand and brought her close. "Please don't tell anyone. The rebels can't know I was spying on them."

"I think that you should tell Ramos. He won't let anything happen to you. He'll protect you."

He sighed. "Maybe you're right."

He picked up the lantern and stepped out of the passage. She followed him, almost dropping the bag containing the

Crystal Ball when her cloak caught on her feet. He slid the wall back into place.

"I'm glad you're okay," he said. "I didn't mean for anything to happen."

"Thank you again for the Crystal Ball," she said, her cheeks blushing.

She watched him leave. Grant drew a short pocketknife from the folds of his cloak and flicked it open. He carved an X on the wall.

"This way I know which wall slides out to reveal the passage," he explained when he saw her watching him. "I have to make sure King Ramos knows about it."

"Can you take me to my parents now?"

Grant began walking, not bothering to answer. She guessed he was upset that he was unable to hear her conversation with Kiernan. As she followed, clutching the bag from Poklin's, she began thinking.

What had Damon been doing in the backroom at Poklin's? Then another thought hit her. If Damon was at Poklin's, surely Poklin saw Damon. In fact, when she was looking at the Crystal Ball, Poklin joined her from the corner of the shop where Kiernan said he had seen Damon. Why hadn't Poklin given Damon his order at the store?

Grant stopped walking. He stepped back and gestured toward a door. She placed the bag from Poklin's on the floor, dug in her cloak for the leather-bound journal, and tapped the door several times with its spine. *The Book of Mathias* grew heavier with each passing second. She couldn't hear anyone moving in the room and was about to give up when Grant motioned that she should try again. She raised her hand, ready to knock, when the door opened.

"What's wrong?" her father asked sleepily, squinting in the light of the hall.

"I found this," she answered, holding up the journal. "I

think you should read it, and I have some questions about these."

She removed the photographs from the book and held them up. It took a moment for him to comprehend their significance, but once he did, he immediately snapped awake and grabbed them from her hand.

"Where did you find these?"

"I found the pictures in the trunk at the foot of my bed," she answered, hoping he wouldn't press her on the journal's origin.

"Of course," he said as he thumbed through the photographs. "The cloak you're wearing was your mother's. I should have recognized it."

"Why is Contlay with Alderic in these pictures?"

Her father looked to the floor and answered, "Grant, please take Lana to her bedroom."

She was so mad she couldn't think straight. Her father sensed her anger and rushed to explain.

"I'm going to get King Ramos and Contlay. We'll meet you there."

She grabbed the journal and photographs from him and reluctantly followed Grant back to her bedroom. She closed the door and sat on the floor. When she tired of waiting, she withdrew the Crystal Ball from the bag at her feet. As she glanced into the globe, trying to distract herself from her thoughts, she saw a gray cloud form in the center.

She felt as if she were in a trance as the cloud formed an image. A skinny man with wild brown hair and bloodshot eyes looked back at her. Suddenly, the image shifted, and the same man was now standing in front of a legion of cloaked figures. The look on his face was pure evil.

The feeling in the pit of her stomach was enough to convince her this man was her birth father, although he appeared different than in her dreams. Tears gathered in her eyes as she threw the Crystal Ball at the wall—although the images were still imprinted in her memory and would be the rest of her life. Instead of breaking, as she hoped it would, it bounced off the wall and rolled back to her, stopping at her feet.

At the noise, Grant sprang into the room, and she wiped the tears from her eyes.

"This is beautiful," he said, picking up the Crystal Ball and handing it back to her. "Crystal Balls are extremely hard to break."

"Wait," she called out before he left. "Will everything you see in them come true?"

"They're only toys," he answered, then narrowed his eyes at her. "Did you see something?"

Lana shook her head. She didn't want everyone to think she was crazy. She glanced at the Crystal Ball before kicking it to the wall again. Grant walked back to the door as her parents, Ramos, and Contlay appeared.

Once Grant left the room, Ramos quickly said, "Lana, I need to see that book."

She removed the photographs from the journal and gave it to him. She saw that he was dressed in a long white robe and had dark circles underneath his eyes. It was also the first time she had seen him without a crown.

"Whose journal is it? Who's Mathias?"

He opened the leather-bound book and glanced at the first page. His face paled, and his fingers began trembling. She thought that he was going to drop the book.

"Mathias is your father," Ramos explained as he sat on the bed. "That's his middle name."

"Why does he call himself Mathias?"

"From what I've heard, he only went by that name within the Rebellion," he answered. "Hundreds of years ago, there was a great King of Medora named Mathias. Alderic looked up to him. Plus, it was another way to distance himself from his family."

"Where did you find that book?" her father asked.

"Damon's room."

Ramos stiffened. She felt terrible and wished she hadn't found the horrible book. She realized she had been the Princess of the Rebellion. She had been the baby girl referenced.

She turned to Contlay. "Were you friends with him?"

"Yes," he answered.

"And no one thought to tell me this?"

"We're doing our best to let you adjust to everything," Ramos said, still looking through the journal.

"I was one of his best friends, Lana," Contlay said softly.

She was stunned. This was something she wasn't expecting.

"I know I should have told you sooner," he continued. "I didn't know how you would react."

"Who is the other man in the picture?" she asked.

"That's your uncle, Gavril," Ramos answered.

"You have another brother?" she asked, curious why she had yet to meet him. "Where is he?"

"Actually, he was your mother's brother," Ramos answered. "He died eighteen years ago."

She remembered reading Gavril's name in Alderic's journal. She tried to remember what it said but too many thoughts clouded her, fighting for space in her already occupied mind.

"He mentioned Gavril in the journal."

"Gavril, Alderic, and I used to be inseparable," Contlay said. "It wouldn't surprise me that he was mentioned."

"Your mother and her brother, Gavril, came to Bridian with their father," Ramos explained, standing from the bed and joining Lana on the floor. "Your mother was fifteen, and Gavril was sixteen. Alderic fell in love with her. Six years later, they married, a few years later, everything fell apart."

"Gavril was in love with a girl from Altaris named Marianna," Contlay said. "She was already betrothed though, to Gwendolyn's son."

"Gwendolyn is Queen of Altaris," her mother jumped in. "The Altarians are mermaids, a very special breed that once had the ability to live underwater or on land. Once Alderic began poisoning them, they lost this ability."

Contlay exhaled loudly, as if in pain. "On the night before Marianna was to be married, we went to Altaris. Gavril wanted to convince her to run away with him. Ronan, Marianna's betrothed, killed Gavril out of jealousy. Gavril was lured into the lake. There was a fight, and he drowned. Alderic tried to save him, but their army attacked us."

The room fell silent, as if remembering the dead.

Finally, Contlay continued. "We brought Gavril's body back to Bridian. Your mother was grief stricken. Alderic immersed himself in dark magic, traveling to Medora. No one knew where he was going until it was too late. Not that I'm giving him an excuse for the atrocities he would later commit."

"He was no longer the brother I once knew," Ramos added sadly.

"What about my mother?" she asked in disbelief. "Why did she stay with him?"

"She was too consumed in her own grief to see the signs from Alderic," Ramos answered. "She loved him very much, but part of her died with her brother."

"She should have left him. That's no excuse for my father either! He killed innocent people."

"When your mother finally did see the enormity of your father's actions, she decided to leave," her mother said, wiping a tear from her eye. "By the time we had everything set, she was killed."

"Were you friends with her?" Lana asked, looking at her in a whole new light.

"She loves you very much," her mother said, tears pooling in her eyes. "Just because someone isn't with you physically doesn't mean they aren't still with you. She's with you every day, every moment of the day, and is very proud of you."

"Who killed her?"

"It was an accident," Ramos answered.

"So, he just wanted revenge on the mermaid people?" Lana asked, trying to understand Alderic's motives.

Ramos looked to the floor before answering, "As the future King of Bridian, he wanted to expand to other kingdoms. Our father didn't agree with this. We were at peace, and he wanted to keep it that way. Alderic began recruiting people to help him overthrow our father. He killed those who got in his way."

"What happened to the mermaid people?" she asked. "The Altarians?"

"He poisoned them," Ramos said.

Lana's hand flew to her mouth. "What was he going to do with me? He referred to me as the Princess of the Rebellion? He said I would release the demons. Demons are real?"

Ramos nodded. "Where there is good, there is evil."

"I don't understand," she stammered. "How was I supposed to release them?"

Ramos was silent for a moment, as if searching for the right words. "My father interrupted them during a ceremony. I believe he was luring the demons with the magic infused in you. Two infants were taken from the rebels that night. You and Terris."

"Terris?" she repeated in surprise.

"His parents are rebels," Ramos explained. "His mother disappeared years ago, and his father is imprisoned alongside my dear brother."

"Is that why he's living in the castle?"

"He needed a place to live. His only other adult relative,

Alexander, couldn't care for a child. He doesn't have to work here, he wants to. I think it keeps him busy."

"Alexander?" she repeated, suddenly remembering her friend's sadness at seeing Alexander's death.

"Yes," Ramos answered. "Terris barely knew him though. Alexander was his father's brother."

Lana was silent. She twirled a curly tendril of hair around her finger.

"What kind of magic is in me? It seems like there's magic around everyone here?"

Ramos drummed his fingers on his leg. "There is magic in Telorian. Most of us can use our minds to move objects. Our sense of intuition is stronger. Alderic wasn't happy with that. He wanted more."

She sat in silence, waiting for him to continue. He hadn't answered her question. Her mother clasped her hands in her lap. Her father watched Ramos.

Contlay cleared his throat. "We grew up hearing stories about the Revatto."

"Maris told us about them. They were healers, right? For Medora?"

Ramos nodded. "They were known as healers. Those with the greatest magical abilities were recruited into the Revatto. They used their knowledge to aid the ruling family. My brother made you a conduit using their teachings. He needed an inno-cent to tether the demons to our world so he could control them."

"I read about that in the journal," she said. "It couldn't be him, so he chose me. Sounds like father of the year."

Ramos closed his eyes for a moment. When he reopened them, he said, "The Stones of Medora held little power over you because the same magic that runs through them is in you. We sent you to Mt. Sinclair because there's no magic there, nothing for you to draw from. Now that you're back, we'll have to wait and see what manifests."

"How did the Stones work in Mt. Sinclair?" she asked, trying to come to grips with everything.

"They were infused with magic in Medora and brought to Mt. Sinclair," Ramos answered. "Even though there's no magic in Mt. Sinclair, they'll hold it until it's expended."

"When we brought you to Mt. Sinclair we couldn't leave the house." Her mother looked out the window sadly. "You made things levitate. If you wanted something, it would just appear. It took a good year before all of the magic was gone."

"What about the orbs?" Lana asked. "Or the mirror in my bedroom? They seem like magic."

"That's not magic," Ramos answered. "Not in the same sense that we're talking about. They're just portals. Mass energy in very high concentrations. Think of them as doors."

Lana didn't understand. Four days ago, she had been an ordinary girl. It just didn't seem possible that her life could change so drastically in such a short amount of time.

Ramos stood up. When no one said anything, she looked at her uncle again and saw his brow furrowed. She bit her lip, remembering Kiernan's story. She wanted to tell her uncle that Kiernan had seen Damon but wondered if it would make things worse since he had voluntarily left.

"You should get some sleep," Ramos said, rubbing his eyes.

Her parents and Contlay stood up, and she decided to wait. She knew it would only worry him, and he needed the sleep. She hoped Kiernan would talk to him tomorrow.

Without looking at anyone, she made her way to the bed, too confused and consumed in her own thoughts to protest. As she shut her eyes, she heard Grant addressing Ramos. She knew that Kiernan's passage was about to be revealed. Soon the confusion and exhaustion of the day overtook her.

Hours later, Lana awoke to the sound of knocking. It didn't seem as if she had gotten any sleep, but a quick look out her window revealed bright sunshine. She groggily stepped out of bed and answered the door. She wasn't surprised to see her cousins.

Deliah and Dominic pushed their way into the room. Deliah was dressed in a long gown, her hair in a complicated updo that crisscrossed into a neat bun at the nape of her neck. Dominic was wearing a black top underneath a white vest and black dress pants.

"Angelica came back last night!"

Lana glanced out the door, surprised to see that Grant was gone. Another soldier was in his place.

"Where was she?"

Deliah shrugged and glanced from the unmade bed toward Lana. "Did you just wake up?"

Lana nodded. "Why are you so dressed up? Do we have lessons?"

"Get dressed and meet us in the dining hall." Deliah sighed. "It's my dad's birthday."

Dominic marched out of the room, mumbling something about the time. Deliah turned on her heel and followed her brother. As she shut the door, she let all thoughts of last night subside. She didn't want to think about Alderic, the rebels, demons, or magic.

Half an hour later, Lana was showered and dressed. She decided to wear a pair of dark blue jeans and a black Mt. Sinclair High School T-shirt from one of the boxes Contlay had brought. After she laced up her black and pink sneakers, she threw on Kalinia's cloak, which covered her foreign clothes perfectly.

She ran a comb threw her wet hair and left it down and curly. Her stomach felt heavy when she remembered the conversation from last night. She had been infused with dark magic, the same magic that made the Stones of Medora. Was that why levitation seemed so easy? Was that why she had seen both Alexander and Alderic in the Crystal Ball?

When she opened the door, she saw Grant. She hadn't walked far when she heard her cousins' loud voices. She knew no others who could carry on arguments as they did. She turned the corner, and her suspicions were confirmed. Deliah and Dominic were standing in front of an open door, arguing very loudly as Angelica danced around Deliah's feet. When Dominic saw her, he threw his arms up in frustration.

"That stupid doll is driving me crazy!"

Angelica danced towards Dominic, but Deliah picked her up and began whispering in her ear.

"I thought we were meeting in the dining hall?"

"We were on our way there, but then that *thing* found us, and Deliah wanted to bring her back to her bedroom, as if she couldn't make it there herself."

Lana watched Angelica for a moment. Where had she been the last few days? Her cousin placed her on the floor, and with one last look at Dominic, the doll marched into what she assumed was Deliah's bedroom. She would have suggested going inside so she could see her cousin's room but didn't want to be anywhere near Angelica.

Dominic glared at his sister and angrily stomped away. Lana and Deliah reluctantly followed Dominic to a staircase.

"Where are we going?" she asked. "This isn't the way to the dining hall."

"We're going to our hideout," Deliah explained. "The dining hall was just a good place to meet. Breakfast was already served hours ago, so you'll have to wait until the party."

She followed her cousins up the stairs. When they reached the top, she noticed they weren't alone. A man and a woman were dancing by the huge window that overlooked the forest surrounding the castle. What scared her was the fact that these people were translucent and dancing a few feet above the floor. She was looking at two ghosts.

Her knees buckled. She glanced at her cousins and was surprised to see them ignoring the apparitions. Deliah realized she hadn't been walking with them.

"Come on," she said impatiently, tapping her foot on the ground. "What are you waiting for?"

"Hurry up," Dominic added.

"What are they?" she asked, watching the two figures. "Are they ghosts?"

"Ghosts aren't real." Deliah rolled her eyes.

"They won't hurt you," Dominic said.

"They're not even here that often," Deliah added.

"But why are they here?" she asked, somewhat relaxing and taking a step closer to the figures.

"The dimensions aren't as stable as everyone would like to think," Grant explained. "Usually when people think they've seen a ghost, they've just seen people from other dimensions."

"Is that what these are," she asked, gesturing to the figures, "people from other dimensions?"

Grant shrugged his shoulders. "Because these apparitions appear here frequently, they're probably shadows from the past. These two people have danced here before, in this exact spot, and somehow, their movement was recorded. Now the moment randomly plays back due to the natural breakdown of the dimensions."

The two dancing figures vanished into thin air, leaving behind a white swirling mist. She was going to ask more questions but Deliah and Dominic had already begun walking down the hall. She reluctantly followed, nervously checking behind her every few steps for the ghostly figures. They came to a large room with a beautiful view of Bridian Square.

Lana stepped up to the window. Grassy green hills were in the distance dotted with tall trees, their leaves blowing in the wind. The sky was a clear blue, and she studied it, looking for any differences than the sky she always gazed at in Mt. Sinclair.

She heard people in the hall, their voices echoing, and turned to see Terris and Randy run by the room. When they saw Deliah, Dominic, and Lana, they stopped and joined them. They were both carrying huge burlap bags filled with candy and toys.

"Look at all this!" Randy shouted, dumping his bag at his feet.

Multi-colored candy fell out of the opening. Lollipops, gummies, and hard candy rolled away, and Dominic bent down and picked up a blue and green box.

"Where did you get all of this?" Deliah asked.

"Well," Terris began. "My uncle died."

Lana looked to the floor. She wasn't sure who knew that Terris's uncle had been Alexander and felt uncomfortable knowing all that she did.

"Why is that something to be happy about?" Deliah asked, her brow wrinkled in confusion.

"Don't get me wrong, I'm sad about that." Terris dug his hands into one of the burlap bags. "Apparently, he set up a fund for me, but I couldn't access it until his death. The conservator came by this morning. I had no idea."

"And you don't have parents to tell you what to spend it on," Dominic said.

"That was harsh," Randy said, calling out his insensitive comment.

She saw Terris flinch, as if taken aback. She couldn't believe Dominic had said that. She was learning that both he and Deliah lived in their own bubble, but that had been cruel. She smiled at Terris, and he dropped his bag to the floor.

"Is all this from Poklin's?" she asked, changing the subject.

Terris nodded. "I got some things I've always wanted to try."

Dominic didn't seem to notice the change in Terris as he

tore open the box of candy in his hand. He turned the box upside down, and a bright orange candy spilled into his palm. He then tossed the box to Lana.

"Try these," Dominic said. "They're good."

She caught the box and examined it curiously. In blue lettering was *Poklin's Popping Poppers-Popalicious!* She turned the box around and read the tiny handwriting.

Warning-This product may not be suitable for children. The candy may not stop popping once swallowed, causing slight discomfort. This should only last a few minutes. In rare cases, the candy has been known to not stop popping for three to five days.

"Have you read the back of these?" she asked, holding up her box of *Poklin's Popping Poppers.* "They look dangerous."

"Who reads the packages?" Dominic asked, a wide grin on his mouth.

"Have you known anyone who didn't have the popping stop?" she asked. "The package says it could last days."

"No." Dominic rolled his eyes.

Lana opened the box and poured out one of the huge candies. When she put it in her mouth, the candy popped, hurting her cheeks where it hit. Try as she might, she couldn't swallow it and gagged. She opened her mouth to spit the candy out, and it flew down her throat, stopping the flow of air for a moment.

Once she was able to swallow the candy, popping the whole way, she took a deep breath. The popping sensation continued down into her stomach, causing her to double over from pain. The room exploded into laughter.

"Why did you lie to me?" she exclaimed. "I almost choked to death!"

"You were fine," Dominic said, leaning against the wall for support. "You didn't almost choke. I was watching. You were still breathing."

"Why didn't you tell me it would hurt?"

"Because then you wouldn't have tried it," Dominic answered. "And you have to admit that once you get past the popping, it's worth it."

"That's enough fun." Grant stepped into the room. "We have a party to attend. Terris, leave the bags. You can pick them up later."

She reluctantly followed Grant to the first floor. The hall was so congested with people that they lost Grant and Randy. She smiled when she saw Maris.

"There's Maris." She pointed to their instructor.

"I hate lessons," Dominic groaned. "I just want to be a reaper. What do I need lessons for?"

"You still need lessons to be a reaper," Terris said.

"All you need to know how to do is find the people you've been hired to find and bring them to the Bone Yards," Dominic answered.

"What are Bone Yards and reapers?" she asked as Grant shoved his way next to her, pushing an old man out of the way in his haste to get near her.

"The Bone Yards is a dimension that serves as a prison for really horrible people," Terris answered. "Its actual name is Bonawickham Yards, but everyone just calls it the Bone Yards."

"Reapers are hired by the Council of Elders to find the bad guys and escort them to the Yards," Dominic said proudly.

"What's the Council of Elders?"

"They oversee the dimensions," Dominic explained. "The Yards is such a terrible place that it has to be a unanimous decision on the part of the Elders to send someone there."

Someone bumped into Lana from behind. She was beginning to sweat from the pulsating crowd and wished she could leave.

"Come on, we're going in," Dominic said as he wiped the sweat off his brow. "We shouldn't have to wait."

She followed her cousin through the crowd. Dominic pushed his way to the guard at the door.

When the soldier didn't move, Dominic demanded, "Do you know who I am?"

Grant stepped up to the guard and said something she couldn't hear over the roar of the crowd. The guard pushed the door open, revealing Charlotte and Ramos across the huge room. Once they stepped inside, the guard closed the door again.

"Charlotte, this is ridiculous!" Ramos shouted.

"It's too late to cancel," she heard her aunt answer in mock sweetness. "Everyone's here!"

"Damon's still missing." Ramos threw his hands down in frustration.

"I'm not living my life in fear anymore, and I'm sure Damon's fine!"

Deliah's eyes grew wide, and Dominic mouthed, "I can't believe they're fighting again."

"We should leave," Lana whispered.

"How long have you been here?" Ramos turned toward his children.

"We just got here," Deliah stammered.

"We shouldn't have to wait outside like the rest of them," Dominic said, crossing his arms over his chest.

Ramos sighed. "Have a Choclochino. We'll be opening the doors for everyone else in a moment."

Charlotte scowled and asked, "Terris, shouldn't you be working? I'll take a glass of dandelion tea."

Terris stopped walking. "I have the day off."

"Charlotte, leave the boy alone," Ramos scolded.

Terris's face turned red with embarrassment, and he stepped backwards. She saw a seating area to their left and made her way to it, motioning Terris to follow. She sat down,

Deliah next to her. Terris stood awkwardly to the side, playing with the hem of his cloak.

"Are you going to sit?"

Terris nodded and sat slowly, as if unsure if he should. Ramos opened the huge doors, and the crowd filed in, smiling and shouting happily. Soon the room was crammed to capacity. Soft music filled the air, and even Ramos put on a happy face.

"Where did Dominic go?" Deliah asked, scanning the crowd for her brother.

"With Carter and Ivan by the doors," Terris answered forlornly, still playing with the rip in his cloak.

A hand clamped down on her shoulder, and she jumped. When she turned around, she saw Poklin staring at her. He was still wearing rope suspenders over a shabby white shirt and scuffed brown pants, and she giggled.

"Hello, Lana," Poklin said, handing her a bright purple candy. "It's nice to see you again, under better circumstances."

"What did Damon order that you couldn't give him in the backroom of your shop?"

Poklin looked away from her. "I don't know what you mean."

"I know he was in your store the night he disappeared."

"Be careful, you don't want to anger the wrong people," Poklin warned before walking back into the crowd.

"What were you doing?" Deliah asked in disbelief once Poklin was out of earshot.

"Something's not right with him." She threw the candy over her shoulder. "I can't place it, but something's off. The whole time I questioned him, he didn't even look at me. Did you see him? His eyes were darting all over the place."

"So?" Deliah asked. "Maybe he doesn't like looking at you."

"You can tell someone's lying if they don't look at you when they talk."

"I've never heard that before," Deliah said. "That's ridiculous."

"What was Poklin doing over here?" Kiernan asked, joining them, Dominic and Carter trailing along behind him.

"Lana was giving him the third degree," Deliah answered.

"Did you tell Ramos yet?" she whispered.

"Not yet."

She turned from Kiernan when an older woman stumbled towards her. She was wearing a bright orange dress and matching hat that had a tall feather sticking straight into the air. To her astonishment, she was also wearing orange feathered glasses.

"Hello, my name's Samoa," the woman said excitedly.

"Nice to meet you," Lana muttered, trying to remember where she heard the name before.

"The pleasure's mine," Samoa squealed as she clapped her hands together. "Oh, where is Margot? She would love to meet you!"

She searched her mind, thinking of an excuse to leave the hysterical woman.

"Sorry, Samoa," Kiernan said, as if reading her mind. "We're on our way to see King Ramos."

Samoa frowned and removed the feathered glasses from her eyes. She searched Lana's face for a moment then broke into a smile.

"Oh, that's no problem," she said.

Lana watched her walk away and remembered where she had heard her name. The day her parents took her to see the fountain of Bridian, her mother mentioned seeing someone named Samoa. The doors slammed open, and she turned to look at who had joined them.

"Damon!" Ramos called as he opened his arms wide, as if to embrace his son from across the room.

Deliah and Dominic looked up, curious to see their

brother. As the crowd parted, she had a clear view of her cousin and someone in a black cloak with the hood covering the head. Something was wrong. She could feel it in the air. The music stopped, and she tried to find her parents in the crowd.

"How nice to see you again, Father," Damon said, smiling.

"Come join the festivities," Ramos said, still with his arms stretched open, longing for an embrace. When it became clear Damon wasn't going to move, Ramos asked, "What's wrong?"

Lana felt something crawling on her arm and was disgusted to see a fly. She brought her arm closer to her face and watched it for a moment before flicking it off.

"Who's with you?" Ramos asked.

The person standing next to Damon chuckled loudly and withdrew a bony hand hidden underneath the sleeves of his cloak. Suddenly, the screaming became even louder as Damon's friend removed his hood. Ramos stumbled backward, and she heard Charlotte hit the floor in a dead faint.

When the crowd parted, Lana had a clear view of the one person she hoped never to see again. Alderic was standing next to Damon. His face was pale, his long hair was messy, and he had a mad look in his eyes.

"How nice to see you again, my brother," Alderic cackled.

Damon laughed as Alderic withdrew two Stones of Medora from his cloak. Kiernan took a slow step in front of Lana and raised the hood of his cloak over his face. She slid to the floor. Terris moved next to Kiernan to help block her from harm.

"How did you get in?" Ramos asked over the uproar of his guests. "We have soldiers at every entrance."

"You have a very bright son," Alderic snapped. "Go ahead, Damon. Tell your father what you did."

Damon glared at Ramos. "I had two illegal mirrors made. When I was allowed inside I set up my mirror."

"And I traveled through the mirrors," Alderic spat.

"Granted, it was a tight squeeze, but if you want something bad enough, you'll be surprised at what you can do."

"Damon," Ramos called in a quivering voice. "My son, how could you betray me like this?"

"Actually, it was rather easy."

Ramos looked as if he was going to be sick, and Lana felt for him, betrayed by his own brother and son. The lights flickered, and she hoped the electricity wouldn't go out.

"Where are the soldiers?" Ramos asked, looking around frantically.

"They've been taken care of." Alderic stepped forward. "Do you think I would have walked in here without a plan?"

"How did you escape?" Ramos asked.

"That wasn't as easy," Alderic explained. "But, again, I have Damon to thank for that as well. A few reapers were influenced to release me during my cell transfer."

"Your transfer was days ago," Ramos said, trying to understand. "The Council told me it had gone as planned."

"My cell isn't empty," Alderic spat. "I imagine they'll realize their error soon. I've been in Bridian for two days. Damon's disappearance was set by Poklin to divert attention from us. I was even able to take care of the man responsible for my imprisonment. But I don't have to tell you that, I heard you already saw what became of poor Alexander."

The room was absolutely silent. She looked for Grant and found him a few feet away, slowly making his way towards her.

"Enough of this idle chitchat," Alderic raised his voice. "Where's my daughter?"

She froze. Kiernan and Terris stepped closer to her, shielding her from view. Everyone in the room began searching for her, and she frantically prayed that no one would find her.

"Alderic, she's not here!" Ramos shouted, trying to draw his brother's attention from the crowd.

"Nonsense," Alderic spat. He then turned towards the mass

of people again and shouted, "Come out, Carlecia. Your father's here to see you."

Lana held her breath.

"Come to me!" Alderic hissed.

When no one did or said anything, Alderic grabbed a young man from around the neck and lifted him into the air.

"I'll kill him," Alderic snapped. "Give me my daughter, Ramos!"

A woman shrieked, screaming for the young man dangling from Alderic's arms. All around her, people began running for the doors.

"No one move," Alderic shouted. "My rebels are in this room. They've been my eyes and ears these past fifteen years. It's time to come out of hiding."

Damarius Pilkins, along with a dozen men and women, defiantly stepped up to Alderic.

"I want all of you," he spat.

Half a dozen people stepped up to him, including Poklin and a few soldiers.

"Much better," he hissed, throwing the man to the ground angrily.

"ALDERIC, I WILL NOT STAND FOR THIS!" Ramos shouted over the cacophony of noises around him. "THINK OF KALINIA."

"Don't ever say her name again." Alderic threw his hands into the air, flinging a Stone of Medora right at his brother.

Her breath caught in her throat when Ramos fell to the floor. Alderic called her name again.

"Look for my brother and sister," Damon said a moment later. "Lana will be with them. In fact, I see them now."

10

THE UNFORGIVABLE BETRAYAL

In her entire life, Lana had never been so scared. Neither of her attacks in Mt. Sinclair nor her forced removal from Poklin's by Alexander compared to how she felt now. She shut her eyes, hoping to draw herself away from Damon's fierce gaze.

"Deliah, Dominic," he called. "Where's Lana?"

The crowd turned toward the young Prince and Princess of Bridian as a harsh silence filled the room. She reopened her eyes in fear. While she was glad that Terris and Kiernan blocked her from the crowd, someone was bound to see her with time. She caught herself holding her breath and exhaled nervously, terrified that Alderic would hear her tremble.

"I don't know where she is." Dominic stepped into the crowd, effectively drawing attention from Terris and Kiernan. "Why are you doing this, Damon?"

"ENOUGH!" Alderic interrupted. "I know she's here, and if I have to kill every single person in this room to find her, I will."

She frantically looked around the room again, looking for her parents. She had to find a way to escape but couldn't think straight. When she caught Grant's eye, he shook his head, as if to tell her to stay calm and hidden. The room was hot, and the air felt thick.

Alderic ran towards Deliah and Dominic. He narrowed his eyes at his niece and nephew as he pushed his way through the crowd around him. Suddenly, Grant sprang to life, charging him. Alderic withdrew a Stone of Medora and threw it at Grant. He toppled to the floor as Damarius and Poklin subdued him.

Kiernan looked back at her, winked, and ran into the crowd. Time seemed to move in slow motion. When Alderic saw Kiernan, he ran after him, thinking he was chasing his daughter. The crowd gasped. She was too stunned to move. She couldn't believe he had been so foolish.

A moment later, someone's arms wrapped around her torso as complete pandemonium broke out. Through her confusion, she saw Terris lifting her to her feet. When she was standing, he pulled her toward the doors. She looked behind her to see if Kiernan was all right, but too many people separated them.

With Terris's help, she found herself outside of the room. They had to push their way through the crowd, but they managed to stay together.

"He's going to kill him," Deliah mumbled as she stopped running, trying to catch her breath.

Lana couldn't believe what had just happened and hoped her cousin was wrong. She didn't think she could dislike anyone more than Nick, but Alderic topped the list. He had killed before and there was nothing stopping him from killing again.

"Where are we going to go?" Deliah fell to the floor, holding her arms to her chest.

She struggled out of Terris's grasp. Her common sense told her that rebels would be stationed at every entrance and knew it would be foolish to try to leave through them. Then she remembered the secret passages.

"What's closer, my bedroom or the basement?"

"Why would we go to your bedroom?" Dominic asked. "We'll be trapped!"

"Trust me," she said as those near the doors followed their lead, creating a miniature stampede of frightened people.

"We can't go to your bedroom," Terris explained, as if finally awaking. "Your father probably has rebels waiting for you there."

"Take me to the basement then. I have a plan."

Dominic pulled his sister off the floor, and they began running. She turned and saw two men chasing them. They hadn't appeared frightened. Rather, they looked determined, and she knew they were rebels. Deliah and Terris ran through a mirror. Dominic stepped aside so she could go through first.

Lana felt nauseous as she effortlessly slid through the cold glass and landed on the floor. Before she had time to sit up, Dominic leaped through the portal then pushed the mirror to the ground. When it only cracked, he smashed his elbow against it, finally breaking it.

She sighed with relief when she realized the rebels wouldn't be able to follow them, until she saw the blood. Dominic had cut his elbow. Before she could help her cousin, Deliah pulled her off the floor, and she saw that they were in the kitchen. Cluttered counters with an assortment of dishes took up most of the room. She nervously looked around, trying to see if any rebels had been waiting for them.

"Why did you want to come down here?" Terris asked.

"I know a way out of the castle," she answered, nervously looking around the room again. "At least, I did."

No one caught her last sentence, or if they did, chose to ignore it. Terris walked across the room and slowly pushed the doors open. As they walked, she strained her ears, hoping to hear if anyone was following. Every little noise made her jump.

When she saw a familiar stone staircase, she led the group to the passage. She placed her hand on the cold wall when they finally reached the tiny X that Grant had carved into the stone. She pushed the wall to her right. She stepped into the room and kneeled, running her hands along the dusty floor in hopes of finding the entrance. After catching her fingers in a tiny hole, she lifted the trapdoor and motioned everyone in.

Once everyone was in the passage, Lana slid the wall closed, effectively concealing their escape route. She jumped in the passage after them and took a moment to catch her breath before leading the group through the dark tunnel. She was relieved that no one was following them but wondered where they were going to go. There was no telling who they could trust anymore.

When they reached the end of the passage, she pushed the exit open. Once she saw that no rebels awaited them, she carefully crawled out. She looked up at the clear sky and counted her blessings. They had been lucky that Alderic and his rebels had not captured them. A warm breeze made the leaves on the trees shake, and the birds sang, oblivious to the chaos within the castle. She wanted to get as far away as they could.

Dominic took off his cloak and threw it to the grass. He then removed the vest over his dress shirt. He wrapped the vest around his arm, trying to stop the trickle of bright-red blood. He put his cloak back on.

"Let's go." He stepped toward the forest.

"Wait," Lana called. When everyone turned toward her she continued, "The crowns. We need to leave them."

She removed her crown. She heard Deliah protest, but Dominic forcefully took it off her head. Lana placed the crowns in the passage and closed the door, covering it with leaves.

"My father told me we have to go to some falls." She searched her mind, trying to remember where he told her to go. "To someone named Emery."

"Emeric?" Deliah said. "Ganyon Falls?"

"Yeah. Do you know where that is?"

Deliah nodded. "I know how to get to Ganyon Falls, but we've only been to his house a few times. I don't know if I remember it."

"One problem at a time. Lead the way."

"Don't worry," Dominic added. "I remember his house."

Lana was scared. She was in a new world, and although it appeared like Mt. Sinclair, she hadn't lived in Bridian long enough to know the differences. She wished her parents were with her.

"How's your arm?" she asked Dominic.

"Couldn't you break the mirror without cutting yourself?" Deliah stepped up to her brother.

"Don't start, Deliah," Dominic snapped. "If I hadn't done anything, those rebels would have caught us!"

Terris cleared his throat. Deliah, Dominic, and Lana turned toward him.

"You have to be quiet," Terris warned, flinching under everyone's gaze. "The Shadow Splinters will find us if you're too loud."

"No one's seen them in ages," Dominic scoffed.

"What are Shadow Splinters?"

"They aren't around anymore," Dominic said. "They're extinct."

"They're not extinct," Terris said.

"Don't listen to them," Dominic said. "They're gone. They've been gone for years."

"How long do you think it will take us to get to Ganyon Falls?" she asked, changing the subject before a fight broke out.

"A day or two," Terris answered. "I've never walked there before."

"We usually take horses," Dominic explained.

Lana knew she was in for a long couple of days. The sun was slowly making its way to the horizon, and it would be dark soon. The forest was quiet, and she was thankful that they had yet to encounter anyone. The wind blew around her, eerily whispering into her ears. She listened for any sign that they were being followed but didn't hear anything besides birds and the rustling of leaves.

She wondered where they were going to sleep. She didn't know what kinds of terrifying creatures lived in the forest. For all she knew, these Shadow Splinters could still be around and, while she didn't know what they were, was scared, nonetheless.

As the sun set, making the forest even darker, she shivered. Every little noise made her jump. She was eager to find shelter and rest. Lana stumbled over a tree branch and fell, landing in a puddle.

"Are you all right?" Terris ran to her. When she nodded, he continued, "We're almost to the pond. There are Lambrinios there."

"What's that?" she asked, standing up. "Someplace to sleep?"

"Plants," Dominic answered.

"Their paste prevents infection," Terris added.

"Is that like aloe?" she asked, remembering when her mother had used aloe on her cuts in Mt. Sinclair.

"I've never even heard of that," Terris chuckled.

"What do you think happened to everyone?" Deliah asked.

The silence was deafening. She hoped that no one had been hurt. She hoped Ramos and her parents were all right.

As they walked, she twirled Kalinia's ring around her finger, trying to keep her mind off Alderic. A few minutes later, lights appeared before them. She stared at the bright lights dancing before her. Clustered around a large pond were little fairies, no bigger than her thumb. What was even more extraordinary was that the lights had been coming from the fairies.

Miniature houses had been built into tree trunks, complete with tiny windows, doors, and chimneys. About twenty fairies were gathered around the pond, either sitting on leaves that hung over the calm water or flying. Five smaller fairies were even playing underneath mushrooms that were growing in a patch of weeds near the water.

Lana couldn't take her eyes off them. Was she dreaming? Their wings varied in color, and their skin seemed to be illuminated by tiny flecks of multicolored sparkles.

"We need to get to the water," Terris whispered, startling her from her revere. "Lambrinios grow near water."

"Leave the fairies alone," Dominic warned.

As if they heard Dominic, the fairies scattered. They fluttered into the tiny houses or underneath gigantic green leaves.

"Well, that takes care of that problem." Terris walked into the clearing. "They must have heard us."

Lana stumbled in the dark after Terris while Deliah stayed with her brother, hidden behind an enormous tree trunk. When she reached her friend, she found him cupping his hands into the pond. Terris lifted his hands to his face and glanced at the water.

"I don't think you should drink that." She sniffed the water in his hands. "It smells."

Terris released the water, watching it spill back into the pond. The fairies were slowly returning, which gave Terris light to look for Lambrinios. She couldn't take her eyes off the tiny creatures and continued to watch them, forgetting about the search.

"We're not here to hurt you," she whispered. "We're looking for Lambrinios."

"Over there," the nearest fairy spoke, as she pointed across the pond, in a voice that was soft and sweet, almost melodious.

Terris ran to the other side of the pond while she remained transfixed by the fairies. The one who had spoken landed on her hand. She brought the tiny fairy to her face, surprised to see that it looked exactly as a miniature human would, except for the glittery wings and bright purple eyes. A soft purple hue lit up her wings, and she was wearing a white satin dress that tapered near her ankles then flared out at her feet. Long sleeves covered her little arms.

"I found a patch!" Terris exclaimed, waving a green leafy stalk.

Deliah stepped out from the forest and slowly walked to Lana. The fairy fluttered to Deliah, settling on her thumb. Once the other fairies saw they meant no harm, they too joined them.

"They're so pretty," Deliah said as the fairies gave the pond a haunting glow, making it appear as if they were sitting in a shower of multicolored lights. "I've never seen them before."

Terris walked up to her and took her hand. He squeezed the Lambrinio stalk, and a cold green paste landed in her palm. She glanced down and curiously rubbed the thick paste with her fingers as Terris threw the stalk over his shoulder, walked back to the pond, and cupped his hands into it again. When he rejoined her, he let a few drops of water trickle on the paste, then scooped the concoction off her palm.

Terris nudged her in the arm, gesturing his head toward the forest when she looked at him. When she didn't move, Terris sighed and rejoined Dominic. While Terris tended Dominic's elbow, Lana and Deliah remained transfixed by the fairies.

"You can't stay long."

She jumped when she heard the tiny fairy. She waited for her to speak again.

"We'll take you somewhere safe."

"Why can't we stay?" Deliah tilted her head to the side.

"You'll draw the Shadow Splinters," the fairy answered in a sweet voice, almost child-like.

"I told you they're still around, Dominic!" Deliah shouted toward the forest.

Lana looked at Dominic and Terris, wondering what these Shadow Splinters were. She saw that they were both waiting for the girls to rejoin them, but she was reluctant to leave. She didn't want to go back into the dark forest.

The fairy fluttered off Deliah's hand. Deliah reluctantly stood up and waited for Lana to join her. She didn't want to leave. For some reason, she felt safe with the fairies and closed her eyes, savoring the moment. Something perched on her nose. When she reopened her eyes, she came face-to-face with a fairy. They were surrounded.

"I don't like this." Dominic joined his sister.

"We'll help you," the fairy on her nose said, his wings fluttering in the air.

The fairies tightened their enclosure around them. The one that landed on her nose flew to another and took a green gemstone from her hands, which seemed to have just materialized. She felt so transfixed with the jewel she held out her hand for the apple-colored stone.

"This is for you." The handsome fairy held out the jewel, only to pull it back when she almost had it in her grasp. "But only if you follow us."

"To a safe place," another fairy added as she dropped a single gold coin to Deliah.

Deliah lifted the coin to her eyes, examining it from the light of the fairies. Dominic plucked it from her and threw it into the pond.

"Why did you do that?" Deliah asked.

"Come with us," the fairy near Lana said as he held out the apple-green jewel to her. "We can help you."

Lana lifted the gemstone out of the fairy's hands. She knew they were very lost, not to mention cold, hungry, and tired. As she looked deep within the jewel, she came to the conclusion that they needed help, and since the fairies were offering theirs, they might as well take it.

"Let's go with them."

"What's wrong with you?" Dominic asked. "Did you forget that we were just attacked by your crazy father and his rebels?"

"I want to go with them."

"I can't believe this," Terris said, making his way toward them. "We don't have time for this."

"Snap out of it!" Dominic jumped in front of her.

Two fairies, one male and one female, immediately surrounded Dominic and began whispering in his ear. Terris ran to Dominic, hoping to reach him before they had him in their grasp, but was too late.

"Let's go with them."

One-by-one, the fairies flew away. Deliah, Dominic, and Lana followed them without question. Once Terris realized there was nothing he could do or say to convince them otherwise, he too followed until they came upon another clearing in the forest, not far from the pond. A thin canopy of leaves hung over an enormous pile of gold coins and shiny jewels. She saw emeralds, rubies, sapphires, and diamonds.

"Look at all of this!" Deliah squealed as she clasped her hands together in delight.

A fairy flew down to Lana and said, "It's all yours!"

Dominic jumped into a pile of gold coins, stopping only to cradle his injured arm.

"What's wrong with all of you?" Terris watched them in complete awe. "It's like you forgot everything that happened and that we're on the run! What are we going to do with all of this? We can't take it with us."

"Calm down," Dominic said, his eyes wide in amazement.

"I will not calm down!" Terris exclaimed but stopped when a fairy began to fly around his head, and he tried to push it away.

She picked up a sapphire. It sparkled from the light of the fairies. She finally felt safe and was going to sit when the fairies disappeared, leaving them in darkness. She heard something behind her and turned around. She flinched when a woman in a deep scarlet cloak materialized before her.

She glanced at her friends and saw them huddled together under the watchful eyes of three more women all dressed in the same scarlet cloaks. The woman in front of her lit a match against a tree trunk, giving her enough light to see her face. She had shiny black hair, striking green eyes, and the reddest lips she had ever seen. The woman motioned her to stand up, and she promptly complied. It felt as if she were under another spell.

They were surrounded, and there was no escape. As the match flickered, the woman with the shiny black hair pushed her to begin walking. A moment later, they reached another clearing a few yards away.

Five women were in the clearing sitting on cut tree trunks, flat sides on the ground. They were gathered around an enormous fire that seemed to have a life of its own. The woman leading them motioned that they should sit on an empty trunk. She was so tired she was the first to comply.

"The fairies do their job well. They're strong allies."

Without warning, the fire popped, and the women transformed before her eyes. They were no longer pretty but wild looking. Their eyes were sunken and bloodshot. Their bodies were wasted away, and their perfect cloaks were tattered and torn.

Lana tried standing but found she was rooted to the tree trunk. She turned toward Deliah, Dominic, and Terris and found them in the same predicament. When she looked at the women again, she was astonished to see that they appeared as they first had.

"We know who you are."

"You're Alderic and Kalinia's daughter," another cackled as she pointed her long blood-red nails at her.

"How do you know who I am?"

Suddenly, and to her utter astonishment, Angelica walked into the clearing. She was dressed in a miniature scarlet cloak, identical to those worn by the women, and was carrying a tiny bundle of wood. While smiling at Dominic, she stepped up to the fire.

"Angelica, what are you doing here?" Deliah gasped.

"This is my family," she answered as the fire lit up her porcelain face.

"What?" Deliah sneered. "You don't have a family. You're my doll!"

"No," one of the women snapped. Lana couldn't tell which one because she couldn't take her eyes off Angelica. "She belongs to no one."

"Your father made us what we are today because of Angelica."

Angelica took another step closer to Deliah.

"My parents were rebels," she spoke slowly. "Two of Alderic's strongest allies. That is, until the day they decided to leave the Rebellion. He murdered them within an hour of learning their intentions."

"Angelica," Deliah snapped. "This isn't funny! You're my doll, start acting like it!"

"I'm not a doll," she said, ever so sweetly, as she turned to face Deliah. "My spirit has been trapped inside this doll for sixteen years."

The woman with the long black hair and striking green eyes winced. She looked back to Angelica, waiting to hear more of the story.

"After their death, your father ordered mine," she continued. "I was only a few months old. He didn't want their so-called traitor blood within his Rebellion."

"We knew he was going too far," the woman with the shiny black hair explained. "We took Angelica and the only possession she owned, the doll you're looking at."

"But he found us," another said as they changed into the horrible creatures once again. "He has many spies."

"We had committed the Unforgivable Betrayal," the woman with the shiny black hair continued. "We deliberately disobeyed his command. We tried to protect Angelica, even after he ordered her death. After banishing us from the Rebellion, he cursed us into the monstrous beings we are today."

"Then he stabbed Angelica in the stomach and left her to die."

Lana didn't want to hear any more of the awful story and couldn't believe her father was that evil.

"But he forgot we have our own magic," a woman with curly red hair added to the twisted tale. "He taught us well. Even after the curse, we were able to transfer Angelica's soul into her doll, and she's been with us ever since."

"I knew something wasn't right with her!" Dominic said angrily.

"All the times she disappeared," she thought aloud.

"She came back to us."

"But why was she sent to me?" Deliah asked.

"To be our spy," the woman with the blood red nails explained. "We knew the Princess would come back one day."

"I'm so sorry," she apologized as a single tear fell down her cheek. Oddly enough, she felt responsible for Alderic's actions. "He's a horrible person."

"We'll have our revenge on him," the woman with the shiny black hair snapped as they changed into the horrible monsters once again.

"You're different."

"We can feel it," the woman with the curly red hair said as she walked around the fire, blowing shimmering gold dust into Terris, Deliah, and Dominic's faces as she passed. "In time, you'll have the power to change us back."

"For this, we'll help you," another added.

Lana looked at her friends and found them slumped over, as if sleeping. As the fire crackled, she wondered how they had managed to fall asleep. Angelica remained silent. She looked to the women again.

"You have important things to do," the woman with curly red hair continued. "You must not fail. Don't let your friends distract you."

"Tomorrow, you must go east until you come to the river," the woman to her right spoke, pointing presumably to the east. "Follow it downstream, and you'll eventually reach Ganyon Falls."

She didn't know how they knew she was going to Ganyon Falls and wasn't about to ask. Instead, she shuddered as they changed before her eyes again. Now they looked as they had when she had first seen them. In the light of the fire, she saw that all the women were very pale and had dark red lips that appeared bloodstained.

"Beware the Shadow Splinters that lurk in the forest. You mustn't travel in the daylight."

"Only the night," another continued. "For that is when you cast no shadow."

"It's important that you remember what we told you," the woman with the curly red hair added.

"Now, it's time you sleep as well," the woman standing in front of her whispered, blowing sparkling dust within her left hand into her face.

She was about to protest when the rest of the women transformed back into the horrible creatures she knew had become their true forms. But she didn't care anymore. She sank into a deep sleep to the sound of their voices.

11

THE CITY AT THE BOTTOM OF THE LAKE

Lana awoke to the sound of birds chirping. As images of the previous day flashed through her head, she wondered if it had all been a horrible nightmare. She hoped that when she opened her eyes, she would be in Mt. Sinclair, snuggled in her warm bed. But then she felt the hard dirt beneath her back.

She heard someone stirring next to her and opened her eyes. Beads of sweat dripped down her face, and she rolled over to get a better look at her surroundings. As she sat up, she saw that the fire had gone out. She leaned against the bench she had been sitting on the night before.

"What happened?" Terris asked.

She saw he had dark circles underneath his eyes and was covered in dirt. During the night, he too must have fallen off the bench he had been sleeping on.

"The Outcasts found us last night," she whispered, flinching when she found her throat dry and scratchy.

"I know that," Terris said. "What I'm trying to figure out is why we're still alive."

"They wanted to help us."

Deliah sat up. She rubbed her eyes and shook Dominic until he awoke.

"Sleeping dust," Dominic grumbled. "I didn't even see it coming. Your doll betrayed us, Deliah!"

"It wasn't her fault," Deliah shot back.

She couldn't believe her cousins were fighting again. While she was relieved that they had survived their first night in the forest, they wouldn't make it through their second if her cousins continued their squabbling. They had to avoid drawing attention to themselves.

Lana looked at Terris and found him watching Deliah and Dominic's fight with half-hearted interest. When he realized she was watching him, he smiled at her. As she returned her friend's smile, she remembered the warning she had received the night before.

"We should wait until night before leaving."

"That's ridiculous," Dominic scoffed.

"That's what the Outcasts told me." She stood up and brushed the dirt off. "They said something about shadows."

"I told you yesterday, they're not around anymore," Dominic said, throwing his hands down in frustration. "I don't know anyone that has ever seen them before."

She sighed. "Just because you don't know anyone that's ever seen them, doesn't mean they're not still around."

Lana had seen too much to believe her cousin's last statement. A week ago, she had never known anyone who had been to other dimensions or seen fairies, but now, she knew they existed.

"I guess it all depends on who you know," Terris said, following her thoughts.

Dominic stood up and began walking, calling over his shoulder, "I'd rather take my chances with the Shadow Splinters than be captured by the Outcasts again."

"As much as I hate to say it, Dominic's right," Deliah said.

"We should get as far away from the Outcasts as we can. They're rebels."

"No," she corrected. "They used to be rebels. They're not anymore."

"Once a rebel, always a rebel," Deliah called over her shoulder.

Lana reluctantly followed her cousins. She didn't want to become separated, but she had trusted the Outcasts. They had risked their lives to save Angelica, which made them different from Alderic. She also knew that if they wanted to hurt her, they could have last night.

They had only walked a short distance when they found themselves in the clearing where the fairies had led them the night before. It was empty, except for where the gold coins and gemstones should have been. In their place were piles of leaves.

"Where'd it go?" Deliah asked sadly.

"Just my luck," Dominic said. "We could have taken it."

"What would we have done with it?" Terris asked angrily. "We couldn't have carried it with us!"

A strong gust of wind blew past them, scattering the leaves. She nervously looked for the fairies, expecting them to reappear behind a tree. The forest was eerily silent as they walked. In fact, the only noise to be heard was the crunch of leaves from their passing feet.

After walking many miles without incident, they came upon a section of forest filled with dead trees. The sun warmed her face. She closed her eyes and held her arms out, taking in its warmth, when she overheard her cousin's conversation.

"He would never purposely hurt us," Deliah whispered, leaning close to her brother.

"Deliah, give it up. He's not who we thought he was."

"There has to be some sort of explanation," Deliah trembled. "Maybe he's been brainwashed."

"He chose the Rebellion over his family." Dominic looked to his left, away from his sister.

"He's still my brother," Deliah said, crying softly. "I know he was set up."

Lana ducked underneath a tree branch. There were times she had been sad that she was an only child and seeing Deliah and Dominic made it worse. Even though they fought a lot, they loved each other. Ava and Trevor had become surrogate siblings. They had been so close. As she thought of her previous life in Mt. Sinclair, a thought came to her, and she stopped walking, trying to think clearly.

"Do you know who Damon stayed with when he visited Mt. Sinclair?"

Dominic turned to look at her and asked, "Why are you eavesdropping?"

"Sorry," she apologized, her cheeks flushing. "But did you know he wasn't given permission to go?"

"No," Dominic answered.

"Where did you hear that?" Deliah turned on her.

"I overheard your parents talking about it. I think he met someone in Mt. Sinclair who brought him into the Rebellion. That would explain why he changed when he came back."

Lana began walking again, trying to piece together her thoughts. She knew she was right. Had he met Marty or his accomplice in Mt. Sinclair? They came to a small clearing and stopped walking.

"Damon would never voluntarily join the rebels." Deliah crossed her arms defensively over her chest.

She looked to her feet, then said, "I found something the day we searched Damon's room."

Dominic turned to look at her, his eyes narrowed quizzically.

"I was sitting by his bookshelf." She rushed to explain.

"There was a board covering the bottom shelf, I moved it and found some books on black magic and a journal of Alderic's."

Dominic's eyes grew wide, and Deliah began crying. Lana walked up to her cousin, hoping to comfort her. Deliah stopped crying, wiped the tears from her eyes, and jumped on her. They fell to the ground, and Dominic pulled his sister off her.

"Why didn't you tell us before?" Deliah demanded as she went limp in her brother's arms.

"Be quiet!" Terris whispered with such urgency no one talked.

Deliah stopped crying and wiped her bloodshot eyes. A moment later, Lana heard it. It sounded as if strong gusts of wind were blowing in every direction. Terris's eyes were wide, and his lips trembled. Deliah started crying again, only softer, and Dominic's face turned the palest shade of white.

Lana looked to her feet and found her shadow, clear as day, mocking her. Then she saw it, standing before her and emitting a black swirling mist and awful sulfur smell. She took a step backwards, and then three more of the horrible creatures popped around her, emitting the same black mist and awful smell.

The creatures had them surrounded. They looked like huge wolves that were able to walk on two feet. Their hands and feet were completely covered in thick, dark-brown fur. Two beady yellow eyes peered out from deep within their hoods.

As the beasts surrounded them, she noticed they were wearing dark robes, the hood covering their heads, leaving most of their face in shadow. She flinched when one of the creatures shakily stepped up to her and drew its nails on her cheek, drawing blood. Another let out an ear-piercing howl that sent chills down her spine.

Lana looked at her friends and saw that they too were surrounded and scared. Terris fell to his knees, and one of the

Shadow Splinters yanked him back to his feet, growling and hissing. One of the creatures grabbed her while another took hold of Deliah and Dominic. The rest disappeared around them.

Thick black smoke filled the air. She covered her eyes and held her breath, unsure if the smoke would harm her at all. When she felt like she couldn't take another moment of not being able to breathe, she reluctantly opened her eyes and took a deep lungful of air, relieved to find that the smoke didn't appear to harm her in any way.

The beast holding Lana began growling, snapping its long, pointed teeth in her face. She began kicking, but it clutched her skin and dug its sharp nails into her even harder. Blood trickled down her wrist from the creature's tight grip.

The remaining three Shadow Splinters pushed them through the woods. Their captors were very quiet, so much so that it terrified her. She was too scared to think. She tripped on a rock and fell to the ground.

The beast behind her let out another ear-piercing howl and grabbed her, pulling her back to her feet. She caught her balance and continued walking, too afraid to wipe the dirt off her cloak. Deliah began whimpering, and she turned to look at her, which angered her captor. It walked up to her, and she had nowhere else to look but at the horrifying beast and nearly fainted when it removed its hood. Its face was a twisted mass of bone and fur, and its eyes stared at her, as if it saw something next to her she couldn't.

They walked for hours. Occasionally, one or two Shadow Splinters would join them, emitting the awful sulfur smell when they transported. At least half the day dragged on this way, without any stops at all, and Lana's legs were beginning to feel like jelly.

A small animal jumped in front of their path. The beast

behind her disappeared and reappeared next to it. She didn't know what it was but knew something terrible was going to happen. She gagged as thick black smoke surrounded her again. The Shadow Splinter grabbed the animal by its bushy tail, and it began screeching, trying to escape. The beast swallowed it whole.

Lana began running. She felt awful for leaving her cousins and Terris behind, but before she had a chance to hide, the Shadow Splinter appeared in front of her. It grabbed her hood, dragging her back.

They continued walking in silence. Dead trees dotted the landscape as far as she could see, their limbs reaching for her. She had never heard a forest so silent, as if completely devoid of life. She didn't know how much longer she would be able to take it when they finally stopped at a camp.

A half dozen Shadow Splinters were in a clearing by a fire. The beast behind her pushed her toward a huge tree where another began tying her hands together with thick rope. She struggled to keep her hands as far apart as she could so she could slide her wrists out if given the chance.

When the monster finished tying Lana, it left her to help secure the others. The Shadow Splinters then left them to sit by the fire. She felt sick to her stomach, and Deliah, who was sitting next to her, continued sobbing.

"Deliah, shut up!" Dominic said. "If I'm going to die, I at least want some peace and quiet."

"No one's going to die," Terris said, afraid to take his eyes off the Shadow Splinters. "At least you know they're still around."

"What do you think they're going to do to us?" Deliah asked.

"How should I know?" Dominic snapped.

She began working on her ropes, loosening them so she would be able to wiggle her way out of them. Terris leaned into the tree.

"This is your fault." Dominic turned to Deliah. "You're the one who was making all the noise before we got caught."

"No." Deliah wiped her dirty and tearstained face on her shoulder. "It was Lana's fault. She provoked me."

She started laughing, not because what Deliah said was funny or because where they were was funny. It was merely out of desperation.

"I told you what the Outcasts said! We should have listened to them!"

The Shadow Splinters stopped moving. It was getting darker, and a cold rain fell on them.

"They won't be able to see us once the sun sets," she whispered, remembering the Outcasts' warning.

"Too bad that doesn't help us," Dominic said. "We're still tied up."

She continued to pry at the ropes around her wrists. They were becoming looser by the second. Her skin ached, it was red and raw, but she was close to freeing herself.

All of the sudden, there was a swish of air beside her. One of the creatures appeared next to her, sniffing. She stopped fumbling with her ropes and stood still. The Shadow Splinter put a hairy finger on her cheek and scratched the skin, drawing blood in tiny trickles. It leaned over and licked the blood off her face. She screamed as another beast appeared next to the first and dragged the monster away with an earsplitting screech.

With renewed fervency, Lana began working at her ropes again and let out a sigh of relief when she finally managed to untie herself from the tree. Very slowly, she crept over to Dominic and untied him. While she moved to Deliah, Dominic untied Terris, and soon they were all free from their bindings.

Slowly, they got up and walked deeper into the woods, away from the light of the fire. She held her finger to her mouth, hoping no one would make any noise, when she stepped on a branch. When it snapped, the creatures went silent and blindly looked around their camp.

She stood very still. One of the Shadow Splinters disappeared and reappeared where they had been tied to the tree. It let out a horrifying cry, and the rest of the creatures began disappearing and reappearing at random.

She began running as the Shadow Splinters appeared all around her, howling. She had no idea what the creatures would do to them if they were caught again. She tried to catch up to Terris, but it seemed as if the rain was weighing her down.

"Did you hear that?" Terris called over his shoulder.

Lana tried to listen but couldn't hear anything except the pounding of the rain.

"I thought I heard people," Terris continued.

She kept running, every few feet looking behind her to make sure her cousins were still safe. Moments later, a Shadow Splinter materialized before Dominic. She stopped running, and the horrible creature blindly reached for her cousin. Out of pure luck, it grabbed his cloak and dragged him back towards their camp.

Lana heard Deliah scream and realized that she had been recaptured as well. She turned to look at Terris and saw a Shadow Splinter a few yards from her, sniffing the air. She stood still; she didn't even think she could move if she wanted to. The creature slowly turned to face her.

"Look out!" Terris screamed, drawing the attention of the horrible beasts.

Terris pointed to the trees. Even in the dark, she saw three people crouching within the foliage, holding bows and arrows. One of the men blew into something, sounding an alarm, the low frequency echoing around them. She found she still couldn't move. Her brain didn't seem to be working.

A second later, she heard the release of an arrow. It

narrowly missed her and pierced the nearest beast in the chest. It let out a horrible scream and fell to the ground.

Terris ran to her, grabbed her hand, and began running. She heard more arrows and terrible cries. She let out a sigh of relief when she saw that her cousins had escaped. The few Shadow Splinters who had not been slain had disappeared.

A lake was before them, the moon reflecting off the still water. A row of older houses sat on the opposite bank. They looked neglected, paint peeling off in long strips.

Two men jumped out of the trees, landing near them. Before she could do anything, what looked like a dozen more men and women emerged from the murky depths of the lake. They were slowly changing before her eyes as they stepped out of the water. Their slimy and wrinkled bodies were drying at an accelerated rate.

They slowly made their way to land. She gasped when she saw that they had two slits on either side of their necks that were gradually closing. As they stepped out of the water, they began heaving for breath as these slits slowly disappeared within their skin.

The man closest to Lana sucked in a mouthful of air and smiled. His eyes were the palest shade of green. His skin looked yellow, almost as if it would fall off his body at any moment.

She realized that the slits on either side of their necks were gills. She watched wide-eyed as those who had joined them from the lake tried to breathe, appearing to suffocate as they inhaled for air.

"These two are children of Bridian," one of the men who had jumped from the trees said, pointing to Deliah and Dominic. "Their cloaks give them away."

"Is that right?" another spat as he pulled Deliah's head back by her hair. "Who are the other two?"

Lana looked to the ground. The last thing she needed was for one of them to recognize her. She was glad that she had worn Kalinia's cloak instead of the royal purple her cousins had been wearing.

"What's your name?"

"Lydia," she answered, using the made-up name Kiernan had used at Poklin's.

"Why are you with the youngest Prince and Princess of Bridian?"

"We're friends," she said, omitting the fact that they were related. "We're just passing through."

"We'll be on our way now," Dominic said, stepping backwards.

"Where are you going to go?" one of the men asked as he put a slimy finger underneath Deliah's chin, pushing her head up to his. "You're very far from Bridian."

"Queen Gwendolyn will know what to do with them," a woman interrupted, looking within the lake.

The name the woman spoke sounded familiar. Her mouth dropped open when she realized they were in Altaris. She looked at the lake and her stomach clenched. This was where her uncle had died.

"We should be on our way," Terris said.

"Oh no, the only place you'll be going is down there."

"No!" Deliah exclaimed. "I can't breathe underwater."

"You'll have to hold your breath then."

The man who had questioned Lana grabbed her around the waist and dove into the icy-cold water. She opened her eyes, hoping to find her way back to the surface, when she saw light. Her eyes stung as she looked deeper within the lake and saw buildings and houses nestled at the bottom. The city gave off a haunting glow.

She struggled in her captor's grip when something caught her eye—the man's gills had reopened again. She brushed against his slimy skin and felt sick. She was quickly running out of air. She was lightheaded, and her lungs were on fire. She didn't even have the energy to struggle and lay limp.

When she couldn't hold her breath any longer, the Altarian holding her lifted her head and brought her mouth to his own. She tried pushing away, but the man held her in his grasp firmly. His gills moved as he placed his mouth over hers, careful not to let water in, and breathed air into her. She gave a startled jump as his warm air passed into her deprived lungs.

Lana felt dizzy. Even though she had been given air, she had been holding her breath for too long, leaving her lightheaded. A school of brightly colored fish, the size of her fist, began biting her legs. She had no energy to knock them away, but to her surprise, her captor flicked them off.

They passed through huge pillars at the entrance of an algae covered castle. She felt her lungs ache and shut her eyes, imagining herself back in Mt. Sinclair. When she reopened them, she saw a woman a few yards away sitting on a gray-green throne surrounded by a dozen men and women armed with spears. The woman narrowed her eyes at her uninvited guests and slowly extended her left arm, pointing. Their captors took the order and continued swimming with their prisoners.

Moments later, she found herself above water. She gasped for breath. Deliah and Terris immediately began breathing, but Dominic remained still. She crawled to her cousin when he suddenly opened his eyes and began coughing up murky water. She fell to the floor in exhaustion. She looked around the dark room and placed her head in her hands.

"Yes," a harsh voice said. "They're children of Bridian."

Lana looked up. Standing in front of her was the woman who had been sitting on the throne. She had long gray-green hair, pale green eyes, and wrinkled skin. The gills on her throat had already disappeared, and she was slowly walking towards

Dominic, who was still heaving in short breaths. The woman looked at him how her Aunt Charlotte looked at Terris.

Lana listened to the water dripping off their bodies and watched the woman. Her skin seemed sicklier and more scabbed than the others. When she realized that she was looking at her, the woman took a calculated step forward.

"Who are you?" the woman asked, looking into her eyes. "Why are you with children of Bridian?"

"My name's Lydia," she answered. "I work at the castle. It was attacked, and I escaped with them."

The woman cocked her head to the side before turning to Terris, who was sitting on his knees, looking at everything but the Queen. She reached out and took his head in her hands, lifting it so that he was looking at her.

"And you are?"

"Terris," he answered. "I work at the castle."

Gwendolyn pinched her forefinger and thumb into his neck. Lana ran toward him, but an Altarian grabbed her from behind, holding her back.

"Who are you, really?" Gwendolyn asked. When Terris didn't answer, she threw his head back. "Kill them."

She couldn't believe what she heard. She struggled in her captor's arms.

"You can't kill us," her voice cracked. "We're just kids."

"If you won't answer my questions, then I must assume you're here to hurt us." Gwendolyn stepped closer to her. "I'm protecting my city."

"We're not here to hurt you," she pleaded. "This is the last place I want to be. My uncle was killed here. Let us go, we'll leave and never come back."

Gwendolyn turned back to Lana. "What did you say?"

"We'll never come back," she repeated. "I promise."

Gwendolyn looked into her eyes again, her lower lip dropping. She took another step closer, so she was standing mere inches before her.

"Alderic's daughter," Gwendolyn said, studying her in a new light. "I've heard you came back."

She didn't answer. She heard Deliah crying and turned to look at her. Dominic and Terris were huddled next to her.

"Do you know who I am?" the woman asked, her eyes narrowed.

"Gwendolyn."

"Queen Gwendolyn."

"Please. We need help."

"There was no help when your father poisoned us," Gwendolyn said, her voice low.

"I didn't have anything to do with that! In fact, I don't want anything to do with him."

Gwendolyn laughed, sending chills skittering down Lana's spine.

"In a few years, you'll be just as powerful as he is, and there's no telling the evil you'll cause."

"I'm not my father."

"It doesn't matter. Whether you like it or not, the enchantment is running through you. Soon, it will overpower you, and you'll be just like him. Such a shame too," Gwendolyn said coldly, taking her chin in her cold hands. "You're so pretty. You look like your mother. I heard she had a difficult time getting over Gavril."

Gwendolyn walked away. Lana's insides burned with anger.

"We used to look like you," Gwendolyn continued a moment later. "Before he poisoned us."

Lana heard someone join them from the water. She turned, straining her eyes in the dark room, and watched a man struggle for air as his gills closed. He crawled out of the water and sat at the edge.

"What are you going to do to them?" he asked.

"Exactly what you think I'm going to do."

"They're children. This is all my fault. Let them go."

"Go back, Ronan," Gwendolyn sighed, pointing to the water. "You're not in the right state of mind to handle this."

This was Gwendolyn's son. She remembered the name. He had killed her uncle in a fit of jealousy over Marianna.

When Ronan didn't say anything, Gwendolyn continued, "When she takes the throne of Bridian, do you think she'll help us? Do you think she'll maintain a good relationship with our people? She'll have the power to destroy us! Don't forget the role you played in this either."

"It was an accident," Ronan said.

"You're wrong," Lana interrupted. "I won't rule Bridian. Ramos is King. Damon's next in line." When the words were out of her mouth, she paused. "Well, he was supposed to be. I guess that means that Dominic is."

"You really think that Damon had an iota of a chance to rule Bridian? Are you honestly that naïve? Ramos was only a temporary King until you were brought back. You're the true heir."

Lana winced. She had no desire to rule Bridian. In fact, it was the last thing on her mind.

"I don't want to rule Bridian."

"I guess you can thank me, since you'll be dead by morning. Whatever air that's left in this room will be gone by then."

"You're just inviting Alderic here," Ronan said. "You know he's looking for her, and those beasts of his saw our people take her."

"No matter." Gwendolyn shrugged nonchalantly. "My mind's made up."

"No!" Ronan interrupted. "Let them go."

Gwendolyn effortlessly slid back into the water. Once she had disappeared, the remaining Altarians, minus Ronan, followed.

"I'm so sorry," he said after a moment of tense silence and then dove into the water, disappearing from view.

Lana leaned against the cold wall and closed her eyes. What was going to happen to them? She tried to process everything she had learned, but it was too much. As hard as she tried, she couldn't imagine herself ever ruling Bridian. That is, if she survived.

"They're guarding us," Dominic interrupted her thoughts.

She looked up and saw him leaning over the water. A moment later, he walked back to his sister.

"Who was that man?" he asked.

"Gwendolyn's son, Ronan."

"What did he mean when he said it was an accident?" Dominic continued. "He seems like the only logical one here."

Lana's hands shook, and she tried to steady her breathing. "Gavril, my mother's brother, was in love with Ronan's betrothed."

"Okay." Dominic narrowed his eyes. "That's it?"

"The day before they were to be married, he came here with Alderic and Contlay. A fight broke out, and Gavril drowned."

Lana let her head droop over her bent knees, wishing it would all be over. She remembered that Ronan had called the Shadow Splinters Alderic's beasts. What did that mean? Were they working for him?

Everyone was quiet, and she closed her eyes. What seemed like hours later, she heard movement in the water and saw Ronan watching her. When he didn't say anything, she took it upon herself to start the conversation. She didn't know what he wanted but had questions that needed answers.

"What happened to Marianna?"

"She died a month after Gavril," Ronan answered. "We didn't love each other. It was an arranged marriage. She loved him. She died of a broken heart."

Lana turned away. If Ronan had just let Marianna be with

Gavril, he would still be alive. Alderic wouldn't have spiraled, and the Rebellion wouldn't have been formed.

"I thought your people couldn't leave the water."

Ronan shook his head. "We choose not to go up very often. Those from above have tried to harm us too many times. I'm so sorry—about everything."

Lana waved him off. This was the absolute worst thing she wanted to hear at the moment.

"I was so jealous," Ronan continued. "I couldn't see why Marianna chose Gavril over me. I can't bring him back, but I can help you and your friends."

"How?"

"You're going to have to swim," he said. "But you should be able to leave without anyone knowing. I already took care of the guards."

She thought about her trip to the underwater castle. She barely survived and was going to have to do it all over again. She was hoping Ronan knew a secret way out. A way that didn't require a lot of swimming.

"Won't you get into trouble for helping us?"

"I know what's right, and the past has haunted me too long," he answered sadly. "I took your uncle from you, and for that I am truly sorry. Perhaps if Gavril were still alive, this terrible Rebellion wouldn't have begun in the first place."

"What if it's a trap?" Deliah whispered. "We don't know what they're planning to do with us."

She looked back at Ronan. He sounded so sincere, and they didn't have any other viable options.

"It's better than waiting to die."

"We have nothing to lose," Terris agreed, standing up.

Dominic lazily waved his hand as if to signify that he was in. They turned to Deliah, waiting for her decision.

"Fine," Deliah muttered.

Ronan dove underwater. Lana sat at the edge of the water,

dangling her feet into the cold lake. Before she could talk herself out of it, she pushed her body off the edge, Deliah, Dominic, and Terris following.

She opened her eyes. The cold had been a shock, and her body felt stiff. Deliah swam past her, toward Ronan, and she pushed herself. She didn't see any other Altarians and hoped that he had been truthful in wanting to help them.

Lana tried to focus on swimming, keeping her gaze on Ronan. Her heart was beating so fast it echoed in her ears. She tried to keep her mind off of what would happen if Gwendolyn caught them.

They followed Ronan through empty halls. She focused all her energy on swimming, putting one hand in front of the other and kicking her feet. She knew if they could just reach the surface, they would be all right.

When they left the underwater castle, Ronan breathed air into each of their mouths, and then motioned them to continue onward. She waved her thanks and began swimming through the gloomy water. Although her lungs still ached, she felt hopeful that they would make it. Dominic and Terris were swimming ahead of her, and Deliah was beside her. She wondered where they were going to go when they reached the surface but knew that anywhere had to be safer than Altaris.

A bright yellow fish swam up to her. She tried brushing it away to no avail. Out of the corner of her eyes, she noticed that Dominic had reached the surface, and Terris was right behind him when another giant fish, this one bright blue, knocked her off course. She suppressed the urge to breathe in a mouthful of water.

She tried to gauge how close she was to the surface when she saw that Deliah had joined Dominic and Terris. Her muscles ached under the pressure, and it felt as if she were going to suffocate. It hurt to keep her mouth shut when all she wanted to do was breathe. Her lungs ached with anticipation.

Lana finally reached the surface, but something wasn't right. She could see the early morning light above her but couldn't reach air. She couldn't break free from the water. Something was holding her in.

In a panic, she started banging the clear barrier above her in desperation. It reminded her of ice, only it wasn't cold. She looked at her friends one last time before she gave up, sinking deeper within the water.

12

GANYON FALLS

L ana sank deeper and deeper within the lake, slowly drifting in and out of consciousness. She saw her friends looking down at her and heard the faint echo of Deliah's frantic pounding on the barrier that had prevented her from taking a much-needed breath of fresh air. She shut her eyes and allowed herself to be taken down into the abyss of shadows once again.

A moment later, she felt something next to her. When she reopened her eyes, she was surprised to see Ronan. He wrapped his arms around her and kicked them both to the surface. When they reached the clear barrier, Ronan searched for an opening.

When she finally found fresh air, she inhaled deeply and started to cough. Ronan dragged her to the edge of the lake, pushing her out of the water with the help of Terris, who set her on the cold grass.

"Lana, are you all right?" Terris crouched near her.

She nodded. She was unable to speak because her lungs were still screaming for air. She curled into a ball and listened to the conversation around her.

"Why couldn't she get out?" Terris asked.

Ronan looked to the lake before answering, "My mother's creating a barrier around our city. Once it's complete, no one will be able to enter or leave Altaris. She reached that barrier."

"I don't see a barrier." Dominic stood up, looking into the calm water.

"You can't see it," Ronan answered. "Only a quarter of the lake is uncovered. It's taken many years to get that far."

Lana couldn't stop shaking. The water had been very cold, and she was nervous that Gwendolyn was going to find them. She didn't want to get caught again.

"We should go," Terris said. "We don't want to be here when they find out we've escaped."

Lana slowly sat up. Her cloak felt heavy, and she took it off. Terris helped her stand, and she wrung the excess water off before putting it back on.

Ronan stepped to the edge of the lake. "I can never go back."

"Well, you won't be missing much," Dominic scoffed, not noticing that Ronan had been talking to himself. "They're not the nicest group of people."

"They're still his family," Terris whispered, then turned his attention to Ronan. "Where are you going to go?"

"I don't know," he answered, "but you should leave. They've probably already discovered that you're gone."

"Thank you," Lana said. "You sacrificed a lot for us."

"I'll divert attention from you. We don't go too far from the water anymore, so you'll be safe."

They made their way into the forest. Lana's feet slid in her wet sneakers, and her jeans felt stiff. She heard rustling in a nearby tree and turned, expecting to see the Altarians with their bows. Instead, a brightly colored bird spread its wings and took flight.

A moment later, her thoughts turned back to Ronan. What was going to happen to him? The fact that he was giving up his family, his life, made her realize that he was truly sorry for what happened with Gavril. She thought of her family and hoped she would see her parents soon.

They walked for many miles. No one talked for fear that the Altarians, or Shadow Splinters, were hunting them. A low rumble of thunder broke the silence, and she looked around, searching for shelter before a storm broke out. As a cold rain began falling, Dominic stepped up to a field to their left.

When a flash of lightning lit up the forest, she saw what had drawn his attention. A group of people all turned towards them. Dominic began running toward Lana, Deliah, and Terris. Her stomach lurched; the people were all wearing long black cloaks with a small silver dagger on the chest.

She turned and began running but was too tired to gain much speed. She kept her eyes peeled in front of her, following Deliah and trying to avoid the many traps forests held, when her cousin disappeared.

"What happened to Deliah?" she asked.

Before anyone could answer, Terris was also gone. One second in front of her, the next not. She looked behind her when the forest was replaced with a long dirt road scattered with stones. It was no longer raining but hot, muggy, and very sunny.

Dominic ran into her and pushed her to continue moving. Small, red houses were before them, and she wondered if people lived in them. She ran to the closest house, hoping to find shelter from the rebels. She heard her cousins and Terris behind her. Without stopping to knock, she threw open the door and rushed past a woman with long brown hair braided down her back. She searched the room, spying a countertop, which faced the door and would sufficiently hide them from the rebels. The woman stared at her uninvited guests as two children, a boy and a girl, entered the room.

"Mama, who are they?" The little boy pointed.

The thud of boots on the porch interrupted them, and she looked pleadingly at the woman, silently urging her not to reveal their hiding place. The front door flew open, and she held her breath. The woman put her wooden spoon on the countertop and ushered the children into the next room.

"What do you think you're doing?" the woman said, turning to her second set of intruders.

"We're searching for four fugitives," a man's gruff voice answered. "We're searching every house in the vicinity."

The woman remained silent for a moment.

Lana wondered if the woman was going to turn them in or not when, to her great relief, she replied, "There's no one here, gentlemen, except for myself and my children. Now if you excuse me, we're on our way out."

"Ma'am, with all due respect, we're looking for very dangerous people," another man explained as he walked to the counter and placed his hands on it.

"Well, I'm sorry, but there's no one here," she answered nervously. "Please leave."

"You're all alone?"

Lana jumped when she heard the voice. It sounded like Damarius Pilkins. This question enraged the woman, who immediately took up her wooden spoon and strode out of her line of vision.

"Leave," she said, her voice rising. "You should be out looking for these fugitives instead of harassing my family."

Lana heard the door open and close, followed by the sound of retreating footsteps on the porch. She let out a slow breath.

"I don't know who you are or why you're running," the woman whispered once she was sure the men had continued their search elsewhere. "I just hope I did the right thing."

"You have," Deliah began but was interrupted.

"The less I know, the better."

"Where are we?" Deliah asked.

The woman ignored Deliah's question. "Go out the back way."

Lana crawled out from underneath the counter and looked at her friends, too afraid to leave the house. The woman remained by the door, waiting for them to leave. The little boy stepped into the room.

"Mama, I'm hungry."

"Please," the woman trembled, tears streaking her face. "Don't make me regret helping you."

When they heard a woman's scream from outside the front door, Lana ran to the back door. She slowly opened it and looked out. When she didn't see anyone, she stepped outside. Dominic pushed past her and began running in the direction they came.

Deliah grabbed Lana's hand and began running after Dominic, who was sprinting back to the spot where they had crossed. She nearly tripped on the beaten dirt road when her foot went into a crater. She scanned the road in front of her and breathed in the hot, musty, stale air.

"It was around here somewhere," Dominic said.

"I think it was over there." Deliah pointed to a spot farther down the road.

Terris took off running again, looking for the portal that would bring them back.

"We have to hurry," Deliah exclaimed, looking behind them nervously. "Someone's going to see us."

Dominic caught up with Terris, stopping in what they believed to be the spot where they had left the forest. When no one disappeared, she used the time to catch up with them.

"This was where we came from," Deliah panted.

Lana took a moment to scan their surroundings. When she looked behind them, she saw two rebels. She heard Deliah and Dominic arguing over where the portal should be.

"We have company."

The rebels were gaining on them, and they began running again, Terris in the lead. A moment later, he vanished, followed by Dominic. Deliah ran even faster and vanished as well. Suddenly, she once again found herself in the forest, surrounded by lush green trees.

"Hurry up," Dominic screamed when she regained her composure from traveling between dimensions.

Deliah and Terris were already several feet ahead of her. When she finally caught up to her friends, she covered her face with her hood, trying to keep warm. Despite the warmth of the other dimension, her cloak was still wet from the trip to Altaris, and the cold rain and harsh wind sent chills down her spine.

Terris ran back to Lana and took her hand, forcing her to run faster. She felt a sharp branch catch her arm, cutting the skin, but continued running. She knew the rebels were right behind them. Terris pushed her to the ground behind an enormous bush. She felt sick from fear, and her throat ached. Terris threw his hand over her mouth, trying to stifle the sound of her heavy breathing.

She clenched her hands tightly as the rebels drew near, silently uttering a little prayer that they wouldn't be found. Moments later, they ran by their hiding place without a second glance. Once the rebels had passed, she remembered her cousins and hoped they were safe.

Terris removed his hand from her mouth, and Lana exhaled deeply. She was reluctant to move, too afraid that the rebels would come back. Deliah and Dominic emerged from behind a tall tree and joined them. Her mind was working in overdrive. She could hardly think straight.

They sat behind the bush for hours, too afraid to move, until Dominic's stomach rumbled with hunger hours later. As they walked, they didn't talk for fear Damarius and the other rebels were close. Birds chirped, and small animals ran across their path. To pass the time, she had begun naming the animals in her head, then gave up when she saw the animal with the bushy tail the Shadow Splinter had devoured.

When she heard the sound of running water, she thought she was imagining it. She was thirsty, and her tongue felt heavy.

"The river!" Terris exclaimed, running.

Lana ran after him, the burble of water growing louder. Suddenly, she saw the shallow river beyond a line of trees. They excitedly ran to the river, and she scooped her hands in the cold water and drank. She didn't even care that she was making a mess as the water dribbled down her chin.

Deliah pointed past the river. "Look."

She stood up, looked where her cousin was pointing, and saw houses. After they drank their fill, they followed the river and the sound of children playing merrily. When they stepped into the city, Deliah and Dominic hugged each other when they realized they had made it to Ganyon Falls.

When Dominic began running toward a house at the end of the road, she grew excited, hoping it was Emeric's. She saw that every curtain was down, preventing them from looking inside. Deliah ran up the stairs and began knocking, but no one answered. Dominic, who had been leading them, followed a stone pathway to the backyard.

When they reached the back of the house, they found those windows had been covered as well. Dominic stepped up to the backdoor and knocked. When no one answered, he tried the handle, but it had been locked.

"Where do you think he is?" Deliah asked nervously. "Do you think he's coming back? What are we going to do if he doesn't?"

"How should I know?" Dominic turned on his sister, still clinging to the doorknob, as if it would open if he held on long enough.

Deliah began crying, and Lana knew she wouldn't be able to stand her cousins much longer. She didn't know where she was going to go or what she was going to do if she couldn't find Emeric.

"Are you sure this is the right house?"

"I think so," Dominic answered. "It's been years since we've been here though."

"What do you think is down there?" Terris asked, pointing to a dirt path leading into the woods.

Lana began walking down the path, but stopped when she saw only Terris had been following. She turned to look at her cousins.

"Are you two coming?"

Deliah shook her head no, and Dominic answered, "I'm not going back into the woods."

Lana sighed and continued walking. Purple and white flowers lined the way. They hadn't walked far when she heard the sound of rushing water. A moment later, they stepped into a clearing separated by the river.

"Do you think that's him?" Terris asked.

Lana looked where her friend was pointing and saw an old man standing near the water. For some reason, she had imagined Emeric being the same age as her father. The man was wearing small glasses, perched atop his nose, and a long red-velvet cloak. She listened to the haunting tune he was whistling as he mixed a soapy substance in a large silver basin.

She looked at Terris, waiting for him to do something. A moment later, a voice called out to her. She looked at the man and saw he had set his basin down and was waving to them. She took a step forward, but then paused.

"How do we know that we can trust him?" she whispered.

"You're the one who told us we had to find him!" Terris exclaimed.

"Well, I was wondering when I would finally see you again," the man called, peering at her from behind his tiny glasses.

Lana made her way closer. When they reached the water,

she didn't know what to say, so she wiggled her toes in her wet
socks and glanced nervously into the sky. The clouds were
getting darker by the second, and it looked as if it were going to
rain again. She pulled her cloak tighter across her body and
watched the man before her.

Finally, Terris broke the silence and asked, "Are you
Emeric?"

He nodded while packing his belongings into the basin.
"Let's get out of the cold."

Emeric carefully walked up the path to join them. She knew
she should be happy that they made it to Ganyon Falls, but she
had an uneasy feeling. Emeric walked past them, and Lana
watched him.

"What am I supposed to do now?"

Emeric called over his shoulder, "Stay alive. But we'll speak
of that once we're inside and everyone is comfortable."

"About that," Terris began. "There are two more of us
waiting by your house."

"Yes, yes," Emeric said distractedly. "The young Prince and
Princess of Bridian are sullying my windows as we speak."

"How did you know that?"

Emeric ignored her question. "Another of your friends is
staying with me as well."

Lana's heart beat faster. Was Kiernan staying with Emeric?

"Ivan Pilkins found his way here last night," he continued.

She felt all the air escape her. She couldn't believe Ivan was
staying with Emeric and that he hadn't let them inside. When
they approached his house, they found Deliah atop Dominic's
shoulders, peering into the windows, her dirty hands on the
glass.

"I think someone's in there," Deliah said, her face pressed
against the window.

"Someone is in there," Emeric said, startling Dominic who
nearly dropped his sister.

"Ivan's here," Lana crossed her arms over her chest.

Emeric lifted Deliah off Dominic's shoulders and said with genuine affection, "It's lovely to see you two again. I wish it could be under better circumstances though."

Once Deliah was safely on the ground, Emeric pulled a thin skeleton key out of his pocket. When he unlocked the door, he allowed everyone in. Lana was surprised when she stepped into the house. It was much larger on the inside than it originally appeared from the outside.

Silver chandeliers hung throughout the hall, and the dark wood floors had recently been polished. They followed Emeric down the hallway; past huge pictures of what she assumed was his family. Portraits of men in dark blue top hats and long cloaks were hung to the left side of the hallway while women in periwinkle robes hung on the right side.

Emeric led them to a huge room with a high vaulted ceiling and motioned them to sit. She sat in a cushy red chair and looked around the room as Emeric left.

"He's crazy," Ivan said, joining them from somewhere within the house. "If my father hadn't told me to stay with him, I would have left already."

Her stomach clenched at the mention of Damarius. She looked away from him.

"Don't worry," Ivan said. "I had no idea he's a rebel."

"Why didn't you let us in when we were knocking?" Deliah glared. "That wasn't nice."

He grinned. "Emeric told me not to let anyone in."

"You should have let us in," Dominic said.

"Do you know what happened to my parents? Or Ramos or Contlay?"

Ivan sat on the couch. It was so big his feet didn't touch the floor. He looked at Lana and said, "You know he killed your mother, right?"

"What?" Her voice cracked.

"Contlay killed your mother."

"You're lying."

"No, I'm not," Ivan said, shrugging his shoulders. "You're probably the only one who doesn't know."

She looked to her cousins. Was it true? Had they known all along? Deliah's eyes were wide. Dominic looked at Ivan, one eyebrow raised, as if he hadn't believed him.

"I didn't know," Terris spoke up.

"Of course you wouldn't know," Ivan snorted. "No one would tell you anything important."

Emeric rejoined them. Lana bit her lip, trying to remain calm. Ivan was only trying to provoke her. It couldn't be true. There was no way Contlay killed her mother.

"This is an amazing house," she said to Emeric, trying to stay calm. "It looks so small from the outside. You couldn't tell how big it is."

"It's always the big houses that are vandalized," he said without further explanation.

Lana didn't know what to say to that, so she remained silent. Deliah started giggling, and Dominic elbowed her, whispering to be quiet.

"But," Emeric added, looking around the room, as if it were the first time he had seen it. "How do you know what you see isn't different from what everyone else sees? The color red," he added, pointing to the chair she was sitting on. "Do you ever stop to think that what you perceive as red someone else may perceive as pink or orange?"

She nodded, trying to make it look as if she were following. Terris was watching him in fascination, taking in every word he spoke. Ivan rolled his eyes. Deliah and Dominic looked at each other.

"Now follow me," Emeric said, abruptly changing thoughts. "You must be hungry."

He led them to the kitchen, pausing briefly in the hall to

adjust a crooked mirror. She was going to ask if it was a portal, but then decided she really didn't want to know. When they entered the kitchen, he passed out plates, telling them to eat whatever they could find.

Ivan placed his plate to the counter and said, "Don't bother. The only thing he has to eat are vegetables."

"Eat them raw, they're better for you that way," Emeric explained, moving aside the curtains to look out the kitchen window.

Lana devoured a plate full of carrots and cucumbers. All they had eaten since her uncle's birthday party two days ago was what they could find in the forest—nuts, berries, and leaves from a tree that had a distinct cinnamon flavor, and they drank whatever water they could find. They ate in silence, Deliah, Dominic, and Terris just as ravenous as she was.

After drinking a tall glass of water, she left her plate on the table. She walked into the hall, looking at the pictures as she made her way to the living room, stopping when she came upon a huge portrait of a dark hallway. The funny thing was, she thought she saw someone in the picture on the way into the kitchen. Dominic came up behind her, chewing a piece of celery.

"What are you looking at?" he asked, looking down both sides of the hall nervously.

She started to answer but was cut off.

"I don't care what you're looking at!" Dominic whispered. "I just don't want anyone to hear me. He's crazier than I remember."

"You mean Emeric?"

"He doesn't make sense," he said. "Why wouldn't I see what you see? And who only eats raw vegetables? Hey, do you think Contlay—"

"I know what Ivan said," she cut him off, not wanting to

hear the awful lie again. She lowered her voice and said, "I don't believe him. Ivan's not the most reliable source."

"Well, I don't know if we should trust *him*," Dominic added, gesturing to Emeric who was now walking down the hall towards them.

"Who else are we going to trust?"

"Just because you want to trust someone, doesn't mean you should," Dominic whispered, finishing his stick of celery. "I don't remember him being this weird."

Lana looked at the picture again and jumped back.

"There's someone in that picture who wasn't there a moment ago!"

"What do you mean?" Dominic asked, not really listening but studying Emeric, who was making his way towards them.

"That lady with the funny hat wasn't in that picture before!"

"That's a portal to the Council of Elders," Emeric said when he joined them. "Look, she's gone."

Lana looked at the picture again, and sure enough, the woman had vanished.

"Where did she go?"

"That's a portal disguised as a picture," he explained. "The mirror has been enchanted to reflect the hallway leading to the Council. I need to keep in constant contact with them."

Emeric turned and left them, heading back towards the kitchen. Dominic walked in the opposite direction, towards the living room, and she followed her cousin. When they reached the living room, she saw Terris reading a book. Across the room, Ivan and Deliah were talking. Dominic made his way toward his sister and sat on the couch next to Ivan.

She sat next to Terris. "What are you reading?"

"The most amazing book." Terris snapped the cover shut. "Emeric wrote it."

Lana listened to her friend explain the book but, after a minute, felt her eyes close. When she reopened them, she was no longer at Emeric's or Ganyon Falls. She was in a dark room with an enormous fireplace. Even in the dark, she could see the familiar engravings.

The room looked as it had in her previous dreams, and it felt oddly comforting to be back. The thrones were still in the middle of the room, and the jeweled map was hanging on the wall. Out of the corner of her eyes, she saw someone approaching, the thud of footsteps echoing around her. A flash of lightning lit up the sky, and a huge beast landed on the window ledge. It began scratching its huge talons across the glass, as if trying to get inside.

The thunder shook her awake. She glanced around the room and saw that everyone had fallen asleep. Terris was on the floor, the book he had been reading still open on his lap. Deliah was curled a few feet from him, Dominic was sleeping next to his sister, and Ivan was slouched on a chair.

She heard talking and sat up. Curious, she got off the couch and crept toward the hall. She heard familiar voices and held her breath.

"What's going to happen now?" her mother asked.

"You know what she has to do," Emeric said. "The Crystal has to be destroyed."

"There has to be another way." Her father exhaled loudly. "It'll kill her."

She heard someone step into the hall but didn't have time to hide.

"Join us," Emeric said, motioning her into the kitchen.

Lana stepped into the kitchen and found her parents. She ran to them. Her mother hugged her, stroking her hair, as if she couldn't believe it was really her. Tears streamed down her cheeks. Her father joined their hug, and she had never been happier.

She wiped the tears from her face. She wanted to tell them everything that she had been through, the Outcasts, Shadow

Splinters, Altarians, but couldn't find the words. She saw Contlay standing across the room, his arms crossed over his chest, watching their reunion.

"Ivan said you killed my mother."

"We should talk about this later," her mother said, wiping tears from her eyes.

"Why can't we talk about it now? It's not true, right?"

Another tear slid down her mother's cheek. "Not now, we've all been through a lot."

Emeric sat at the table. "She should know."

Contlay uncrossed his arms, stood up taller, and said something she wasn't expecting.

"I did."

Lana didn't know what to do or say. She was speechless. Ivan had been right. She hadn't believed him.

"I mean, it was an accident. I loved your mother. She was family to me, and I would have done anything to protect her."

Contlay looked into the distance, as if lost in his thoughts, while her father put a protective arm around her, hoping to somehow shield the pain. She pulled out a chair and sat next to Emeric.

"I was aiming for Alderic," Contlay continued, "but I missed. He was a threat to everyone in the room. After he stabbed King Nicodemus, something had to be done, but she got in the way."

Lana held her hand up to signify that she had heard enough, but Emeric said, "There's something else you should know."

"I don't think now is the time to tell her," her mother said.

"No, she needs to know," her father agreed, and Emeric continued.

"Now that Alderic has regained control over Bridian," he began gravely, "he's searching for the Crystal."

When no one continued, she asked, "What's that?"

"Alderic wanted to bring demons into our world," Emeric said.

Lana nodded. She knew this already.

"He wanted to control them," Emeric continued. "They almost released them but were interrupted by your grandfather, King Nicodemus. As a result, the demons were imprisoned in the nearest solid object—a crystal from the Caverns of Medora. In fact, I believe that young man in my living room was to be a sacrifice to the demons that night, once they were released."

"A sacrifice?"

Lana's eyes grew wide, and she felt sick. She couldn't believe Alderic had been going to sacrifice Terris. Her stomach lurched again, and she took a deep calming breath.

"It's quite remarkable that you found each other again," Emeric said.

"So, he's looking for a Crystal? That's the weapon?"

"Yes," Emeric confirmed. "After King Nicodemus disbanded the rebels, the Crystal was hidden until he could figure out what to do with it."

"Where is it Lana?" Contlay interrupted.

She looked at Contlay, noticing the slight change in his voice. "I don't know where it is. I know everyone thinks I do, that it was imprinted in my mind, but I don't. Even if I manage to find it, what are we going to do with it? Can it be destroyed?"

"We'll figure that out once we find it," Emeric answered.

Lana was silent as she processed everything.

"You're the key to breaking it," Emeric continued. "They were called into our world using your magic. You're the only one that can break it. Alderic needs you to release them."

"I don't think I have the magic everyone is expecting me to have." She slouched in her chair, her mind working in overdrive. "I feel normal, except for levitating a few things and seeing things in Crystal Balls."

"It's in you." Emeric smiled.

"You should go back to bed," her father said after a moment of tense silence, looking at her. "You'll be staying here for a while until we figure out where you'll be safest."

Lana fumbled with her hands while she thought of what she had been told. While she knew that Terris had also been taken from the rebels that night, she had been shocked to hear that he was to be a sacrifice.

"How's Ramos?"

"I don't know," her father answered sadly. "We haven't seen him since we escaped."

Lana said goodnight to her parents and walked back to the living room. She was exhausted and just wanted to go back to sleep. She sat on the couch and covered her legs with a blanket. Before she had a chance to get comfortable, she heard glass shattering.

She sat up, and Emeric ran into the room, pulling her off the couch, and dragging her to a mirror at the end of the hallway. He was just about to push her through when another earsplitting crash of glass shook the house. She stepped sideways, barely missing Emeric's shove, and looked around the room in confusion.

"Wait!" she whispered as her father joined them. "I need to find Terris."

"You have to leave!" her father said as Contlay ran into the room, watching her. "They're here for you."

"Not yet," she shouted as she pushed her way past them.

Lana found her cousins awake, looking out a window with Ivan, and ran past them. She saw Terris sitting on the couch with a blanket pulled up to his face. He was the key. She hadn't been the only one taken from the rebels that night fifteen years ago.

"Lana, what's going on?" he whispered.

"You have to come with me." She pulled him off the couch.

They ran down the hall toward her father, Contlay, and Emeric.

"You'll be all right," her father whispered. "We won't let them follow you."

Before she could ask where the mirror led, Emeric pushed her into it. She walked through the silver sea, Terris by her side. She stepped through the opening when it appeared. The room she found herself in looked familiar, but before she had a chance to look around, Terris stumbled out after her.

"Where are we?" he asked, looking around the room in confusion.

A familiar figure was asleep on the couch in front of them. She spun around and desperately threw her hands on the mirror they had stepped out from. She realized they were trapped. Someone must have broken the mirror in Ganyon Falls.

Lana looked around once more and groaned. She couldn't believe that she was in Mt. Sinclair, standing in Nick's living room, and he was asleep on the couch.

13

MT. SINCLAIR

Nick did not stir. In fact, it hardly looked as if he were breathing at all. Lana grabbed Terris's hand and led him to the front door. They were almost to freedom when Terris tripped on a stray tennis shoe, sending him careening to the floor. Nick opened his eyes, and Terris jumped up. She opened the front door and ran outside.

"Where are we?" Terris asked as she led them past her former house and into Frazier Woods, trying to lose Nick, who had begun chasing them.

"This is where I grew up," she answered, carefully sidestepping a twisted mass of tree roots. "We're in Mt. Sinclair. I used to live in that yellow and blue house we passed."

"Do you know that boy who's chasing us? I think he's calling your name."

She heard Nick but didn't want to stop to talk to him. She was hoping that he would give up and leave her alone. She was still mad that he and Laurie had lied to her, told her that her father wanted her to walk home, leading to her near abduction.

When they came upon the creek, she stopped, remembering the afternoon she had been attacked by rebels, the afternoon that marked the beginning of her new life. She looked behind them, thankful that she didn't see Nick. Lana carefully crossed the shallow creek. When they made it to the other side, she led them up the muddy embankment. Terris was quiet, struggling to keep up with her. She saw a flash of silver on the grass, the sun reflecting off a shiny object. As they got closer, she recognized her cell phone and ran to pick it up. She tried to turn it on, but the battery had died.

"What's that?" Terris asked.

She put the phone in her pocket and explained what it was as they continued walking. A few minutes later, they stepped out of the woods.

"These people," Terris said. "What are they wearing?"

A dozen men and women were walking down the street in business suits or jeans, nothing out of the ordinary, until she remembered where she had just come from. She looked at her dirty, wet clothes and knew she stood out like a sore thumb. A car drove by and Terris jumped. She saw an elderly man coming up the sidewalk and broke into a trot to catch up with him.

"Excuse me, sir!" she shouted. "Please, can you tell me what day it is?"

The man stared at her for a moment, finally smiling. "Am I on hidden camera?"

She shook her head no and asked again, "What day is it?"

"I know all the tricks. You're going to have to find someone else."

She stared at the man as he continued on his way, mumbling something about crazy reality television.

"It's Tuesday."

A young woman with honey-blonde hair was sitting on a bus stop bench a few feet away.

"That's what I thought," she said, but then stopped. "What time is it?"

The woman looked at her curiously, her eyes raised as she watched Terris staring at the cars in amazement.

The bell tower chimed, and Terris ran to her, clutching her arm. "What's that sound?"

Lana counted the chimes alerting the hour. It stopped at three. She took Terris's arm and ran, calling back to the woman, "Thanks for the help!"

She crossed Main Street and ran to Mt. Sinclair High School. She raced through the parking lot towards the manicured bushes near the entrance. When they were hidden, Terris sprawled out on the grass while she peered around the bushes, hoping to catch a glimpse of her friends, Ava and Trevor. Using the free time until students were released from class, she explained everything to Terris.

"The bell should ring any minute," she looked at her bare wrist, as if checking a watch.

"Isn't there someplace else we can go?" he asked, fumbling with his necklace.

The shiny pearl caught Lana's attention. She remembered her dream. The dragon on the fireplace had been missing a pearl eye. Her heart raced. Could that be the key? A clue to the Crystal's hiding place?

"Where did you get that necklace?"

Terris shrugged. "I've always had it. It might have been my mom's. I never really knew her."

Lana was quiet as she sat on the grass. She knew both his parents had been rebels, his dad was imprisoned, and his mom had disappeared. Was it a coincidence that he had a pearl necklace?

She remembered the last time she had attended school in Mt. Sinclair and realized it had been exactly a week ago. Why had Nick been home on a school day and, more importantly, why did he have a portal to Emeric's in his house? A moment later, the final bell rang to dismiss students from class, sending her out of her thoughts. She jumped up and looked over the bush, only to crouch back down again when Laurie Huntington and Bill Polanski walked by.

"Everyone is dressed the same!" Terris exclaimed, looking at all the students wearing the standard white shirts, navy-blue pants, and white sneakers.

"Something I don't miss."

Lana stood up when Ava walked out the double doors. She hadn't really thought out her plan. She wasn't sure how she was going to get Ava's attention without drawing unnecessary attention to herself.

"Ava!"

A few people looked at her, including Ava, who walked to the bush slowly. The crowd of students scattered, walking toward the line of buses or waiting cars.

"Lana?" Ava said incredulously. "You're back?"

"We need a place to stay for a while."

"My mom got a letter from your mom saying you moved to Florida. I was so upset you didn't say goodbye. You haven't been answering your phone."

"I'll explain later," she said. "We need to get out of the open before anyone sees me."

"We'll go to my house," Ava said. "My parents are working."

"Both of us." She gestured to Terris.

Ava finally noticed Terris and asked, "Who's he?"

"This is Terris. He's a friend," she explained, readjusting the hood over her face. "Where's Trevor?"

"He joined the technology club today." Ava led them across the parking lot towards Main Street. "He has meetings every day after school now. Today is his first one."

Lana nodded. Although she was glad to be back in Mt. Sinclair, it no longer felt like home. She missed her parents and wished they were with her. Their reunion had been too brief.

When they reached Ava's two-story white stucco house, she

was relieved. At least they would be out of the open, although Mr. and Mrs. Graham were very strict and watched every move their daughter made. They would surely know that Lana and Terris were there.

She followed Ava up the concrete steps to the front door, thinking of happier times. If only life were that simple again. She used to wish for an adventure, something to break the monotony of her life, but now that she was living one, she wished she could go back to her dull life. At least it had been predictable, and she knew she would be alive at the end of each day.

"Are you okay?" Ava asked when they reached her bedroom on the second floor.

She nodded and began telling her friend what had happened to her and where she had been. Ava listened in fascination until she heard a door open downstairs.

"Your parents are home! Where are we going to go?"

"They never come up here," Ava whispered as she stood up and opened her bedroom door. "I'll be right back. I'm going to tell them I have a big test to study for."

"Please, don't tell them anything!"

Ava smiled. "I won't. I'm your best friend. You can trust me."

"Thank you."

"I'm not even sure *I* trust you," Ava said, almost as if an afterthought, her hand hovering on the doorknob. "Although, your family did disappear."

"It's all true."

Ava opened the door. Without looking back, she went downstairs, closing the door behind her. Lana was so exhausted she lay on the bed.

"What are we going to do now?" Terris asked. "How are we going to get back?"

"I don't know."

When Ava rejoined them, she brought snacks. She set a

plate full of cheese and crackers, baby carrots, and dip on the floor near Terris.

"I called Trevor," Ava said. "I didn't tell him anything. I want it to be a surprise."

Ava began to fill her in on the happenings of Mt. Sinclair High School. Nick had stopped going to school. Ava said she hadn't seen him since the day after she disappeared. Laurie had begun dating an eleventh-grade football star, Bill Polanski's brother, George. When she finished, they heard a thud.

"Is that a rock?" Ava asked, stepping up to the window. "Uh oh, Lana, you want to see this."

She ran to the window. Standing below a huge evergreen tree in Ava's front yard was Nick. He had changed since she had seen him earlier. He was wearing jeans and a gray T-shirt, a blue baseball cap on his head.

Ava opened her window and shouted, "What do you want?"

"I know she's up there," Nick answered. "I want to talk to her."

"Who's up here?" Ava asked innocently.

"Don't play stupid, Ava, Laughs is up there, and I want to talk to her."

"Who's Laughs?" Terris asked, joining Ava at the window.

Lana tried dragging Terris away from the window before he could be seen but was too late.

"That's him!" Nick shouted. "That's the boy I saw with her! Let me talk to him."

"Goodbye, Nick," Ava said, closing the window.

"No! I just want to talk to her."

"What's going on out here?" Ava's father shouted from the front door.

"Can I come in and talk to your daughter?" Nick asked.

Lana couldn't breathe. Nick was going to find her. Ava flew downstairs. She tried listening at the door, praying she wouldn't let Nick in. She didn't want to talk to him. The less people that knew where she was, the better chance she had at hiding from the rebels.

After a very tense moment, she heard people coming up the stairs. She stood up, searching for a place to hide when Ava and Trevor came into the room. Ava was carrying three bottles of water, and she tossed one to Lana.

"Look who I found on my way to kick Nick out of my front yard," Ava said cheekily.

"Lana?" Trevor said as he squeezed his friend so hard she could barely breathe. "We thought you moved."

"It's complicated," she answered when Trevor finally released her.

"Wait until you hear her story," Ava added.

"Who are you?" Trevor asked Terris, who on being addressed skittishly knocked over a pile of books on Ava's nightstand.

"This is Terris. Terris, this is Trevor."

"I'm so happy to see you. We tried calling you, but you never answered."

Lana began to tell her story again, only this time with frequent interruptions on behalf of Terris when he saw fit to either describe the castle or add his thoughts on instances that concerned him. When the tale was finally over, again, she reached for her water and drank the whole thing, soothing her tired throat. Trevor expressed his doubts but finally relented when she was adamant that it was all true.

"You've never lied to me before," he said, then turned to Ava. "What do you think of all of this?"

Before Ava had a chance to answer, Lana had an idea. "I can prove it."

Ava and Trevor looked at their friend, waiting for her to elaborate. She looked around the room nervously. She had to find something to levitate. Once Ava and Trevor saw that she could levitate objects, she knew they would believe her. Plus, she wanted to see if it would work—if she was really a conduit since there was no magic in Mt. Sinclair.

Terris cleared his throat, waiting for her to do something. She was so nervous she didn't even think she would be able to levitate anything but had to try. She saw a math textbook on Ava's nightstand.

She cleared her head, envisioning a beach while pushing aside all negative thoughts of Alderic and the rebels. The room was silent, and everyone's eyes were on her. She opened her eyes and focused every ounce of energy on the book, willing it to levitate. She imagined two invisible hands reaching towards it and lifting it into the air.

Very slowly, the book started to rise. Out of the corner of her eyes, she saw Terris smiling. Ava's face was pale, and she had her hand to her chest, as if she couldn't believe what she was seeing. Lana lost her concentration, and the book fell back to the nightstand.

"I believe you," Ava said, her voice shaking.

"How'd you do that?" Trevor asked. "That was the coolest thing I've ever seen!"

Lana couldn't believe it worked. She sat on the bed. Trevor filled her in on his week. He aced his pop quiz in math and wasn't picked last in gym. He then told her about his first technology club meeting. When they were done catching up, Trevor looked at his phone.

"I have to go," he broke the silence. "My mom's home, and I have homework to finish before school tomorrow."

"You can't go to school tomorrow." Ava threw her hands down. "We need to help them."

"You need to go to school."

"Don't be silly." Ava sat on her bed. "We're going to help you."

After a moment of consideration, Trevor finally relented. "I still have to go home though. I'll come over in the morning, and we can brainstorm."

When Trevor left, Ava gave her clean clothes and a toothbrush. Once she was clean, she felt like a new person, like she could accomplish anything. Ava gave Terris a pair of blue shorts and a gray T-shirt and put their dirty clothes in the wash.

When Terris fell asleep, Lana and Ava stayed up talking for hours. It almost felt like the past week had been her imagination, that everything was normal, until she heard Terris's snoring. Lana didn't remember falling asleep but awoke to the sound of Ava gathering her coat and backpack off the floor.

"I thought you said you weren't going to school?"

"I'm not, but I have to make it look like I went," Ava said. "Your clothes are on the chair. I stayed up last night to make sure they were clean before my mom saw them."

Lana stood up and walked to the window, surprised to see the screen on the floor. Terris mumbled something about a Choclochino and rolled over in his makeshift bed by the closet. She watched Ava walk out of her house and run to the evergreen tree. Ava climbed it easily and stepped through the open window. She replaced the screen and sat on her bed.

"I already said goodbye to my parents," Ava whispered. "They think I'm on my way to school now."

"Why didn't you just tell them you were sick?"

"That was way more fun," she said, looking at her watch. "They should be leaving in twenty minutes."

As Ava predicted, twenty minutes later, her parents left for work. Lana went to the bathroom and dressed in her clean clothes. When she was done, Terris got dressed. Ava was watching a video on her phone when Trevor opened the door.

"I hope you don't mind, I let myself in," he said as a way of greeting. "I saw that the cars were gone."

"Saved me the trip downstairs." Ava shrugged her shoulders.

"Did anyone think of a plan?" Lana asked hopefully.

"Well, obviously you have to find the Crystal," Trevor said. "First, we should try to figure out how you can get back."

"I don't understand why there's a portal in Nick's house," Ava said. "It doesn't make sense."

"I don't know. I guess portals can be anywhere. Maybe it was a coincidence? Or they put one next door in case of an emergency?"

"We should cut and color your hair," Ava said. "Maybe these rebels won't recognize you with a new look."

Ava's cell phone rang. She looked at the display and quickly answered.

"Hi, Mom," she said, holding her forefinger to her mouth, letting them know to be quiet. "What's wrong? I'm at school."

Lana could hear Ava's mom's response even though she wasn't on speaker. "Ava Ann Graham, I just got a phone call from the school and need to know where you are! I'm on my way home. You better be there when I get there."

"I don't feel good." Ava coughed into the phone. "I came home early." She pressed a button on her phone then tossed it to the bed. "She hung up on me."

"She sounded really mad. We'll go."

"Where are we going to go?" Terris panicked.

"You can come to my house," Trevor said. "My mom's working."

"I'm so sorry," Ava said, hugging her friend. "Hey, do you think my parents can help?"

"The less people who know, the better. Please don't tell them."

Lana followed Ava downstairs. After they said goodbye, they followed Trevor to his house. They were quiet. She used the time to think of a plan. She knew she had to get back to Bridian. When they reached Highland Road, she stopped walking.

She looked at Terris. "We're wasting time."

"Did you think of a plan?" Trevor asked.

"Hopefully we'll be able to get back the same way we came."

"There has to be a reason they had a mirror," Trevor agreed. "Even if they don't know anything, maybe there's another portal."

Terris was quiet. Lana looked at Trevor again, realizing this may be the last time she would see him. She wished she had thought of that when she left Ava's.

"I'm going to miss you," she said, a tear sliding down her cheek.

She quickly wiped the tear away and looked at her feet, trying to keep from crying. Trevor frowned.

"I can come with you," he said.

"No. That will just delay our goodbye. We'll come back if it doesn't work."

Trevor nodded. "I'll tell Ava you said goodbye."

Lana led Terris to Nick's house, which was only three blocks away. She hoped that Nick wouldn't be there. She didn't want to talk to him. When they turned up Crescent Avenue, she slowly made her way to his house.

Standing in front of Nick's house made her uneasy. Maybe it was the fact that the house she grew up in was right next door, or perhaps it was because she didn't want to do what she was going to do. Looking at Terris one last time, she mustered all the courage she had left, marched up the front steps, and rang the doorbell.

A tall woman with long blonde hair answered the door. She was dressed in dark blue jeans and a bright pink shirt.

"There you are, Lana." Mrs. Jacobs smiled. "Richard and I have been looking for you. Nick told us that he saw you come out of our mirror."

"Wait, you know about the mirror?"

"Why don't you come in, and we can chat," Mrs. Jacobs said as she stepped into the foyer and held the door open. "Are you hungry? I was making Nick's lunch."

"I'm starving," Terris exclaimed as he patted his stomach in eager anticipation.

"Well then, come in, and I'll make some more sandwiches. You can eat with Nick," Mrs. Jacobs said. "We recently told him about Bridian, and he's taking it kind of hard."

Lana stopped listening. The last thing she wanted to do was eat a meal with Nick. All she wanted to do was see if they had another portal in their house.

"We don't really have time to eat," she tried explaining but stopped when Nick came out of the kitchen.

"What are you doing here?" he demanded as he pulled a gray sweatshirt over his plain white T-shirt. "Thanks for running from me yesterday."

"Nick, we're going to eat, and then we can talk." Mrs. Jacobs led them into the kitchen.

Lana took a seat on a barstool, Terris next to her. She played with the hem of her cloak, and Nick grudgingly took a seat across the bar and stared at her, slowly twisting the top off his water bottle.

"Lana, who's your friend?" Mrs. Jacobs asked, looking at Terris curiously.

"This is Terris."

"What's your last name," she asked as she removed five cups from an overhead cupboard.

"VanDriesen," Terris answered.

Mrs. Jacobs dropped the cups. The porcelain shattered, and she turned very pale.

"Mom, what's wrong?" Nick asked, jumping off his chair.

"Nothing, I'm just clumsy today."

Nick sat down while his mother found the broom and began sweeping the shattered pieces into a pile.

"Really, kids, I'm fine," she explained as Mr. Jacobs rushed into the room. "I haven't heard that name in a while."

"What happened down here?"

"Everything's fine," Mrs. Jacobs explained to her husband. "I dropped a few cups."

Mr. Jacobs moved to the bar but stopped when he saw his guests. "Lana, we've been looking for you."

"I heard. This is my friend Terris."

Mrs. Jacobs set a plate full of peanut butter and jelly sandwiches on the bar. Nick glared at her as he picked up a sandwich. As she ate, she allowed herself a moment to forget about everything else.

After everyone ate and the dishes had been washed, she explained everything that happened. It didn't look like Nick believed her. Mr. and Mrs. Jacobs excused themselves for a moment. She yawned and looked out the window that faced her house, jumping when she heard Nick slam his fist on the table. He stormed out of the room, leaving them alone.

"What's wrong with him?" Terris asked.

"How should I know?"

A moment later, Mrs. Jacobs rejoined them. She went to the sink and filled a glass with water from the faucet. She took a big gulp and placed the cup on the counter.

"I don't have much time. I need to get back," she said when Mrs. Jacobs turned to look at her, hoping to convey the urgency she felt. "We actually came back through the mirror in your living room. I was wondering if there are any other portals in your house."

Mrs. Jacobs nodded and began tapping her long acrylic nails on the countertop. "You must have been in Ganyon Falls with Emeric. Nick was hysterical when he saw you emerge from the mirror. That's why we finally told him the truth last night."

"Why do you have a portal to Emeric's?"

"Richard and I are from Bridian too. When you were sent

here, we accompanied Jacqueline and Grayson. Nick was born shortly after," Mrs. Jacobs added. "He's not a citizen of Bridian, but due to the unusual circumstances behind it, I'm sure that can be changed once we return."

"You're coming back?"

"Yes," Mrs. Jacobs answered as Mr. Jacobs rejoined them. "I mean, once everything is settled over there."

This answer seemed to satisfy Mr. Jacobs, and he continued to putter about the kitchen, finally pausing long enough to pour himself a cup of coffee.

She shifted uncomfortably in her seat. "Well, that's why I need to get back."

"Nonsense," Mr. Jacobs exclaimed. "You're safer here."

"I have to go back," she repeated as Nick walked into the room again and threw his backpack to the floor.

"I don't see why I have to go to school tomorrow if we're moving to that other place," he whined.

"You're going to school, Nick," Mr. Jacobs said, placing his coffee cup in the sink. "We might not be going anywhere."

At this remark, Mrs. Jacobs spun around and glared at her husband. "Think of the opportunities Nick will have. He could be an ambassador!"

"Margaret, he can't be an ambassador. He wasn't even born in Bridian!"

Lana jumped at his exclamation.

Nick took a seat next to his mother. "I don't want to be an ambassador anyway! I still have no idea what's going on and why she's in my house."

"We've been through this already, Nick," Mr. Jacobs said. "We're no longer needed to help Jacqueline and Grayson, and this is our home."

"You can't be serious!" Terris exclaimed. "Granted, I've only seen a little of this dimension, but there's no competition! I already miss the Choclochinos."

"Don't I have a say in this?" Nick asked.

"There's no telling how long this war is going to last," Mr. Jacobs explained. "I don't want anything to do with it. I've put in my time!"

"Doing what?" Mrs. Jacobs questioned.

"This is our home," he countered.

Mrs. Jacobs laughed a dry laugh. "And you think Alderic is going to stop with Bridian? You know as well as I do that he won't."

"Well, isn't it for her?" Nick asked insolently. "Let's just give her to them and make it all stop."

The room grew so quiet she was sure she would be able to hear a pin drop. Mrs. Jacobs looked furious, even Mr. Jacobs looked mad.

"Don't say that."

Nick leaned forward on the countertop and looked right into her eyes. "Even when you leave you screw things up."

"That's enough, Nick!" Mr. Jacobs said.

"I need to find a way back," she interrupted. "Please, tell me, are there any other portals?"

Mrs. Jacobs nodded. "What are you going to do?"

"I have a plan," she answered. "I just need to get back."

She knew the first thing she had to do was return to Bridian, to the castle. She had a feeling the fireplace in the abandoned hall would lead her to the Crystal.

"Maybe you should wait here for your parents," Mrs. Jacobs said. "I can't keep you here, I'm not your mother, but I would feel better if you stayed."

Lana thought about her offer. It was tempting to stay in Mt. Sinclair to wait for her parents, but she didn't even know if her parents would be coming for her.

"We'll be fine. The rebels who attacked Emeric's house are looking for me now, probably in this dimension. They know we left through his mirror."

"You're right," Mr. Jacobs said as he removed his glasses and began wiping them with his shirt. "It isn't safe here either."

"We have a mirror to Altaris," Mrs. Jacobs finally said.

"That's the only one?" Her stomach turned, remembering their time in the underwater city.

"The portal to Emeric's is broken," Mrs. Jacobs said. "I imagine they broke it after you went through."

Mr. and Mrs. Jacobs led them down the hallway and up the stairs to the second floor. Lana paused when she reached Nick's school pictures hanging on the wall at the bottom of the staircase. They started from kindergarten. What struck her was how innocent Nick appeared in his younger years. What had changed to make him so angry and bitter?

"Keep moving, Laughs," Nick whispered so his parents wouldn't hear. "This doesn't change anything. I think we'll be moving to that place after all."

She ignored him. Just what she needed. Not only would she have to deal with Ivan, but Nick as well. She ran up the stairs and stepped into the third doorway to the right. The spare bedroom was immaculately cleaned, the bed was made, and the windows were polished. Mrs. Jacobs walked to a full-length mirror next to the window, took a rag that was hanging off the side, and began wiping it.

"What are you doing?" Nick asked.

"Wiping the protective film off the glass," Mrs. Jacobs answered.

When the mirror was completely wiped, Mrs. Jacobs stepped back and looked at Lana, waiting to see what she would do. She walked up to the mirror, placed her hand on the cold surface, and jumped when her hand went through the glass.

"Are you ready?" she asked Terris, pulling her hand out of the mirror.

When he nodded, she turned to Mr. and Mrs. Jacobs and thanked them for their help.

"No problem," Mrs. Jacobs said. "I'm just worried about what you're going to do when you get to Bridian. Maybe we should go with you."

"No. We'll be fine. I know what I'm going to do."

Nick whispered, "See you later, Laughs."

Lana stepped into the mirror. The swirling sea of silver engulfed her once again as she made her way to the rectangle of light opposite her. When she approached the light, she tried looking through the mirror, hoping to see where they were going to step into. All she saw was the thin layer of dust coating the glass. Her stomach sank as she remembered that it could be difficult to travel through a dusty mirror.

Taking a deep breath, she pushed herself through the mirror. She threw all her weight against the glass but couldn't break free. Terris ran into her, propelling them through the dust-covered mirror.

Lana sat up. They were in a small house with no furniture. The room was empty. She tiptoed to the nearest window and peeked out.

"The lake's right outside the door!" she whispered.

Terris shrugged his shoulders and opened the door. Two rebels greeted them. They grabbed her arms and pushed her down the stairs. They had walked into a trap.

14

THE REBELS' SLAVE

The rebels pulled Lana down the steps. They began shouting, screaming that they captured her, and a dozen more joined them from a house to their left.

"He'll be so happy," someone squealed, pushing his way closer. "We'll be rewarded."

As the rebel wrestled his way toward her, another stuck his foot in front of his path, tripping him. They burst into laughter when the man's hood fell off, revealing his face. She recognized Poklin.

All laughter stopped the moment a tall rebel stepped forward. As soon as he spoke, she knew it was Damarius.

"He'll be very pleased to have his daughter back."

"What should I do with her?" the man holding her asked, adjusting his hood and allowing her a clear view of his scarred face.

"Am I the only competent one here?" Damarius thundered, his eyes shifting crazily over the group. "Keep a firm hold on her! We're going to have to walk."

Damarius turned toward her, removing his hood. He spoke in a soothing voice.

"How's my son? I hear he was found in Ganyon Falls but managed to escape. Others were not as lucky."

Lana couldn't believe that he was asking about Ivan. It was as if he had no soul. Then again, with his work in the Rebellion, he may have lost it years ago.

"You're lying," she said, her heart beating so fast it hurt to breathe.

"Let's just say we have who we need. How do you think we found you? Not that we couldn't without their help, but they made it so much easier."

Tears formed in her eyes, and she clenched her fists. She saw a lone figure standing apart from the rest of the rebels and grew frightened. She knew Damarius was acting as their leader, but the other figure was actually in control. Lana glanced at the lake. It was so calm it looked like glass. She expected to see the Altarians rise above the water, shattering the peaceful illusion.

After walking many hours, she had given up hope of escape. The rebels didn't miss an opportunity to display their need for destruction. When trees blocked their path, they were easily set on fire. They didn't care how much damage was done as the fire from one tree spread to another.

When they stepped out of the forest, Damarius faced the trees, watching the thick black smoke. She looked for Terris but couldn't find him. They made their way across the barren field to an enormous wooden fence that encircled an ancient cemetery.

The fence wound its way around the entire site. Huge spikes were set atop the individual posts, and the entrance was blocked by two enormous wooden doors with an even bigger padlock that looked as if it required a key. The wind howled as Damarius stepped up to the lock.

The lock broke instantaneously, and the doors swung open. The group wound their way around crumbled tombstones and huge monuments that were engraved with names of those whose life they marked. As they began the steep ascent to the second tier of the cemetery, she saw Terris and gave him a strained smile, hoping to give him courage.

When they reached the top of the hill, she looked behind her and nearly tripped. Tall trees devoid of leaves dotted the landscape, giving the whole scene an even creepier feel. She stumbled forward when someone pushed her from behind.

As they wound their way past more monuments and head-stones, she realized where they were going and felt an ache in the pit of her stomach. They were headed to a freshly dug gravesite, loose dirt surrounded the headstone instead of grass. Lana stepped up to the grave and nervously looked at the inscription. She read the stone marker again—*Alexander VanDriesen*. She looked at Terris, but he had not seen his uncle's name yet.

A moment later, Terris finally caught her looking at him and seemed to understand that he was missing something. He read the inscription on the marble tombstone. Recognition dawned on his face, and he dropped to the muddy ground on his hands and knees.

A group of rebels pushed their way to the tombstone. With their bare hands, they began digging up the freshly packed dirt, throwing it over their shoulders. Damarius stood next to her with his hands folded across his chest. Terris crawled over to her on his hands and knees. The hair on the back of her neck prickled as the silent rebel watched her from across the gravesite, daring her to make a run for it.

Lana continued to watch as they dug up the loose soil. She even strained her neck when the coffin had been revealed, trying to see inside. Terris looked as if he were going to be sick. The rebels were covered in dirt, and when they reemerged from the hole in the ground, with smiles on their faces, their hands and nails were dirty.

Damarius pushed his way forward and held his hands out

for silence. Nothing stirred, not even the wind. She had never heard such utter silence before, and it filled her with a sense of dread. He stepped up to the hole that had been dug, the tips of his feet hanging off the edge. He threw his hands in the air, and the casket's lid flew off. She slowly edged her way closer, curious to see what was going to happen. The rebels shrieked with delight at Alexander's emaciated body, which was writhing in shock. The rebels released her and joined Damarius at the edge of the grave.

"This is what happens to our enemies!" Damarius shouted.

A moan escaped Alexander's lips, and she couldn't believe he was alive. She stepped closer, trying to see what they were going to do to him. Damarius jumped into the hole in the ground. She began crying as he took hold of Alexander.

"I don't understand. He died days ago."

"Alexander didn't die. We have very powerful drugs. Some that even mimic death."

"Why bury him?"

"To keep up appearances," he answered. "We don't want anybody knowing he's alive. That would ruin our plans. Since everyone thinks he's dead, he can be our slave, and no one will be the wiser." Looking around the cemetery, he added, "I heard it was a beautiful ceremony though."

Lana flinched. She needed to get far away from them as fast as she could. She inched her way backward, toward Terris, and tripped over a small headstone. She sat in the mud and watched the rebels drag Alexander out of his coffin.

A moment later, through the light drizzle of rain, she saw something flying towards her. She braced herself, fearing the worst. She heard Terris inhale sharply as the object approached. The orange and black entity slowly settled on her leg, and with a startled gasp she saw it was a butterfly, although it looked half dead. The rain had injured the delicate creature's wings.

"It's a butterfly!" Terris whispered, suddenly hiccupping. "That's good luck!"

"Why is it good luck?"

"Butterflies are said to be the souls of the dead," Terris explained between hiccups.

Lana looked at the butterfly again and felt a renewed sense of purpose. She had to go on. She had to fight. The horrible atrocity taking place in front of her made her realize it all had to stop. Too many people were living in fear. The butterfly flew towards the lone rebel.

She turned toward Terris and whispered, "We have to get out of here."

"That's my uncle," he said sadly. "I thought he was dead."

"We all thought he was dead," she reassured him, realizing that everyone was engrossed in Alexander's excavation. "No one's paying attention to us right now."

"That's because they're digging up my half-dead uncle to be their slave!" Terris said loudly.

She held her hand up to his mouth, hoping he would keep quiet. "We'll figure out how to save him later, but first, we need to save ourselves."

Lana stood up, relieved that the attention wasn't on her. She looked towards the lone rebel across the gravesite and saw the beautiful butterfly flying towards him. In one swift move, he grabbed the frail butterfly and crushed it in his hand.

"No one's coming for us," she said coldly, watching the rebel wipe his hands, and the butterfly's remains, on his cloak.

"What's your plan?" Terris asked, slowly raising himself to his knees.

Lana looked around, feeling hopeless. They didn't have much time. Soon the rebels would lose interest in Alexander.

"What if we climb the tree and jump to the other side of the fence?" Terris whispered.

She looked at the tree. It looked easy enough to climb. The

only problem was that they would be back in the forest with absolutely no idea where they were; and that was only if the rebels didn't catch them.

Before she could talk herself out of it, she hoisted herself up the tree just far enough so she could jump to the other side of the tall fence. She landed on both feet and turned to help Terris, but he had already landed next to her on his hands and knees. Without looking back, they broke into a run, scrambling over branches and puddles of mud.

"That was too easy," Terris panted.

He was right. She turned around, expecting to see rebels chasing them. She heard the sound of their raucous laughter, taunting Alexander.

In an attempt to keep her friend's spirits up, she said, "I think we just got lucky."

Lana kept running until her lungs ached. She was sure she heard the snap of a twig behind them but was too scared to turn around. She hoped they weren't being followed.

"Do you have any idea where we are?"

"No," Terris panted, "but I need to rest a minute."

She stopped running, grateful for the break but nervous that the rebels were right behind them.

Terris began some mental calculations in his head, mumbling every so often, "We were in Altaris," "Bridian to the North or South?" "East maybe?"

She used the time to catch her breath when she heard the crunch of leaves to their right. She turned to look but didn't see anything. Beads of sweat dripped off her face only to be carried away by the softly falling rain that managed to penetrate the thick canopy of leaves overhead. She looked at Terris, who pointed to her left and began running. She followed, hoping that the crunch of the leaves was only an animal.

When she felt that her lungs would explode, she slowed to a walk. She leaned into her side, trying to ease the muscle cramps. Terris had his hands on his knees, bent over as he steadied his breathing.

"Bridian shouldn't be that much further," he panted.

She nodded, still trying to catch her breath.

"Look over there." Terris pointed to their left. "I think I see a trail."

Lana followed his gaze and saw a clearing beyond a patch of trees. She knew they should get out of the forest, if only to figure out where they were. She began walking towards the clearing and heard Terris follow. The grass was tall, and she had to watch her step.

When they reached the clearing, she saw not only a large trail, but a house. Her breath caught in her throat when she saw five people seated at a long wooden table in the yard of the small house.

"Follow me." Terris stepped past her.

Two girls, about her age, were sitting with their backs to her but had turned to look at them when they heard Terris. Both girls were petite with long curly blonde hair, brown eyes, and pale, well-worn dresses. An older woman, with hair that reminded her of her aunt Charlotte's, looked up as well. The small boy didn't bother but rather used the break to devour his food. At the head of the table, a large man with thick, curly black hair eyed them suspiciously.

"What town is this?" Terris asked, glancing hungrily at the food.

"Sumner," the elder man answered.

"Sumner," Terris repeated, confused.

"No one's familiar with our little town," the man laughed. "Although, given its rich history, you'd think people would remember."

Lana looked at Terris, wondering if they should leave. She didn't know what Sumner's rich history was and didn't care to learn either.

"Many years ago, Sumner was founded by citizens of Bridian and Medora. They didn't agree with the Medoran War," one of the girls answered, as if reading from a textbook.

"I guess I must have missed that." Terris scratched his head.

"Probably not," the older man said as he chewed his food. "Their plan didn't work. It just angered King Nacaro."

His wife rolled her eyes, having heard the story too often.

"Do you want something to eat?" the man asked. "You two look famished."

Terris nodded eagerly. The two girls slid over on the bench, making room for them to sit.

"The name's Henry," the man said. "And this is Ned," he added, pointing to the little boy who was eating like there was no tomorrow. "These two beauties are Karla and Nadia." The two girls smiled, and Henry pointed to the woman. "And this is Madge, my wife."

Lana said hello while Karla ran into the house for more plates. She noticed that Karla was barefoot. She discreetly looked under the table and saw they were all barefoot. She listened as Terris introduced them. She hoped he knew enough not to use her real name.

"I'm Lydia," she said before Terris disclosed her name.

Kiernan's made-up name for her had stuck. She was starting to think she might as well just change her name to Lydia.

"What I'd like to know is where you two came from?" Henry asked.

Lana heard Terris answer but felt as if he was talking from a distance. She looked up and found herself staring into the dark red eyes of a large beast. It was sitting on its hind legs, its black furry hands in front of him, reminding her of a large cat.

The creature looked into her eyes, as if searching for something. She glanced around the table but no one else seemed to be aware of its presence. In a panic, she desperately tried to get

Terris's attention, but he was too engrossed in his conversation with Henry. Madge had been staring at her with a scowl on her face, oddly resembling her aunt Charlotte again. Little Ned was still eating, and Karla and Nadia were whispering excitedly, looking at Terris.

She felt dizzy, so dizzy that everything around her blurred together. All she could see was a mesh of colors. She stood up, uncertain of what to do, when the monster lunged at her, its long talons poised for attack. Fearing the worst, she frantically dove underneath the table.

"What's wrong?" Terris asked.

Lana looked past Terris and saw the creature had disappeared. They were alone. She could hear Henry and Madge whispering above her but couldn't make out what was being said.

"Nothing, I—I—I'm all right," she stuttered, crawling out from underneath the table.

"What happened?" Madge asked.

She didn't answer. She was unsure herself but guessed she must have fallen asleep. She rubbed her forehead in frustration.

"I'm just so tired."

"Yes, we know all about your travels, Lydia," Henry said. "Terris was just filling us in."

Lana's cheeks flushed. She couldn't believe that Terris had told them everything.

"You told them?"

"Yes," Terris answered. "I told them all about your father."

Lana couldn't believe her ears. She looked around the table when she realized they were still calling her Lydia.

Terris saw the look on her face and rushed to explain, "I told them all about your father's death."

She breathed a sigh of relief. When she finally looked up again, everyone was looking at her. Even Ned stopped eating.

"My father," she said, feeling horrible for believing that Terris would betray her. "I miss him so much."

"Well," Henry began. "It's a good thing your distant cousins are able to support you. Although, it's too bad Terris was the only one able to accompany you to Bridian. With the reemergence of the rebels, nowhere is safe."

Karla and Nadia looked frightened as they pushed their plates away from them.

"It is too bad. We really must be on our way before it gets worse."

"Nonsense," Henry said, shaking his head. "You can stay here for the night. I hear Bridian's a virtual ghost town anyway. Madge has family there, and we heard that everyone has packed up and left. Too bad Alderic's daughter, Princess Carlecia, ran off."

Lana looked up. "What do you mean?"

"She's the only one that can stop it," Henry explained. "But she's missing. Probably hidden away. Or maybe she joined the rebels. It's bound to happen anyway."

"What makes you think that?" she asked nonchalantly, trying to make it seem as if she didn't really care.

"Everyone knows about her past. From birth, she's been surrounded by too much evil."

"Bridian's in all sorts of turmoil now that she's back," Madge said.

"I have faith in her," Terris said after a long silence.

Henry went back to eating his meal. She was too nervous to eat. She didn't like sitting in the open and nervously watched the forest, expecting the rebels to find them. When Terris finished, she stood and picked up her plate.

"Leave them," Madge said. "I'll take care of everything."

Lana waited for Terris to say a polite goodbye. She knew something wasn't right with the family. The way Madge kept looking at her was odd.

They walked for many miles without talking. Every few feet she looked behind them to make sure they weren't being followed. What seemed like hours later, Terris explained that they would be arriving in the Square shortly.

"Have any plans yet?" he asked.

"How does one go about destroying a Crystal that contains demons?"

Terris didn't answer. When she saw the castle, she was both excited and nervous. Excited to find the Crystal and nervous because she didn't want to face Alderic or any other rebels.

Lana knew the best way into the castle was through the passage they had escaped from. It was the closest entry point. When they reached the trapdoor, she lifted it open. Terris began pacing.

"What if there are rebels down there?" he asked, pulling his cloak tighter around his body. "I'm surprised we haven't run into them again. I wouldn't think they would abandon the castle."

She knew he was right. She stood up and ran her hands along her cloak. She was going to turn around, formulate a new plan, when she saw her crown. She had forgotten about it.

"I'm going, but you don't have to."

"What about the necklace?" he asked nervously.

"You can give it to me now. I'm not even sure it's the key. In fact, I'm not even sure the Crystal's here at all. It's just a guess."

"I'm scared," he whispered, as if saying it too loudly would make it worse. "I'm not like you."

"I'm scared too, but I know what I have to do." She looked to the ground as tears filled her eyes again. "There's a chance I won't make it out of here alive. Well, probably a very good chance."

"Then why do it?" he asked.

"It's the right thing to do." She jumped into the passage and picked up her crown. "I can't sit idly by while he hurts people. If there's a chance that I can stop him, I'll do it."

Lana put the crown on its rightful place atop her head. Terris jumped in the passage after her. They slowly made their way through the dark tunnel in silence. She let out a sigh of relief when they reached the end, pausing when she heard a noise behind her.

"Did you hear that?"

When Terris answered that he hadn't heard anything, she realized she must have imagined it. She knew she was agitated over the anticipation of what was yet to come. She hoisted herself out of the passageway. She placed her hands on the wall and slid it open.

Once they left the passage, they made their way upstairs. The castle was very quiet, and every little noise made her jump. She knew she was being paranoid, but it sounded as if someone was following them.

As if on autopilot, she managed to navigate her way through the castle to the painting of the willow tree and lake. The castle was empty, making it seem even bigger. It appeared as if everyone had been in a hurry to leave, and all possessions were left behind.

With one last glance at Terris, Lana stepped into the mirror. Once she was inside, she looked at the peaceful lake and thought of her cousins.

"This is a little too familiar," Terris said, remembering the day they discovered the abandoned hall with Deliah and Dominic.

She walked to the second mirror and stepped into it. When she was in the abandoned hall, the hair on her arms prickled. Terris joined her, and they made their way to the throne room. The first thing she saw was the broken mirror, still scattered across the floor.

Lana stepped past the shattered glass. When she was in the

room where her mother and grandfather had been murdered, she walked to the enormous fireplace, sidestepping upturned furniture. Terris followed.

She placed her hand on the fireplace. Terris took his necklace off and slowly handed it to her. She placed the pearl in the tiny indentation of the dragon's eye.

It was a perfect match, but nothing happened. Terris shrugged his shoulders. She was so certain that she had been right. Anger boiled inside of her, and she kicked the metal grating. When it fell, a hidden room had been revealed, illuminated by a misty red light. Without thinking, she pulled the grating out of her way and crawled into the fireplace. Once she was in this new room, several things happened in quick succession.

Lana was knocked to the floor as hundreds of demons swarmed the tiny room. They looked like the beast she had seen in Sumner. Their beady red eyes glared at her.

A large Crystal was perched atop a huge silver pedestal to her left. She covered her ears from the harsh wailings of the evil creatures. It felt as if a million thoughts were swimming inside of her head, and she wanted nothing more than to rid herself of them. She placed her hands on the Crystal, and the beasts grew louder. Then everything went silent, even the demons. They seemed to have disappeared within it.

She looked around the room, surprised to hear clapping from outside the fireplace. Someone was applauding her, but she knew this wasn't a congratulatory round of applause. A familiar voice broke the silence.

"I knew you would lead me right to it."

Lana peered into the throne room, searching for the source of the voice. Standing before her, looking into the fireplace, was someone she was not expecting to see. She had been fooled all along.

15

THE CRYSTAL OF MEDORA

Lana was surprised to see the man before her. Something wasn't right. He looked different than how she remembered him in Ganyon Falls.

"I knew you would remember," Contlay said, wearing the long dark cloak of the rebels. "And I knew you would lead me right to it."

She heard Terris gasp but couldn't take her eyes off Contlay. So many questions raced through her.

"I need help," she pleaded. "I don't know what to do."

"Give it to me," he demanded, stepping closer to her. "I'll take care of it."

Instinctively, she stepped backwards. A million conflicting thoughts flooded her. She had a feeling that he was a rebel and had always been one. How he had fooled everyone for so long?

"Leave her alone!" Terris shouted.

Contlay had been stepping closer to her. She looked at the Crystal again, praying that something would come to her. A plan to not only break it but send the demons back to where they came from.

"All I want is the Crystal. All you have to do is give it to me."

"Don't do it," Terris cautioned.

Contlay stepped back, out of her line of vision. She heard a loud noise followed by silence. She slowly stepped to the mouth the fireplace to see what had happened. She grimaced when she saw that Contlay had thrown Terris against a wall. Contlay was slowly walking toward her, his eyes focused on the Crystal.

She instinctively stepped back until she was flat against the wall. Her brain was muddled. She stared at Contlay and forced herself to speak.

"STOP!"

"What are you going to do, Lana?" he asked.

She needed time to think. She had to keep him talking.

"You're a rebel? All this time ..."

He laughed. "Now is not the time for that conversation."

"Well, the way I see it," she locked eyes with him, "is that I have the Crystal, so I decide whether we talk. I want to know the truth."

"Already it's in you, the will for the Rebellion," he said, stepping up to the mouth of the fireplace.

She felt sick. The fact that she had once trusted this man made everything so much worse. Then she realized he had been the lone figure amongst the rebels. He hadn't talked because she would have recognized his voice. He had followed them.

"How did you find us?"

"That was easy," he answered, his eyes boring into her own, as if prying for the last bit of information she might still hold. When she looked confused, he continued, "Did you think that in the presence of that many rebels you would actually escape? I followed you here. The whole thing was a setup. I saw the look on your face in Ganyon Falls. I knew that you remembered. I called off the attack that night. I knew that you would end up at Nick's house and would eventually come back through their mirror to Altaris."

"They didn't set us up?"

"No, they didn't."

Lana's mind continued to race, and she looked past Contlay, into the throne room, hoping help would arrive. When no one came, she turned back to him.

"You weren't aiming for Alderic, were you?" she asked, as if hearing the echo of the fatal bullet from many years ago. "Who were you trying to kill?"

"So, you caught on," he said with an insidious grin, taking another slow step forward. "I thought you would."

"Stay where you are!"

"Or else?" he mocked.

"Who were you really aiming for?"

Contlay looked to the ground, as if remembering the past. "Ramos. Too bad I missed. My aim is terrible."

Lana couldn't believe he had murdered her mother and was talking about it like it was nothing. Like it was just another task that had to be done. She tightened her hold on the pedestal, too afraid to touch the Crystal.

"This doesn't make sense," she said, trying to piece together the puzzle. "You had plenty of opportunities to take me. Why wait all this time? Why pretend like you're helping?"

"It would have been pointless," he sighed. "You hadn't remembered anything, and if I tried to force it out of you, you never would have remembered. It had to come naturally."

"Then why was I ambushed in Frazier Woods?"

"I had to speed up the process. I wanted you to trust me, and I needed you to return to Bridian. To finally leave that wretched place was heaven. Picking up after children all day long is awful."

"How did you have everyone fooled?"

"I played the part. I never quite got it either. I was Alderic's best friend, his partner in crime, you might say. We did everything together."

Something Contlay said struck her as odd. She had to keep him talking. The puzzle pieces were beginning to align.

"You *were* Alderic's best friend?"

"Let's just say that more people are turning to me and abandoning his faded hopes of glory."

A new voice interrupted them. Her stomach sank.

"How nice to see you, Contlay, although you're telling my dear cousin lies."

For the second time that night, she was speechless. Damon was almost unrecognizable. His hair was greasy and disheveled. He had deep bags underneath his eyes, as if he hadn't slept in days.

"Don't lie," Damon spat, sweeping into the room, his long cloak billowing after him.

"I'm not lying."

"If anything, you're hurting our cause!" he said, and she knew that he was gone, too immersed in the Rebellion. "Splitting us in two won't help us against our enemies!"

"Nothing I'm instigating," Contlay said. "It's not my fault that people are coming to appreciate my view, my side of things."

And then, she heard a voice she wished she had not.

"Now, Damon," Alderic said as he too walked into the throne room, giving her chills. "We must not divert our attention from the real matter at hand."

Lana began trembling. She watched Alderic in fear, her mind racing with all the horrible crimes he had committed. She remembered Angelica and couldn't believe her father could so ruthlessly murder an innocent child.

"How nice to see you again, brother," Contlay said unconsciously, almost by rote. "How did you know we were here?"

Alderic chuckled, "Did you think I would leave my home unattended?"

He walked up to the mouth of the fireplace, looking in. His eyes darted past Lana and locked on the Crystal.

"He hid it right under my nose," he said. "It makes sense. The demons had been calling to me that night. I knew they had to be close."

"Who took you in when no one else would?" Contlay turned to Damon. "Who first showed you the way?"

"Why praise the apprentice when you can praise the master?" he answered. "You had nothing to do with it. The only thing you were good for was to give me a break from my pretentious parents."

"I showed you the way!" Contlay spat, as if he couldn't believe what he was hearing.

"You merely guided me in the right direction," Damon said, joining Alderic at the mouth of the fireplace, looking at her. "Something I would have found on my own."

"Enough of this." Alderic turned to face Contlay.

He threw his fist in the air, and a Stone of Medora flew at Contlay, knocking him down. She cringed as Alderic turned toward her again.

"My daughter, we must release them. I know you can see them, feel them."

She stepped backwards. She was so scared it seemed as if she had lost the ability to talk. Alderic turned his back to her and looked at Damon.

An evil smile crept upon her cousin's face as he stepped up to Contlay, now motionless on the ground. In one swift move, he kicked him in the stomach.

"Damon, what happened to you?"

"My uncle, your father, showed me the light."

"How could you betray your family?"

"Betray my family?" Damon repeated, his eyes wide in confusion. "I would never betray my family. My real family, that is. Ramos was never my family. Oh, he did put on a good show though."

Lana couldn't believe how far taken he was. Her hands began shaking as she reached for the Crystal, pulling it to her chest. Her hands tingled, and she clutched it tighter, not wanting to drop it. The room was still very dark, save for the reddish tint from the demon-possessed stone.

"He loves you."

Damon looked disgusted then shouted, "HE NEVER LOVED ME!"

"What do you mean he never loved you?"

"All he cared about was your return," he snarled. "I was never going to rule, to be King."

"I don't want to rule Bridian."

"Exactly why it should have been me," he said, as if stating his case to an invisible jury. "He knew how much I wanted it. How badly I needed it."

Damon paused, as if regaining his thoughts, and for a moment, he looked at her somberly. She thought he was going to pull himself out of the trance he had been in when he continued, "The day I heard him talking about you, I knew I couldn't go on. I couldn't pretend to follow him anymore. To agree with him when he was wrong."

"What day? What happened?"

"The day I overheard him tell his advisors that when you returned the throne would be yours," Damon said, looking to the ground, as if remembering a time in his past that still haunted him. "That it was never intended for me at all. That's when I found the abandoned hall. I found your father's journals and books on black magic hidden in a loose floorboard in his former bedroom. That began my quest for the truth."

"You stayed with Contlay in Mt. Sinclair." She looked at Damon, finally realizing why he had run off.

"I overheard my father speaking about Contlay once, that he was in Mt. Sinclair, protecting you. I knew he still had ties to the rebels. Everyone trusted him, but it didn't make sense. He was hiding something, and I wanted the truth. He connected me with contacts that led me to my uncle."

"And that's what you found," Alderic said, stepping up to Damon. "The truth."

Lana almost forgot that Alderic was there. She saw that he had been listening to Damon's story and looked very proud.

"The truth about the Rebellion and the fact that we are working for the benefit of all," her father added.

"And let me add that my mother didn't make life easy," Damon said.

"So you ran away. Nice job, Damon," she said sarcastically, although she could sympathize with his feelings about Charlotte; she really was horrible. "You find out you can't rule Bridian, so you run off and join the rebels. You proved your point."

Damon was taken aback. He hadn't been expecting her to fight back.

"I don't think that you understand the power we hold right now." Alderic stepped closer to her. "Once the demons are released, we'll be unstoppable. All the innocent people you're trying to protect really aren't so innocent. They deserve this. You have one last chance to join us and be spared, to use your gifts for good."

She was appalled. She had been immersed in the Rebellion unwillingly and didn't want her so-called gifts.

"Step out of the fireplace and look out the window," Alderic instructed, pointing to the huge window across the room. "I promise I will not hurt you, Lana."

She didn't know which part was more unbelievable, that he called her Lana or his promise that he wouldn't hurt her. Since she couldn't think of an alternative, she tightly clutched the Crystal and stepped out of the fireplace. She carefully side-stepped Alderic. He folded his arms across his chest, as if to signify that he would leave her alone.

She looked over at Terris and saw that he was still slumped over, unmoving. She couldn't tell if he was still breathing and hoped he was still alive. She would never forgive herself if something happened to him.

Damon began pacing the room, eyeing the Crystal hungrily. When she finally reached the window, she looked out and immediately wished she hadn't. Through the fog, she saw hundreds of rebels. The castle was completely surrounded.

She had to destroy the Crystal. One look out of the window told her she had to. She looked back at Alderic and saw the huge grin on his face. For some reason, she felt drawn to the window again. When she glanced out for the second time, the crowd of rebels had grown.

"I'm going to show you just how powerful I am," Alderic said.

Damon slumped to the ground. She drew in her breath sharply as Alderic pointed to the huge window behind her. With a wave of his hands, it blew apart, and fragments of glass flew outward and fell upon the rebels below.

A strong gust of wind blew her hair across her face. As if in a trance, Damon opened his eyes and lifted himself off the floor. A crooked smile crept across his face, and without warning, he began running at her.

Still clutching the Crystal, she took a step to her right, and Damon jumped onto the window ledge, laughing as he peered at the rebels below. She knew that her cousin was under the influence of Alderic's evil and was terrified that this would be the last time she would see him alive.

Damon turned his back to the open air. "I hope to be seeing you soon, Lana. On our side."

Alderic flicked his hand, and Damon stepped backward, off the window ledge. She heard herself screaming. She ran to the open window, hoping to see what had become of her cousin, but Alderic drew her attention again.

"Give it to me."

Lana fell to her knees. She was about to give up, to give in to him, when she looked at Terris and saw that he was slowly moving. She forced herself into a standing position, careful to avoid the shattered glass from the broken window. She could feel the cool breeze and longed to be anywhere other than where she was. Alderic followed his daughter's gaze and saw that Terris was trying to stand.

"Leave him alone!"

Alderic turned to her again. "He's just an insignificant being. Look at him. He can't even defend himself."

Terris hid his face. A tear slid down her cheek. She had never felt so helpless.

Alderic stepped closer to his daughter. "Give it to me!"

Lana saw movement out of the corner of her eye and froze. Before she even had a chance to react, Contlay stood up and began running toward Alderic. Too late, Alderic turned around, giving Contlay just enough time to attack.

Contlay landed on Alderic, throwing him to the ground so hard she heard a snap when he landed on his right arm. He struggled to get up, but Contlay stepped on his injured arm, pushing all his weight onto the wounded limb. Alderic let out an awful scream that echoed within the room, and her heart beat so fast she thought she would pass out.

As Contlay walked towards her, she clutched the Crystal so tightly her arms throbbed. She could hear Alderic's anguished cries, but the room was spinning so fast it took all her energy to concentrate on keeping the Crystal within her grip. Without saying a word, Contlay narrowed his eyes at her and began running.

All of the sudden, Terris sprang in front of her, shielding her from Contlay as they both fell to the floor. She knew she had to escape but couldn't leave Terris. Contlay would kill him. Out of the corner of her eye, she saw Alderic moving. He was slowly making his way toward Contlay and Terris. She tried speaking, to warn her friend to get out of the way, but nothing came out.

Alderic stepped up to Contlay, pulling him off Terris and throwing him to the ground with one hand. His right arm was awkwardly hanging down his side, and she knew it was broken, perhaps even dislocated from the shoulder. Alderic pulled three shiny stones from deep within his cloak and smiled.

"This is for Kalinia."

Alderic threw a Stone of Medora at Contlay, cursing him. It bounced off his shoulder with barely enough force to inflict any damage. She ran up to Terris, helping him stand while trying to keep the Crystal within her grip. She knew she had to escape. If she could bring the Crystal to Ramos, he would know what to do with it.

She began running, dragging Terris to the door since he could barely stand on his own. Alderic began shouting in a language unknown to her. The wind was blowing so fiercely the jeweled map fell to the floor with a loud crash.

Alderic screamed. She turned around and saw that Contlay was standing. Alderic threw his left arm in the air, releasing two more Stones, one at Contlay and one at her. Lana couldn't tear her eyes away from the scene unfolding before her.

Contlay pulled something shiny from his pocket. When he held it up, she saw it was a knife. As Contlay sprang toward Alderic, the Stone hit him in the chest. Contlay fell, and she had just enough time to see his knife rip into Alderic's chest before the Stone aimed at her hit the back of her head.

She fell to the ground, dropping the Crystal as Terris slumped to his knees without her support. For a moment, she sat in silence, slowly drifting in and out of consciousness, listening to the sound of footsteps coming closer. The last thing she remembered was someone stepping up to the Crystal and lifting it from the floor.

16

THE REUNION

L ana awoke to complete silence. She couldn't bring herself to open her eyes. Every muscle in her body ached, and she had a throbbing pain in the back of her head, near the nape of her neck. She tried to remember what had happened, but nothing came to her.

She heard shuffling and froze. Like a flood, the memories hit her at once. Where was the Crystal? Were Alderic and Contlay still fighting for it?

She opened her eyes and breathed a sigh of relief. Terris was pacing, every so often looking out the broken window Damon had jumped from. When he saw that she was awake, he stopped walking.

"I tried waking you."

She remained silent. Even if she wanted to talk, she didn't have anything to say. Her head hurt, and her throat ached.

"It's gone," Terris said, wringing his hands nervously. "I've looked everywhere."

Lana sat up. As if in a daze, she looked around the room. She didn't see the Crystal.

"Where is it? Where did they go? What happened?"

He shrugged his shoulders. "I don't know."

"What do you mean?" She stood up. "Where is it?"

Terris looked to the ground, then answered, "When I woke up, it was gone."

"Who took it?" she asked, her thoughts overtaking her. "What're we going to do?"

"I don't know," he repeated, beginning to tremble. "Both Alderic and Contlay were already gone when I woke up."

She looked around the room one last time and ran toward the door. She had to find the Crystal. She remembered it falling from her hands but had no idea who had taken it. When they emerged from the willow tree mirror, they made their way outside.

When they reached the drawbridge, she scanned the horizon. The early morning sky was still very dark, and Bridian appeared deserted. The rebels were gone. She looked around for any sign of Damon and breathed a sigh of relief when she didn't see his body, although that didn't mean he was still alive.

As she stepped into the Square, she heard talking and froze. The voices were coming from behind Poklin's Variety Store. Her knees began to shake, and she almost fell to the ground in fear. The adrenaline seemed to have escaped her. Terris caught her and helped her stand.

The voices sounded familiar, but she couldn't be sure over the roar of the wind. She gripped Terris's arm as the voices grew closer, making their way around the row of stores to the drawbridge. She couldn't believe her ears. She looked at Terris, hoping he heard what she had, when her parents, Ramos, Deliah, Dominic, and a dozen soldiers stepped into the open.

Terris began running, dragging her behind him. She had never felt so happy, and all thoughts of the Crystal vanished. When her mother saw her, she stopped dead in her tracks, almost as if she had run into a wall. Then she ran toward her.

"Lana," her mother exclaimed, wrapping her in her arms. "I'm so glad you're all right."

A moment later, her father was hugging her as well. She was so happy that, for a split second, she felt that everything would be okay.

"Where have you been?" her mother asked, wiping the tears from her eyes. "We've been so worried."

"Why are you standing in the open?" her father added. "It's not safe."

Lana didn't have time to process the questions. When the soldiers spread out, surrounding them, she saw someone she was not expecting, nor ever wanted to see again.

"Damarius," she whispered, too afraid to speak any louder. "He's behind you."

Ramos looked at Damarius and smiled. She realized that he must have been traveling with them. Had they been captured by rebels?

"Damarius isn't a rebel," Ramos said.

"Yes, he is," she stammered, wondering how he had everyone fooled. "I saw him with them."

"Thirteen years ago, he infiltrated the Rebellion," Ramos explained. "He's been our spy ever since."

"No. He's one of their leaders."

"That was all an act," Damarius said. "I had to follow orders from Alderic. I had to fit in."

"Don't talk to me. I saw what happened to Alexander! I know what you did to him!"

"Lana," Ramos said, stepping up to his niece. "Damarius already explained everything to me. He brought us here. The good news is that Alexander isn't dead. When we can spare a few soldiers, we'll rescue him. We're lucky Damarius oversaw that operation and talked your father out of killing him."

"He's lying," she pleaded. "He's a rebel. I know it."

Damarius fell to his knees beside her and took her hand.

"You have to believe me. The past thirteen years have been horrible."

"Without his intervention, the rebels would have freed Alderic sooner," Ramos explained. "He has delayed his release for many years."

"It's okay to trust him," her mother said gently.

Lana's head began to spin. Too many thoughts overtook her. She snapped her hand away from him.

"Does Ivan know you've been playing both sides?"

Damarius didn't answer. The wind blew, and she shivered.

"Only a handful of people know," Ramos said a moment later.

Images of the rebels digging up Alexander flashed before her. She saw Damarius laughing, and heard the moan that escaped Alexander's lips. She thought of all the clues, everything that pointed to the conclusion that he was a rebel.

"You were with Alderic before the castle was attacked. Kiernan said he saw you when Damon disappeared. You were in a house in the forest together. You knew Alderic escaped."

"I couldn't tell King Ramos then," he answered. "It was a test. If I failed, he would have killed me. I wanted to gain more intel. I didn't know he was going to make his move so soon. I thought I had more time."

She didn't believe him. She couldn't believe that Ramos and her parents trusted him. Her mother wrapped her in another hug.

"It's all right," she said. "Don't worry. He told us you would be here. He left the rebels to find us when you escaped."

Deliah and Dominic began arguing. She didn't even know what they were fighting about but smiled. She had missed them.

"What happened in Ganyon Falls?" She turned to them. "How did you escape?"

"Once you and Terris went through that mirror, the rebels

left," Deliah answered, shrugging her shoulders. "We stayed with Emeric for another night, until Dad found us."

"Contlay must have called off the attack," Ramos said, shaking his head, as if he too couldn't believe that he had been a rebel.

Lana turned toward Damarius. "Why didn't you tell them about Contlay sooner? If you were really spying on them, you would have known he was one."

"That's the thing," he answered. "No one talked of him. He hid it well."

"He had us all fooled," Ramos said sadly.

Lana didn't know who or what to believe. It was all too much to comprehend. The past week had utterly worn her out. She couldn't think straight anymore.

"Where have you been?" she asked Ramos, working up the courage to tell him she had led both Alderic and Contlay to the Crystal.

"Luckily, I was able to escape the night of the party," her uncle explained. "After I was attacked, Grant was able to rescue myself and Charlotte. We went to Rochelle; Charlotte has a sister there. When I heard that you were with Emeric, I set out at once but arrived too late. You had already left."

"How did you find us?" Terris asked. "How did you know we'd be here?"

"We were making our way to Altaris," her mother answered. "We were going to join you in Mt. Sinclair. We figured you were still with Nick and his family."

"Damarius caught up to us," her father added. "He told us what happened, and we pieced together that you were on your way back to Bridian."

"The Crystal's gone," she blurted out.

Ramos sighed. "So you remembered?"

Lana began crying. She couldn't hold it in anymore.

"There's more. One of them has it."

Her mother wrapped her in another hug as Terris filled everyone in on what they had been through.

"I'm just glad you're safe," Ramos said. "You're not sure who has it?"

"When I woke up, they were already gone," Terris answered when she couldn't. "And so was the Crystal."

A breeze lifted the hair off her forehead. The sun was slowly rising, and she tried to smile. She was glad everyone had survived but felt too uncertain about the future. In fact, she felt sick thinking about it.

"I'm so sorry. I had the Crystal, but I didn't know what to do with it."

"It's not your fault," Ramos said, placing his hand on her shoulder. "You shouldn't have had to come here on your own."

"We're just glad you're all right," her father added.

She looked to the ground. How long would it be before the next attack? Her eyes felt heavy, and the sting of tears overwhelmed her.

"Alderic must have the Crystal. I led him right to it."

"They need you to release them," Ramos said. "It will be okay."

"Where's Charlotte?"

"She's still in Rochelle. Soon, she'll begin the trip home."

Ramos turned to a soldier, giving instructions to search the castle. Her parents turned to Damarius and began talking softly. Lana shivered as she replayed the night in her head. She saw the Crystal on the silver pedestal, Damon step off the ledge, and Alderic fighting with Contlay.

"We've been thinking," Dominic whispered, stepping closer. "It was probably Contlay who trashed the abandoned hall after Damon disappeared."

Lana thought about it, realizing it made sense. He had

probably been looking for the Crystal. She also realized that things would never go back to normal. Too much had happened. She looked at her cousins and Terris, remembering their journey and everything they had been through.

"The Shadow Splinters are still around." She turned to her uncle. "They're not extinct."

"Deliah and Dominic already told me," he said, his jaw set. "I never thought they were."

"I told you, Dom," Deliah said smugly, looking at her brother. "I was right."

Dominic rolled his eyes.

"Have you heard from Kiernan yet?" Lana asked.

"He's fine," Dominic said. "We saw him yesterday, on our way here."

"He's staying with family," Deliah added.

Ramos cleared his throat. "They're going to do another search of the castle. I'm sure all the rebels are gone. It's just a precaution. Meanwhile, we're going to Poklin's. When we get there, take whatever you want."

She looked at her uncle, waiting for him to continue. He began walking, leading them to the shop.

"Is this a joke?" Dominic asked when they reached the backdoor.

"No," Ramos answered. "Poklin won't be back, and since he publicly admitted that he's a rebel, I'm evicting him. He's four months late on rent. The merchandise belongs to Bridian. What you don't take will be divided among the other children."

Ramos opened the door and continued, "We don't have long."

She walked up the stairs, passing her father who stood watch, scanning the Square for any rebels. Deliah and Dominic ran past her. Before she stepped into Poklin's, her father took her arm.

"It's not your fault," he reassured her. "I'm very proud of you and all that you've accomplished."

"Thank you." She gave him a weak smile.

Dominic jumped the counter and unearthed a dozen burlap bags. She halfheartedly took a bag and began throwing candy into it until she came across a Crystal Ball. As the mist swirled, beginning to reveal a scene, Deliah came up behind her and snatched it off the shelf.

"I'll take that."

Lana made her way down the long aisles toward the back-door. She nervously looked behind her, relieved to find no one in the immediate vicinity, and tiptoed her way to the very back —where Kiernan had seen Damon. When she reached the wooden door, she tried the handle and, surprisingly, found that the door swung open with a gentle creak. The room was dark, but she saw a long wooden table near the door.

When she stepped into the room, she slowly closed the door behind her and knelt to examine a few papers on the table. She soon realized that it was pointless. It was too dark, and she didn't want to turn on a light. Instead, she quickly gathered the papers and shoved them into her bag.

As she stepped back into the store, closing the door behind her, she heard a noise. She saw Damarius.

"What are you doing back here?" he asked, opening the door and looking into the room curiously.

Lana clutched the bag and stepped away from him. Without answering, she quickly made her way to Ramos while Damarius disappeared into the back room. As she walked, she tossed a few boxes of candy into her bag, concealing the papers. When she joined her cousins, she looked around the store one last time.

Ramos stepped up to his niece. "Would you like me to carry your bag?"

"No!"

She didn't want her uncle to see the papers. Any information she found would be given to Damarius, and she couldn't bring herself to trust him. Ramos motioned everyone out of the shop in a hurry. Deliah reached into her bag, pulled out a lime green candy, and shoved it in her mouth. When she stopped chewing, she turned to Lana.

"Do you think Angelica will come back?"

"Deliah, she was a spy," she answered, trying to sound as empathetic as possible. "You know she's not your doll. She never was."

Deliah shot her a blank look, then ran off to join her brother. She looked for Damarius, wanting to stay as far away from him as possible, and saw that he was bringing up the rear. He clutched a bag from Poklin's, probably for Ivan.

"There's something I have to ask you," Ramos said, discreetly stepping up to her. "Was Damon there? I mean, in the abandoned hall. Terris wouldn't say for sure, but I have a feeling he was."

Lana remained silent. She didn't know how to answer him. Finally, she decided that the truth would be best.

"He was."

Ramos faltered. She felt sorry for him. She couldn't imagine the pain of losing a child. Even though Damon may still be alive, she knew that Ramos had lost his oldest son to the Rebellion.

"I'm sorry. I don't know what happened to him."

"There's something I've been meaning to tell you," Ramos said, regaining his composure. "The throne is rightfully yours. I'm only a temporary placeholder until you're of age. You've proven yourself beyond doubt."

"I know," she said but immediately regretted it when he narrowed his eyes at her. "I mean, I assumed so."

He nodded. Lana didn't want him to know that Damon had

been drawn to the Rebellion over the fact that he would never rule Bridian.

"What do we do now?"

"We strengthen our defenses," he answered, nervously looking behind them. "And pray my brother doesn't have the Crystal."

She walked over the drawbridge in silence. Ramos looked at his niece, as if he was going to tell her something, when he thought better of it. She knew he had more secrets that he wasn't yet ready to share—just as she did.

When they were safely inside the castle, the drawbridge was raised, and the doors locked. It felt odd to be in the castle again and wished they could stay somewhere else.

"I have some good news," her father said, joining her in the foyer. "We heard from Nick's parents."

Lana remained silent, waiting for the good news. She needed something to cheer her up. She felt as if she had single-handedly sealed their fate by giving Alderic exactly what he had been looking for.

"They're leaving Mt. Sinclair," he continued. "They'll be living here, in Bridian."

Her heart sank. She had been hoping they were going to stay in Mt. Sinclair.

"Lana," Ramos said. "I need you to tell me everything that happened again. I know you must be tired, but we can talk on the way to your bedroom."

She said goodbye to her parents. When it was just Ramos, Terris, and herself, she began explaining everything that had happened, starting from the night of the party. When she was finished, Ramos remained silent.

"I knew this day would come," he whispered. "I just didn't think it would be so soon."

Suddenly, she thought of something. "Why was Terris given the pearl from the fireplace? It wasn't even the key."

"Yes, but from what I understand, it led you to the Crystal," Ramos said, leading them into her bedroom. "My guess is that it was supposed to jog your memory. My father hoped that one day you would be able to destroy it."

"Everyone assumed you knew where it was," Terris added, as if he had been thinking about it too. "I was given a clue to its hiding place in case you..."

"Joined him," she finished, twirling her ring around her finger.

"Well, in case he got to you first," Ramos said. "You're the only one able to destroy the Crystal and release the demons. It was your magic that brought them into this world. They're tethered to you. I'm sure Alderic is working on a way around this though."

Lana didn't think she was, or ever would be, able to destroy the Crystal. She had her chance and failed.

"But why was it given to Terris? Why wasn't it given to someone else?"

"Don't forget," Ramos began. "Terris is also connected to the Rebellion."

She nodded, smiling at her friend.

"You did everything that you could," Ramos said. "You just weren't ready."

"I led them right to it. I had it. I was actually touching it and didn't know how to break it."

"It's all right," he said, stepping up to her. "Alderic was bound to find the Crystal. Since escaping the Yards, the demons have been calling to him too. He would have found it eventually."

Lana wiped the tears from her eyes. Terris stepped up to her and hugged her. She squeezed him tight, thinking of everything they had survived together, starting as infants.

"It took a lot of courage to stand up to him," Ramos

continued after a moment of silence, looking at Terris as well. "You're both very brave, more so than I."

"Why does everyone think I'll join him?" She wiped the tears from her eyes. "He even asked me to. He said I was bound to the Rebellion anyway."

"Whether you like it or not, their magic is inside of you."

She began crying again. She didn't want to join the Rebellion or have anything to do with magic. She wanted nothing to do with Alderic, or Contlay either.

"It doesn't matter though," Ramos explained, taking her hands in his own. "We're all faced with evil, every day of our lives. It's all around us, not just you. In a very weak moment, my brother made his choice, and it's up to you whether or not you'll follow in his footsteps."

Lana knew her uncle was right. Whether or not she was going to join the Rebellion was her choice, and she had already made it.

"Don't let your fears get the best of you," Ramos continued. "Your crown is a reminder that you're destined for more."

Her eyes stung. She was exhausted and needed time to process everything.

"You should both get some rest. You've been through a lot, and this is far from over. We have a lot of work ahead of us."

Lana nodded and watched them leave, closing the door behind them. She sucked in a mouthful of air, trying to calm her nerves. The air felt electric, and she nervously shivered. Her hands tingled, and she dropped the bag from Poklin's. As candy scattered all around her, the papers caught her attention. She quickly shoved them back into the bag and hid them under the candy again.

She put the bag in the trunk at the foot of her bed, then sank into the soft mattress, pushing aside thoughts of Alderic, Contlay, and the Crystal. Although she was curious about the papers from Poklin's, she was too exhausted, perhaps even a little scared, to look at them. She knew one thing for certain: when she awoke, she was going to devote all her energy to finding the Crystal. She had to fix her mistake. She still couldn't believe she had led Alderic and Contlay right to it.

What seemed like hours later, Lana was finally able to push aside her thoughts long enough to fall asleep. She slept a dreamless sleep, which suited her just fine. The real-life nightmares were just beginning.

ACKNOWLEDGMENTS

Thank you to everyone who has helped make my dream possible! That includes you! Thank you for taking the time to read part one of Lana's story.

To my parents, MaryAnn Taylor and John Battista, for reading countless drafts. To my husband, Chris LeMore, for encouraging me every step of the way. To my Grandma Kay, thanks for being there whenever I need you. To my brother, Kyle Taylor, thank you for the cover art. You can view his work on Instagram and Etsy (@CalamityParty).

A very special thank you to my son, Nello LeMore, for just being you. I love you more than you'll ever know.

ABOUT THE AUTHOR

Jessica R. LeMore is the author of *The Princess of the Rebellion*, the first novel in *The Mirrored Crown* series. Jessica lives in Upstate New York with her husband and son. You can visit her online at www.jessicarlemore.com.

facebook.com/jessicarlemore
twitter.com/jessicarlemore
instagram.com/jessicarlemore

Made in the USA
Middletown, DE
15 March 2021